CW01430873

Calum's Shorts

Short but tall tales of the retired accountant cum adventurer and his acquaintances, that take place in Millport, Isle of Cumbrae and other exotic locations around the world.

Edwin Deas

Other Novels by Edwin Deas

Crises on The Cumbraes; The Unlikely Adventures of a Retired Accountant

Six at Cambridge? The Return of Calum the retired accountant in another unlikely non-accounting adventure!

Keep in touch with the author:

www.edwindeas1.wixsite.com/edwindeas

www.facebook.com/edwindeasbooks

www.linkedin.com/in/edwindeas

Calum's Shorts

Edwin Deas

Copyright © 2019 by Edwin Deas

All rights reserved. This includes the right to reproduce any portion of this book in any form.

Cover design by Bronwyn Jenkins-Deas

Editing by Bronwyn Jenkins-Deas & Dr Helen Ralston French

First printing in 2019

Published with Kindle Direct Publishing (KDP)

ISBN: 9781096308348

Disclaimer: This book is a work of fiction. The characters, incidents, and dialogue are drawn from the author's imagination or are used fictitiously. Any resemblance to actual events, locales or persons, living or dead, is entirely coincidental. However, some events, locales, and persons may have been borrowed, purely for these stories. Fear not, they have not been harmed and will be returned in exactly the same condition as the author found them.

This book is dedicated, once again, to Bronwyn-Jenkins-Deas for she persists in believing and it sure helps.

Contents

Blue Turns to Grey

I heard my mother approaching my bedroom. This would be the final call, I predicted. She and my dad had been packing the big steamer trunk all morning and their voices had got louder and louder as they struggled to squeeze all the clothing and accessories, needed for two weeks, into what had started off as an enormous empty thing that reminded me of a coffin. The beauty of sending a trunk ahead by train to one's holiday destination was that you could travel relatively lightly thereafter. No heavy cases to carry onto trains and more especially between train stations in Glasgow. For my family, these were the days before airline travel and the nightmare of handling luggage in airports. These were even the days before we had a car.

'If you don't hurry up, Calum, and get your toys ready for packing, you will have to do without them. We won't be able to get them into the trunk.'

My dad chimed in, with a louder and less friendly voice from a distance. 'And, if you don't hurry up, there will be no room for you either. How would you like to miss your holidays and have to stay here in Edinburgh, all on your own?'

I had absolutely no intention of missing the annual pilgrimage to Millport on the Isle of Cumbrae in the Firth of Clyde. Conversely, I had no intention of packing too many of my toys. For, I was all too aware that a shortage, or absence altogether, of toys would more than likely lead to me being bought some new ones in the wonderful Aladdin's Cave that was Mapes Cycle Hire & Toy Shop in Millport. I had seen this tendency develop more and more each year that we had journeyed to Millport and I could remember back at least five of my almost nine years. There was definite strategy in my procrastination, although I was not altogether sure what the word meant, having only recently been accused of it.

'Yes, yes. I am almost ready. I can't find my bucket and spade that I got last year.'

'Never mind them. You can always get another set. Just bring through the other things you want to take.'

Bingo! They were already falling for it. A new bucket and spade were on the way by the sound of it. I had actually no idea where last year's set was, really, honest! After all, what use could a bucket and spade be put to in a big city like Edinburgh? They were probably tucked away at the back of my wardrobe. Now, what else did I want to be bought for me? The new Dinky Plymouth Plaza and Corgi Rolls Royce Phantom V would definitely be top of my list. So, I had to make sure I forgot to pack any toy cars. Lastly, if I forgot to deflate my football until it was too late to get it into the trunk; I would be in line for a new plastic Wembley football that everybody in my street seemed to be getting in that summer of 1960.

The doorbell rang and my dad yelled to me. 'That will be the porter from the railway company to pick up the trunk. You have ten seconds to get your things packed or nothing goes.'

Ten seconds later, I had a meagre handful of small toys ceremoniously laid out on top of the clothing and asked in an innocent voice if I could help with the closing of the trunk.

'What about your.....?'

'Do you not want to take your....?'

'Oh, never mind. We need to get this thing closed up. The porter will not wait all day.'

Mission had been accomplished.

This was Tuesday and I now had to wait all the way through until Saturday before it was time for us the catch the train, first to Glasgow, and then to Wemyss Bay. It would have been nice to be going on holiday in our car, just like my best pal Brian was doing at this precise moment (all the way to Whitley Bay in England!), but we had no car in those days. However, I did not miss it because we had never had one. We could get to Cumbrae including the incredible sail on the steamer called *Talisman* from Wemyss Bay to Millport inside one day quite easily, but it took the trunk four days in the goods vans of the trains to get there. However, it would be waiting for us when we arrived. It always was. I would insist that it was opened up the minute we arrived at Barclay House in the West Bay of Millport, where we lodged. After all, I would need my toys right away!

I intended to use the time up between now and Saturday to get myself appropriately excited about the annual holiday. It was basically the same every year. We stayed at the same place. Mrs. Anderson looked after the cooking and cleaning although my mother seemed to help out more often than not. I never stopped to think it was supposed to be her holiday too. The reason she liked to help was that Mrs. Anderson was absolutely ancient! And, that was when I first remember going to her house. She had got a lot older every year since then. I was big for my age and had only one inch to go before I would hit five feet tall. But I knew already I would be towering over Mrs. Anderson this year. I was equal with her last year. She was tiny and always wore the same clothes with long skirts that touched the ground and her silver, grey hair in a tight bun. I had raised a laugh, then received admonishment just a few weeks ago when I had made an observation as the family was watching the brand new film *Kidnapped*, starring Peter Finch, at the cinema, just as an old woman was about to serve the two fugitives a paltry meal of porridge and hard bread, 'Oh look, there is Mrs. Anderson serving the breakfast. I never knew she was thaaat old!'

We always had great food at Barclay House. We sat at a very large dining table that would not have fitted into the kitchen in our small flat in Edinburgh. It seemed like we had bigger meals than we had at home too, served on enormous china plates and in casserole dishes with lids. I was allowed to serve myself, which was a rare treat, and had gradually learned not to be irritated by the caution, 'Don't take too much, Calum, you can always have a little more if you have room for it,' once I knew it to be true. This year, I looked forward to eating as much as I could because I was going to use up a whole lot of energy on all the activities that I was planning.

In truth, there were not really all that many activities to do in Millport and they were mostly the same every year but I never tired of them. There was a world of difference between growing up in Edinburgh and spending two weeks each year on a real island, surrounded by water! Scrambling over the rocks, looking in tidal pools for strange sea creatures, discovering hidden beaches that only my brother and I knew existed. And, that was all before lunch. In the afternoon, we would walk along the promenade, dodging among the throngs of tourists doing exactly the same, looking in all the shop windows with at least half an hour reserved for Mapes where you could never hope to take in all the toys on offer. It was better than any toyshop in Edinburgh even when they got in their big displays at Christmas time. At Mapes, every day was like Christmas time. I remembered last year studying the window every day for the entire fortnight only to notice on the very last day that they had the brand-newly released Corgi toy, which was an American station wagon ambulance, nothing like the uninteresting ambulances we had in Scotland. The problem was I had no pocket money left by the last day and I had used up all my credit with my parents. Caleb, my brother, had just left school and was now working as a laboratory trainee. He had lots of money now. He bought me the ambulance. His standing with me, although we were seven years apart in age, was always high. From that day onward, it was sky high.

This year was going to be hugely different, however. Caleb had gained permission from our parents to stay in Edinburgh with our aunt rather than going to Millport. I strongly feared that the fumes in this chemical lab of his must be systematically rotting his brain. How else could anyone in their right mind opt out of Millport? I wondered how much of a difference his absence might make this year. After all, we always spent most of our time together. Our parents were not really the adventurous or sporty types. My mother could never scramble over rocks even if her life depended upon it and my dad could just about kick a football, but not very well. In addition, he did not know the names of the Edinburgh Waverley players whom Caleb and I sought to emulate in our pretend games. That certainly might be a different kind of match without Caleb. And, what about the beach? We always went to the beach in the afternoon after our window-shopping interlude when our parents finally got up from the lunch table and ventured out mid-afternoon. Our parents, however, never went anywhere near the inviting, but generally freezing, water of the Firth of Clyde. They just wanted to sit in deckchairs and read newspapers or paperback books. Where was the excitement in that? It was always Caleb and I who would race each other to see who could be first into the water. Even though he was seven years older, I always made it first because I was fast; boy was I fast! I had won first place in all my races in the school sports. Perhaps he *did* slow up a bit on the approach to the water's edge, but that did not matter. When we had tired of swimming, we were given money to hire a rowing boat and set off on voyages of discovery. He mostly did the rowing because he seemed to be able to steer the boat in a straight direction. I had a tendency to make it go around in circles and those oars seemed to splash us so much that it was just as well we were only wearing our swimming trunks. We were able to reach the Eileans, the two small islands of inexhaustible mystery, located just off the main beach. It definitely was useful having a big brother. Hmmm. That was going to be different too. I had not stopped to think about it before. Maybe I would not be allowed to go out in a rowing boat on my own.

The four days from Tuesday to Saturday were a troubling mixture of looking forward with excitement and growing doubt. Real doubt. The first doubt I could ever remember that might have an important bearing on me personally.

The journey, as usual, was just as exciting as things would be once we arrived at our destination. I would never tire of the thrill of riding in a steam train from Edinburgh Waverley station to Glasgow Queen Street station. We were in a single carriage with no corridor so there was no ability to walk up and down the train as there would be on the next one. But that did not mean I used the seat that had been purchased for me. I stood for the entire journey with my nose pressed against the window, catching fleeting glimpses of the farmlands and towns as they whisked by and, ever so often, involuntarily flinching from the billows of steam belching from the engine and rushing by the window. Without fail, my dad would say what he always said in this circumstance, 'Don't stand so close to the window, the steam from the engine will make your face dirty.' And, every time I fell for it and stood back momentarily. Just like when I got too close to our little television set at home and if we were watching a swimming contest or a sailing programme, he would say, 'Don't get so close, you will get splashed,' and I would always move back.

I was never much impressed by the fact that we had to change stations in Glasgow, from Queen Street to Central, to catch the train to Wemyss Bay. In a big city like Glasgow, you would have thought that they would have the brains to build one big station instead of two little ones. That means an unnecessary waste of time walking between the two, while risking life and limb crossing the busy Glasgow streets. Glasgow always seemed busier than Edinburgh to me.

The second train of the day was much different from the first. More and more trains were now becoming diesels rather than the wonderful steam variety. So much for progress! However, the one thing the diesels had going for them was that they had a corridor running from one to end to the other. That meant the one-hour trip seemed to take no time because I was constantly walking up and down the train, peering into carriages to see who was sharing my adventure. I assumed, of course, that everyone was bound for Millport but really Wemyss Bay was a destination in itself as well as a hub for steamers to a number of holiday resorts on the Clyde. On this part of the trip, I noticed the first impact of Caleb's absence. Usually I was allowed to wander up and down the train on my own, but Caleb was invariably sent to check on me and eventually ensure that we reunited with our parents as we pulled into Wemyss Bay. This time without Caleb, which had been exciting at first, proved to a bit of a frightening experience. I could not find my parents! As I sensed we were getting closer and closer to our destination, I frantically peered into every carriage to no avail. Had they got off somewhere? No, it was non-stop journey. Just as I was starting to panic, a familiar head popped out of a carriage some way ahead of me.

'Ah, there you are. We thought you had got off. You better come back now. We are almost there.'

I had recovered my composure by the time I took my seat for the first time all day.

The sail on the paddle-steamer *Talisman* was definitely one of life's great joys. Everybody seemed excited to be on board. There was music playing on the open deck when the sun was shining. People rushed to grab deck chairs, but I did not care because my intention, as always, was to explore the boat from top to bottom. This included the packed open deck for, indeed, the sun was shining this day, as my dad had predicted it would be, and the lower enclosed decks, where the less adventurous travellers gravitated. I always sneaked a peak into the very formal dining room where one could spend the entire sail enjoying an extensive meal served on starched, white linen with silver cutlery. Probably quite nice, but I always considered it a waste of precious time when there was so much else to see and do. Likewise, the bar only warranted very a quick look. It amazed me to see mostly men gulping down pints of beer as if their lives depended on it. They could not see or do what I was doing if they were just stuck in a crowded and smoky bar. I left the best for last before I would recommence the whole itinerary if time permitted. The bottom deck housed the engine room including a glassed observation area for the massive, thrashing paddles that propelled the steamer. I gazed in wonderment at the phenomenon of these big pieces of wood churning through the water to make the boat move. As usual, I was joined by lots of other kids, mostly boys, doing exactly the same. I wondered if later in life we all would move upstairs to the bar and another generation of boys would replace us.

Doubts concerning Caleb's absence that I had been wrestling with all week, were extinguished by mid-afternoon, however, once we actually set foot on the magical island. Mrs. Anderson was standing outside Barclay House waving a white handkerchief to welcome us, lest we might miss her and go to stay at another boarding house. Fat chance! My mother noted from a distance that Mrs. Anderson was looking well for her age, then remembering my ungracious observation during *Kidnapped* looked directly me and whispered, 'Don't you even dare,' without even enlarging on her thoughts.

I'd had decided not to wait about for the trunk to be opened and instead just set off, by myself of course, to explore the rock formations in front of Barclay House. I had only half listened to my mother's laboured warnings about being careful on my own. If truth be known, Caleb's absence had suddenly given me a new sense of self-importance. I was master of my own domain. I concluded that years later once I knew what the phrase meant.

Another thing that started in those first hours of independence that I never really acknowledged until several years later was that I started to talk to myself. Caleb was not there but I found I could carry on my usual banter about things we were seeing or things we planned to do as if he were there by simply talking inwardly to myself. That practice has continued to this day and has served me well in reaching the right decisions without fear of contradiction from Caleb or anyone else for that matter.

8

As the days of the first week passed, I found that not only were all the usual activities possible on my own, some were even better because I was in command. I had not realized that my brother had been in charge before. Even hiring a rowing boat had been achieved but at a high cost. My dad insisted on accompanying me on the voyage and somehow the evidence of pirates on the Eileans or the possibility of sharks watching our progress through the gentle waves did not seem to materialize as they had in previous years. Football was not the disappointment I thought it might be, however. My dad showed some dribbling and shooting skills that he had hitherto suppressed, but he was still not much of a goalkeeper and I soon tired of scoring goals. To make matters worse, he kept comparing my prowess to that of Edinburgh Waverley players of yesteryear whom I had never heard of. I definitely could be mistaken for Willie Somebody, who I only learned later in life had been my dad's hero in the 1930s!

I had, of course, been both surprised and overwhelmed with my parents' generosity in buying me several new toys from Mapes, including both new cars that I had previously earmarked. My mother made even me chuckle when she said that I deserved some new toys because they had rushed me into packing back in Edinburgh and it was not my fault that I had ended up short of toys when we had arrived in Millport! Was I clever or what?

One day we did something new! That was quite an event during our annual holidays. I would not be able to go out fishing in the evening because my brother was not here to take me, and my parents had always refused to fulfil this obligation. In truth, I was not too disappointed. It was always freezing cold in the open launch and I had never ever caught a single thing. Even Caleb's gesture one year to give me one of his fish with the promise that we would both confirm it as my catch had not succeeded in placating me. It had only set off a lifelong frustration regarding the hooking of a fish, or more precisely the failure to so do.

Therefore, it was no loss to miss the evening fishing trip, especially as it was replaced by an afternoon trip in the same launch from Great Cumbrae to its sister island Wee Cumbrae, to visit the lighthouse. Just the boat trip in warm sunshine, rather than in the bitterly cold darkening of the evening, would have been enough, but setting foot on the smaller island and scrambling over the rocks to examine the lighthouse and its surrounding buildings was the icing on the cake. Of course, my mother declined the invitation to scramble over the rocks and elected to stay on the launch, but my dad and I were at the very head of the group of tourists. Every night from the bay window of Barclay House, we could see the light swooping around from Arran to Bute to Cumbrae and on to the mainland in consistent circles. But now we were at the source, and a great adventure it turned out to be. The lighthouse keeper welcomed us and explained how it all worked. It seemed like a grand profession and you got your own island to live on to boot, for nobody else lived there permanently. My dad was a policeman and my brother was on his way to joining him on the force but I had no such inclination. For a few days at least, lighthouse keeper was a definite possibility for me.

Just when I thought I had exhausted everything there was to do in Millport, along had come the adventure to Wee Cumbrae. Perhaps inspired by that realization, I decided I would spend the rest of the holiday looing for new adventures to undertake for the first time. Little did I know what I was letting myself in for!

===000===

It all started with a woman. I was later to learn that was generally the pattern to life.

I was not looking for a new girlfriend. I already had one in Edinburgh. Paulina. I had previously sneaked out to the shops, bought a postcard, written it secretly while sitting on the pier, and posted it to her. However, I had some doubts about Paulina, I have to admit. She had been on holiday in Spain of all places and her postcard to me had not arrived by the time I left for Millport. In addition, she was in the year ahead of me in primary school (the beginning of a lifelong fascination with older women) and would now move up to secondary school next month. I would remain in primary school for another year. Would the relationship survive the separation? Maybe the lack of a postcard was the first indication? Anyway, I was more intent on making the relationship work than finding someone else when I spotted the little girl in the blue reefer jacket.

As West Bay Road rises to meet with Cardiff Street, Bute Terrace, and the Golf Road, there were two sets of tenement buildings enjoying a prominent position at the intersection. I was striding purposefully by, on my way to my daily examination of Mapes window, when I spotted her standing outside the door of one of the buildings. Boy was she ever cute! Small and dark haired with the nicest face I had ever encountered. Did she smile at me even? I stopped and tried to pluck up the courage to cross the road and say hello. Internal conversations must have gone on for an eternity because, by the time I had persuaded myself that speaking to her was the thing to do, and Paulina would never know in any case, just as I put a foot on the roadway to cross, an adult stepped out from the doorway and took her hand. The spell was broken. The smile, if indeed there had been one, vanished as she looked up into the stern face of the tall adult with the steely grey hair. I changed course by effecting something of an ice-skater's pirouette manoeuvre and, when I landed back on the pavement, I set off on my original journey as if I had never been interrupted. But, the little goddess in the blue reefer jacket had been well and truly observed and noted.

Over the next couple of days, I managed to pass the tenement building at the intersection at least a dozen times, but she was never standing at the doorway as she had been. Instead, I twice spotted her on the promenade, firmly taken in hand by the adult whom I assumed to be a mother, but I could never manoeuvre myself into a face-to-face meeting. On a third occasion, I definitely blew it. While standing next to Mapes window, I spotted them approaching me. A face-to-face was inevitable. At the last moment however, I glanced sideways and noticed new Subbuteo table soccer teams that had just arrived in the shop that very morning. My joy at seeing Edinburgh

Waverley, my favourite team, displayed was instantly destroyed when I glanced back and found that the little girl in the blue reefer jacket had passed me by. As I spun on my heels, all I could see was the back of her head. Then the head turned to briefly look at me but was just as quickly returned to the forward position by a tug on the hand. The chance was lost, at least for the meantime.

By now, each day was devoted to some of the usual activities and a whole lot of trying to nail a meeting with the little girl in the blue reefer jacket. Even my parents noted how self-sufficient I had become in the absence of my brother. They seldom saw me except for meals. I got the feeling they had been dreading the thought of having to amuse me all day long and that was now obviously not required. I even saw them one day slipping into Frasers Bar for a late morning drink, something I had never seen before. My impression of my parents was that alcohol had been imbibed on Hogmanay and Hogmanay only, a necessary ritual to usher in a prospectively prosperous new year. I was kind of amused and wished Caleb had been present to share my secret.

The Millport of those days was crowded with holiday-makers on their annual two-week break from work and the humdrum of living in big cities, usually located in the west of Scotland. We were unusual in that we came from the east coast. I never met anybody else who came from Edinburgh but that was alright because I was intrigued by the people of the west with their sing-song accents and determination to have a good time. The island people went out of their way to entertain the visitors. There were events, concerts, and competitions every day and I was always determined to participate in as many as I could. One that was I born to be part of, well in addition to the races on the beach and around the island, football matches, treasure trails, and bicycle relays, was the window-shopping quiz. You were given a list of clues and had to locate a specific item in a shop window which was then to be written down next to the clue. As I spent a fair part of each day gazing in shop windows anyway, I was a natural for the competition and could even frequently provide the answer to the clue directly from memory. A completed list and first in your age-group brought the reward of something as simple as sweets or a stick of Millport rock to add to the satisfaction of winning.

On one such quest, I was doing extremely well and had almost completed the list when I ran straight into the little girl with the blue reefer jacket. I immediately noticed she was not doing quite as well in finding the answers and realized that opportunity was knocking loud and clear to make her acquaintance properly.

'Hello. We meet again. How are you doing in the hunt?

'Not very well. There are an awful lot of windows to look in.'

'Have you not been looking in them all week? I have. I can almost recite some of the stuff just from memory. Look at my list.'

'I am not normally allowed out on my own and my mother doesn't have much time for the shops, except maybe the food shops.'

'How about I give you the answers I've got and that will get you completed quicker?'

I was keen to see the effect of this magnanimous gesture on my part, noting with a little unease that I had never even contemplated her having an answer that I did not have. However, this tender establishment of a relationship was instantly dashed without her response ever being forthcoming.

Her mother appeared as if she had been hiding among the crowds just waiting to pounce.

'I think you have had enough time on your little game. Did you enjoy it? Now give me your hand. We need to get to the greengrocer before he shuts for lunch.'

And in an instant she was gone. This one-sided conversation between them had taken place as if I were invisible and, before I could collect my wits; all I could see were their backs. I thought I might have heard a muffled 'bye', but I could not be sure.

The whole enjoyment of the game was lost for me and I think I just let my list fall to the pavement. I wandered aimlessly along the quieter, seaward side of the promenade, wondering just why it was

13

so difficult to get to know someone. I resolved to give up the chase and place all my faith in Paulina. However, by the time I had reached the Crocodile Rock--that brightly painted rock that looked just like a beast emerging from the sea--I had changed my mind. I was not going to give up that easily. I would track down whatever her name was; I did not even know that. Yes, "the normal programme was going to be resumed", as I had heard recently stated on television. In this case, I would resume my search. I even determined to go find my list of answers and resume the game. That was not so easy. By the time I got back to the location of the unfulfilled meeting, my discarded list was gone. Somebody had struck it lucky. A prize almost presented to them on a platter without having to do anything. But I cared not about the game if the little girl could ultimately be snagged.

Well into our second week of the fortnight, the breakthrough came. Well, sort of. On passing the tenement building for at least the fifth time that day, I was taken aback when a blue reefer jacket appeared in the doorway, stopped, and most pointedly stared my way. I hesitated but only for a millisecond; I was not going to blow it this time. A most obvious smile directed my way only reinforced my determination as I strode across the street with minimal large steps.

'Hello there. I have been hoping to meet you again. My name is Calum. When is yours? I mean what is yours? Your name I mean. What is it?' I stammered and felt my face redden.

I was met with the sweetest smile and then a kind of shy burying of the head into her shoulder.

'Go on. Tell me your name. Do you fancy doing something?'

'Ok.'

I never did learn whether the ok was to indicate a willingness to reveal her name or a desire to do something together. At that second, the door swung open and the mother stepped out, took one look at me, grabbed the little girl's hand, and gave forth.

'What do you want? I have seen you hanging about.'

14

Boy, she was even more formidable on this side of the street than she appeared from the other.

If my face reddened before, it felt like it had now gone a deathly pale. I tried for words, but they would not come. I tried a little smile from adult to child and back to adult, but it came out as a cross between a grimace and the precursor to an impending vomit.

I gulped, 'just saying hello.'

'Well, hello....and goodbye. We don't want to be bothered by the likes of you. Off you go now.'

And with that, I was summarily dismissed and left to wonder just exactly what the "likes of me" amounted to. I tried to sneak a last look at the little girl in the blue reefer jacket but only succeeded in looking straight at the adult. The look on that face was enough. I turned tail and made off toward the West Bay, feeling like I had encountered a dragon and, unlike St. George, I had failed miserably to deal with it. I was not even consoled by a little voice;

'Aw mum.'

That voice was quickly silenced.

'Never you mind that nonsense. C'mon, we are late for your appointment.'

With that, they set off at a pace along Bute Terrace, which I was able to confirm, once I had plucked up the courage to look around.

'Fucking Hell' was an expression that had lately come into vogue among my pals back home and it was given out at high volume and to good effect as I suddenly stopped retreating. A passing couple tut-tutted at the profanity without knowing anything about its justification. There and then, I decided to turn around and make pursuit, as I had seen some of my detective heroes do on television. Perhaps this appointment that had been mentioned would shed some light on things.

I soon realized that Bute Terrace, as a fairly straight street, offered little in the way of cover for me. This necessitated me constantly dodging in and out of gardens whenever I thought either

15

of my subjects might be on the verge of turning around. This seemed to be causing consternation to the same tut-tutting couple who unfortunately had also chosen Bute Terrace for their afternoon walk.

'Not only does he have a foul mouth, I would be surprised if he isn't a burglar. They are getting younger and younger.'

Overhearing the assessment, I turned and hoped that a shrug of the shoulders and an innocent smile might alleviate their concern. I suspect it didn't.

Mother and daughter continued their forced march. I could see them approaching what I knew was the island primary school. That seemed odd. Surely, the school was closed for the summer holidays. Sure enough, they walked past and carried on to a group of large stone buildings encircled by a high wall. I could not remember ever noticing those buildings before, even though they were just behind the Garrison House and I had been in there several times to enjoy the delights of Andy's Snack Bar. This was something else and had quite a spooky look about it. I think they call it a gothic look.

They followed the line of the wall for a bit then suddenly disappeared through an archway into the grounds. The day was overcast and even though it was only late afternoon, the grounds had an ominous look about them. I caught up and surreptitiously peered through the archway but could just make out two figures climbing steps and entering the largest of the buildings. Though the heavy door closed behind them, I could not summon up the courage to follow them into the grounds, so I decided to stop at the archway and watch what happened from there.

Nothing happened. I soon hopped from one foot to another because I needed to pee. But I could not risk walking down to the toilets I knew to be in the Garrison House, in case I missed the girl and her mother. Nor could I contemplate a swift pee against the wall because something told me that this was a religious place and the largest building had the look of a strange church about it. I might be a foul-mouthed burglar but there was a limit to the scope of my indiscretions.

Still nothing happened. I had chosen not to wear the watch I had received for my last birthday during the holidays for fear of immersing my hand in seawater during one of my adventures and wrecking it. But I could sense it was getting late. Days were long in July and the sun was far from setting, but it did not seem to be able to find its way into these heavily treed grounds and that made it seem all the later. And, my stomach was telling me that dinner time had arrived if not already passed. And, did I mention my now desperate need to pee? It might have made sense to abandon the surveillance at this stage. Yet, I stayed where I was and maintained my routine of popping my head around every so often to look though the archway toward the door of the largest building. I could no longer see the door in the gloom; in fact, I could only barely make out the outline of the building.

Yet, still nothing happened. I was forced to concede to the demands of the bladder. By now it was getting dark in the street and was quite dark in the grounds, so I quietly entered through the archway. Turning my back to the barely visible buildings, I relieved myself against the wall. As that relief swept across me like someone lifting a heavy boulder off my shoulders, something made me turn around. The door at the top of the stairs to the largest building had been half-way opened and light was now cascading out in a limited beam, but enough to make things out. I decided I better get the business done in double quick time before I got caught by those about to exit the building.

I then heard some rustling of leaves behind me and naturally turned around again. A figure was walking toward me, not from the top of the steps, but instead no more than ten feet away. I could make out a small person, most likely a female, dressed from head to toe in grey, with a white edge to a large hood that was covering the head, including her face. Onward she walked until she was almost within touching range of me.

'Fucking Hell,' emitted for the second time today.

I could not make it to the archway, so I had no choice other than to creep in the opposite direction, alongside the wall and deeper into grounds. The lady in grey stopped and seemed to be staring in the direction of the archway. That was good for me. I ducked down low and made my way toward the steps that led to the half open door, with the intention of hiding behind the staircase. I made it and got down on my haunches, believing myself to be out of sight from anybody coming down the steps and from the lady in grey as she seemed to continue to stare toward the archway and the wall. Surely there was no way she could see the damp patch on the wall in this ever-fading light.

My adopted position was not the most comfortable and I was trying to decide what was to be my next move if nothing else changed when, horror of horrors, the lady in grey suddenly wheeled around and slowly started to head toward the steps. I could not move for fear of being seen and there was a good chance she was going to be able to spot me when she reached the bottom of the steps. Slowly, she walked my way, her head somewhat bowed within her hood and her hands nowhere to be seen as they were enveloped in long, wide sleeves. She was quite small, definitely about the height of the little girl, now without her blue reefer jacket. Had I guessed correctly?

On and on she came as I froze to the spot. Suddenly the heavy door at the top of the steps was slammed shut, causing the light projected on the steps to be extinguished. I glanced up and could barely see, but was pretty sure that nobody had come out so the door must have been shut from the inside. Now, I turned to face the threat from the opposite direction.

The visibility was not good but the lady in grey was nowhere to be seen. She had been almost on top of me and now she had vanished. I needed no second bidding to seize my opportunity for escape.

I took off across the leaf-strewn grounds, under the archway, and down College Street toward the promenade at considerable pace. This was commendable, considering I was simultaneously ensuring that all the important parts were again safely contained within my jeans after my untimely interruption, and I was carrying on an animated conversation with myself.

'She must have become a nun. The little girl in the blue reefer jacket has become a nun. I have missed my chance.'

Once I reached the promenade, I slowed down a bit but still headed for home without delay. It was not as dark out in the open, but I could still see that it was way beyond dinner time.

Even as I rounded Crichton Street, having taken the lower route rather than going by the infamous intersection and tenement at the top of Cardiff Street, I could see Barclay House over two hundred yards away with a small group of people gathered outside. That did not bode well I thought. I wondered if Calum Davies might be on the agenda for discussion.

As I raced up, all heads turned toward me and I could see my parents, Mrs. Anderson, and the local policeman.

'There he is now.'

'Calum Davies. Where on earth have you been?'

'You have missed dinner completely. What were you thinking?'

'Have you been in trouble, son?'

I decided to try to answer all the questions with one explanation that came to me in the instant that I gasped to catch my breath before opening my mouth.

'I am sorry. I went for a walk around the island and I forgot how far it was. It took a lot longer than I remember when Caleb and I walked it last year.'

I could see angry faces transforming into concerned faces, so I added a bit of drama for good effect.

'Then, I got a stitch, so I had to sit down for a bit near the Lion Rock and, of course, that made me even later. I am really hungry!'

At that point, the group broke up and I was ushered indoors with several hands on my shoulders by way of protection and indication that no punishment was about to befall me.

'No harm done this time,' pronounced the policeman. 'But next time, make sure you go with an adult.'

'He is missing his brother. He still wants to do all the same things he usually does on the island, but he is still a bit young,' opined my mother, and my dad nodded.

'The wee lamb must be famished. Good job we kept his dinner in the oven,' announced Mrs. Anderson with by far the most important words of those offered.

Not much was made of my misadventure and, after eating a hefty dinner, I expressed the need for an early night and took off to bed much earlier than normal. Any thoughts I had of a good, long, refreshing sleep were dashed, however. I lay awake for what seemed like most of the night going over and over in my head the events of the day just passed. I knew I had seen the little girl in the blue reefer jacket and her mother go through the archway and enter the building at the top of the stairs, and I also knew that they had not returned because I had never left my observation post. That was, they had never appeared until the nun attired all in grey had approached me. What a fright she had given me! And, what disappointment! I did not know an awful lot about nuns, but I knew they generally did not make good girlfriends, even for a holiday period. My thoughts turned again toward Paulina. I still wondered what was going on there. But I could not get the little girl in the blue reefer jacket out of my mind.

===000===

Next morning, my mother took me aside for a conspiratorial whisper.

'If you want to go another walk today, that is ok. But, why not ask your dad to go with you? He is feeling a little bit left out now that you have become so independent with Caleb not here. I know he would like to be asked.'

It was not a bad idea and I had in mind to find out more about the mysterious walled buildings without creating too much of a fuss, so an innocent conversation on a walk with my dad seemed to be the perfect opportunity. We opted to walk around by the coast road to Fintry Bay and return by the walk through the farms to the golf course and be back in good time for lunch as well. Of course, I was thought to have already covered half of that walk yesterday but neither of them seemed to notice. Millport was the kind of place where repeat activities were inevitable.

The walk to Fintry seemed to pass in no time as I chattered away about everything under the sun, except the key topic which I was reserving for the return trip. I noticed my dad was much more relaxed and chattier than he was at home, where he always seemed to be rushing to do something or other in the little spare time available to him. He worked as a policeman on a shift system, so there were many days when he was at work or sleeping because he had been on night shift. He called it being at his spiritual home when he was in Millport and attributed his relaxed demeanour to that fact. I thought that was a neat description that I might adopt for my own use in the future.

As we headed up the hill out of Fintry on the always muddy farm track, I moved into curiosity mode.

'You know those big grounds with the walls and the buildings inside, on College Street, behind the Garrison House. Do you know what they are?'

'That is the Cathedral of the Isles and it has some sort of religious college attached to it. That is why it is called College Street I suppose.'

'Have we ever been inside?'

'I have, years ago. I don't think you have.'

'And the cathedral is just like a regular church?'

'Well not quite. It is a famous cathedral because it is the smallest in Europe. It has services on a Sunday.'

'How come we never go?'

'Your mother would like to, just like we do at home. But we decided you and Caleb would be reluctant to give up even a small part of your holiday, so we never did.'

'That was a good decision.'

'I thought so too! In any case, it is not the same church as the one we go to. We are Presbyterian or Church of Scotland.'

'You know I was walking by it last week and I thought I saw some nuns. I did not know there were any nuns in Millport.'

'Nuns? I think you must be mistaken. There are no nuns in Millport that I know of. Unless they were on their holidays from someplace else, like us,' he laughed and drew a laugh from me too, although I was none the wiser on the nun in grey.

'In any case,' he continued, 'I think all the nuns are part of the Catholic Church. The Cathedral of the Isles is Episcopalian. They are different from the Catholics and from us, but I don't remember them having any nuns. You were learning about all that stuff in school, remember? The Reformation and all that.'

'Mmm. John Knox and Martin Luther. I maybe need to find out some more about these nuns.'

'I wouldn't lose any sleep over it. I don't think you saw nuns. If it was last Thursday, it was probably a group of women in plastic raincoats. Remember it rained that day?'

As he laughed again, I noticed we had arrived at the foot of the Golf Road. The walk had passed by in no time due to our conversation and now we were at the infamous intersection and the tenement. I glanced sideways and was kind of relieved to see nobody at the door to the building.

I had enjoyed my chat with my dad, even though the mystery remained unsolved. If I had been a bit older, I might have asked if he fancied a pint in Frasers Bar before lunch. Instead, I asked if he fancied an ice cream to which he agreed, and we continued down Cardiff Street to the Ritz Cafe.

The remaining couple of days of our holiday went without incident. In spite of the reality that there was not now likely to be a holiday romance with the little girl in the blue reefer jacket, I still chose to pass by the tenement whenever I was heading to or from the town centre, but I did not see her again. Nor did I see her anywhere else on the island. That appeared to suggest that she had indeed become a nun and was now confined within those high walls. My dad unexpectedly offered an opportunity to confirm that suggestion when he asked if I would like to visit the Cathedral of the Isles on our last full day, to take advantage of a special opening for tourists. To his and my mother's surprise, I readily agreed. Before that, I made a concerted effort to make sure I had done all the things that it was possible to do on the Isle of Cumbrae and within the town of Millport. An exhausting schedule had to be somewhat truncated when the Friday brought rain again. However, I was quite insistent that we should fulfil our obligation to tour the cathedral, with the rationale that most of the tour would be indoors. My dad somewhat reluctantly had to agree and showed some sign of regretting ever having made the suggestion in the first place. But, go through with it we did.

For once, my mother accompanied my dad and me along the promenade toward the cathedral. I was surprised, after we had turned up College Street, that we did not go through the all-so-familiar-to-me archway, but instead continued to walk up the gentle incline until we met a road that turned into the grounds. I was informed that the archway really led to the backdoor of the cathedral and that this road was the main formal entrance. That was news to me. The road wound through the wooded grounds and eventually arrived at a small courtyard onto which the main door of the cathedral, the main door of the college building, and the main door of an adjacent building that sort of looked like it had rows of bedrooms, opened. All along the walk, my eyes had been shifting from side to side, in the hope of seeing the nun in the grey habit, or perhaps some of her colleagues, but the grounds were deserted apart from a couple of other tourists headed in our direction.

We were met by the director of music for the cathedral, who was to be our tour leader. I learned that construction of the cathedral had begun in 1849 and it opened in 1851. The college had come along later and the dormitories later still, to accommodate visitors spending several days in religious study or contemplation. Our guide mentioned the other permanent residents of the complex, of whom there were precious few, but made no mention of any nuns. I did not bring up the subject and was relieved that both my parents chose to keep quiet on the subject too. The tour was quite interesting and the small cathedral itself was quaint, yet in stark comparison to the giant St. Giles Cathedral in Edinburgh, the only other cathedral I had ever visited. However, we were assured that the Cathedral of the Isles had all the necessary trappings that St. Giles had, and its congregation and priests were obviously rather proud of its status as the smallest cathedral in Europe.

At the conclusion of the tour, our guide suggested we could leave the cathedral by the back door and take the steps down to the alternative exit through the archway. Things were beginning to whirr in my mind. Was it possible that the little girl in the blue reefer jacket and her mother had entered by the exit and exited by the entrance, thereby failing to encounter the trusty detective stationed at his chosen spot? I was further confused when we closed the backdoor to the cathedral, and I saw a notice affixed to it which advertised confirmation classes on each of the next three Tuesdays from 4 pm to 5 pm. The great nun mystery had been on Tuesday past and the appointment in the cathedral had obviously been for around 4 pm as far as I could remember. Hmm, curious I thought.

One thing was clear, however. There had been no mention of nuns or any evidence as to their existence. However, that did not change the fact that I had witnessed one, and I thought I knew her previous identity. What was this confirmation all about? I had heard of kids of my age being confirmed, but I did not know what it involved. It was doubtful it was about becoming a nun because one of my pals in Edinburgh had gone through it and he hadn't become a nun, or a monk for that matter. He had said it was just something his parents forced him to do, as usual.

The final night of our holiday climaxed with the long-promised fish suppers from the Deep Sea restaurant. My brother had often claimed that the Deep Sea was the best in the world. How he knew I did not know, but I had never been inclined to argue with him. As my dad and I savoured the delights contained in the newspaper wrappings, and burned our fingers into the bargain, my mother complained that the newspapers made your fingers dirty and would contaminate the food. Such scrupulous attention to detail did nothing to diminish our pleasure, but she seemed to succeed in putting herself off. As a result, she passed her supper to me to finish off and I was only too happy to help her out.

Another wonderful holiday had been enjoyed. I was looking forward to getting home to my pals. I was looking forward, with some trepidation, to finding out what was up with Paulina. Hopefully, my postcard was sitting on the doormat waiting for me. And I was looking forward to regaling my brother with all the neat things he had missed, and I intended to start immediately in altering his thinking about not coming to Millport next year. Two things were sure in my mind: that there would be another year, 1961 in fact, and that there would be another Millport visit.

Next morning, we saw the steamer trunk packed with great difficulty and collected for its four-day trip home. I seemed to have acquired a lot of new clothes and toys in the last two weeks, which caused the difficulty in snapping the trunk shut. We said our goodbyes to Mrs. Anderson. I wondered again just how old she was, but I never imagined for one minute that she would not be there waiting for our arrival next year. She always insisted on giving me a slobbery kiss in spite of my best efforts to get out of Barclay House ahead of everyone else. I failed again this year and then she whispered in my ear.

'Don't you go getting yourself lost in that big city of Edinburgh like you did on our wee island,' she said through a phlegmatic cackle.

I protested that I had never at any time been lost but this was subsumed by the cackle.

As we walked toward the pier to catch the steamer, my dad said we could go the hilly way up to the intersection and down Cardiff Street because we had plenty of time. We usually went around by Crichton Street. I never thought much about the choice of route. My mind was on the steamer and the trains ahead.

We reached the intersection and I looked across the street. There she was! The little girl in the blue reefer jacket, not a grey habit, was standing in her doorway. Our eyes very clearly met. My parents were chatting about something and so I don't think they even noticed her. What would she do? What should I do?

As if to conceal any action, lest her mother suddenly appear as she had a habit of doing, the little girl maintained a stiff arm but gave a little wave of the hand at the end of it. Oh, and she also turned on the cutest smile; and then off again.

Without breaking stride, I reciprocated the stiff-arm, almost secret, flick-of-the-wrist wave. And, I returned the smile, maybe holding it on for a little longer in a brazen act of bravado.

Then we turned down Cardiff Street and headed for the pier.

===000===

I now shake my head in surprise that I would have such vivid recollection of that summer of 1960, and the little girl who spent the entire two weeks wearing her blue reefer jacket, irrespective of the weather - excepting when she might have been wearing a grey nun's habit, trimmed in white around the hood. Here I am sitting in the Crab Pot Pub in Victoria, British Columbia, Canada and the best part of forty years has passed since that mysterious episode.

I am spending a quiet Sunday afternoon all on my own, enjoying a pint and reading a newspaper I have brought along for the occasion. The family members are all doing their own thing, which has become increasingly common, and so it is not unusual for me to head down to the Pot once I have finished marking accounting papers. The newspaper I have brought along and, in fact, the reason why my thoughts have been driven all the way back to 1960, is the Scottish Sunday Post and an unusual story it carries, typical of the stories it carries every week. Little folksy stories of days gone-by in Scotland. The Post does not pretend to be the purveyor of the latest news. It looks backwards with perpetually heavy sentiment and sometimes forward with unbridled optimism and I, like countless Scots at home and abroad, have read it all my life. At one time, it was reckoned to have the largest newspaper circulation per capita in the world. And that did not include the vast number of copies that were recycled to relatives living outside Scotland. My brother Caleb, since my dad passed away and my mother has entered a sad late period of her life where she is not an active player, physically or mentally, has picked up the mantle and now sends me the newspaper every week. It arrives about ten days after its publication date, but that does not matter because the Sunday Post does not dwell on contemporary news much at all.

I turn my attention to my second pint of dark ale. It is good that Canada has finally caught up with Britain and pubs now offer a variety of beers, not just the European pilsner type that was about all you could get in the 1980s when I first immigrated. It tastes so good that I quaff half of it in one swallow. Then I pick up the Sunday Post again to re-read the story that has caught my attention. But I am no more than two lines into the story when my mind wanders back to 1960 again.

I wonder what has become of the little girl with the blue reefer jacket. Even if she did not instantly become a nun, she still had made a lasting impression on me. She is one of two women who have remained with me all my life, even though I have never got to know either one or have never seen either again. The other was Heather Randall in high school. For some reason I have never forgotten them, and they frequently come into my thoughts for no particular reason.

I have to confess that my fears at that time about Paulina were not ill-founded. There was no postcard waiting for me when I arrived back in Edinburgh. I never saw her again that summer and then she was off to the big school in the autumn. One year later, of course, I moved up to the same school, but by then, our relationship had evaporated. Strangely enough, I was later to encounter Paulina for a third time in my life when she joined my accounting firm, Brookes, as a trainee accountant like myself. However, accountancy was not for her and the last I heard was she had moved permanently to Spain, the very spot where the demise of our relationship had first taken root.

I had reasoned that the little girl in the blue reefer jacket may well be a local, not a tourist, if she were attending classes to prepare for confirmation, but in succeeding visits to Millport, though I did not track her with quite the same zeal as in the first year, I never saw her again. It is funny how something sticks with you so long. I was in Millport just last year and could not help looking over to the doorway of the tenement every time I passed it. Was I really expecting a blue reefer jacket attired individual to be standing there?

Many things have changed in my life and yet some have remained exactly the same. Millport is still my obsession as it was as a child. It just takes longer to get there now. My wife and children have been won over, although their enthusiasm to visit every couple of years might be down more to merely humouring me; I am not sure. My brother Caleb has turned out to be an odd one. In spite of his previous enjoyment of our annual holidays, not only did he opt out in 1960, he has never set foot on the island again in his life to date. Somehow he developed other interests and they did not include Millport. I could never quite understand his change in attitude, but I am still able to cherish our earlier memories. Strangely enough, my parents never set foot on the island again either. My dad got sick and after hanging on for a couple of tough years he passed away just as I was becoming a typical troubled and troublesome teenager. My mother has lived a long life to this day, but somehow has never been inclined to do any of the things on her own that she had previously done with my dad, including visiting Millport. As soon as I was permitted, I resumed my visits, and now with the group of pals that had been suitably indoctrinated, but I never saw Mrs. Anderson again. I assume she might have died not long after our 1960 visit, but I could not be sure. I really should have checked into it on one of my visits, but I was content to just let her reside in my memories.

I think back to the little girl. She will be a big girl now. I wonder what she has done with her life. Was confirmation all that she thought it would be? Perhaps like my pal, she had been merely forced into it by her mother. I recall that mother being of the truly forceful type, so that might well have been the reason. At least I now know finally that she did not become a nun. I sort of have the Sunday Post to thank for that. I have never really believed that she became a nun, but I could never be totally sure until now. I doubt that she could have continued to live on the island even if she had been a resident. The population was never that large and surely I would have seen her again, if only one time, on my many visits. So, where might she have gone? Her blue reefer jacket has had a lasting impression on me too. I always promised myself that I would buy myself a similar jacket and even though I have admired them on others and looked at them frequently in stores, I have never done so yet. Perhaps it is destined to remain in the memory and nowhere else.

I shake my head, finish my beer and hold up my glass to signal the bartender for a refill, and proceed to read the story in the Sunday Post again.

In the mid-19th century, a Mrs. Mackenzie of All Saints Church in Edinburgh, founded the Community of St. Andrew of Scotland to do God's work. The Sisterhood of St. Andrew was a small group of Episcopalian nuns associated with that community. There! My dad was wrong! There were nuns in churches other than the Catholic Church. That does not surprise me because I now know the Anglicans and Episcopalians to be quite similar to the Catholics, and their split from Rome during the Reformation was more about differing opinions on management and organization than it was about religious dogma. The group of nuns operated out of various places in Edinburgh, then set up their own headquarters in Joppa, at that time a small village just outside of Edinburgh. Their primary purpose was to provide help and support to the fallen women of the area, of whom there were probably many at that time.

By the early part of the 20th century, the Sisterhood begins to wind down. The story does not reveal why, perhaps a lack of funds, and no new nuns are admitted. The existing members remain for a while in Joppa, in quiet, contemplative retirement, but in 1919 their accommodation has to be sold and the group is dispersed. This is where it gets interesting.

Apparently, some of the nuns are sent to the Cathedral of the Isles in Millport to see out their days. They spend almost ten years there, and because they are now all quite elderly, at least one passes away on the island. In 1927, the remaining members are transferred back to Edinburgh for some reason, and it is reported that the last remaining member of the Sisterhood of St. Andrew dies in Oxford in 1949.

It is the sidebar story to the main piece that really catches my attention. Since those days in the 1920s, it has long been held that the grounds and buildings of the Cathedral of the Isles are haunted by one of the nuns who died there. She is spotted from time-to-time wandering in peaceful contemplation, much in the same way as she would have done when she was alive. The nuns of the Sisterhood of St. Andrew were known to be dressed from head to foot in grey, with a white trim on their voluminous hoods, which were different from most other holy orders. I am almost tempted to utter that expletive that has invaded my story two times already! But I show restraint and merely ruminate about what I have read. I did not dream about the lady in grey. I did not dream any of it. It had all happened. But by 1960, there were no nuns in Millport. Only a reported ghost of one. Ergo, I must have seen the ghost. There is no other logical explanation for it.

I read on. To this day, while the cathedral is famous and much visited by church-goers and tourists alike, the Episcopalian Church chooses not to make much of the legend. Nevertheless, it is well known by locals, and those who have been fortunate enough to have witnessed the apparition that wanders the grounds and buildings to this day.

Well there you are. I must be one of the fortunate ones. I am not sure I considered myself fortunate at the time, but at least it cleared part of my mystery once and for all. My little girl in the blue reefer jacket had not instantly become a nun. I had just seen a ghost while rooted in my stake-out all those years ago. It is as simple as that.

I toast the memory of both ladies and take another drink of ale.

The Strange Case of the Mysterious Engineer

The four band members and their trusty number-one roadie piled out of the London train at Glasgow Queen Street station. Dubus had arrived home. Well almost, they still all lived in and around

Edinburgh. Save for their cherished instruments which they carried by hand; all the rest of their equipment would be making its way north in a van driven by roadie number-two.

Evan Davis was not intent on heading to Edinburgh just yet. He was tall and thin with a curly mop of hair once likened to a wheat field in a storm. He wore a leather jacket over bright red shirt and trousers, as usual. David Rich was the best musician among them, but he was burdened with a very deep personality. He and Evan were the driving force of Dubus and its main composers. He dressed all in black, including a cape that would have been highly pretentious on anyone else, but somehow it fitted in with his dark hair and often dark mood. Alex McCann, who swung between being spaced out and just plain happy-go-lucky, blinked and looked around. He never took the band or anything it did very seriously. He was small, dressed in denim, and looked nothing like a rock star. Brian Rodgers on the other hand worked tirelessly to epitomize the look of a rock star. He always dressed in the latest London fashions, which today consisted of a glam androgynous outfit that looked totally incongruous with the overall image of the band, but that was exactly what was intended. His hair was the longest and he sported a moustache long after the others had gone clean shaven again.

'This is the last chance. Let's just skip going to Millport. I am knackered and so is everybody else. Let's just catch the train to Edinburgh and Gus can take the equipment there,' Brian implored of his mates Evan, David, and Alex.

The leader of arguably Scotland's number one rock band looked from Brian to David and Alex and back to Brian. He could feel a debate coming on as they stood on platform number-two. Fortunately, there were no screaming girls to witness the discord among the band members. Those days were over. Even a passing porter simply muttered, 'Hi lads,' without even giving a hint that he recognized who he was talking to.

'We have talked about this at least ten times. Westview is only available for next two days, then it is booked solid for the next six weeks by Marty Allan and then the Blues Seekers. I really think we should at least lay down the basic track for "Sailing into the Sunset".

33

We are so close to completing the album. We only need two more tracks and then it will be done, and we can have a bit of a break.'

Brian whined on. 'We have been on the road throughout Europe for the last five weeks. We need a break now.'

'Look, the album is overdue. You know this business. Let yourself get out of the market for just a little bit too long and you will be forgotten. Then, it is helluva difficult to make your way back.'

The band frequently went through these kinds of debates. Although childhood friends, they had been making music together now for the best part of six years and, at times, what had started out as just a bit of fun had ultimately become a grind. The singles chart-toppers were now a thing of the past and the transition to becoming an albums band, which was necessary to survive as the new decade beckoned, had been difficult for them. They had also discovered that after the initial euphoria of being on the road, with all that the sex, drugs, and rock'n'roll scene had to offer, had worn off; they had become content to stay home, enjoy their modest riches, and record occasionally. However, sales of albums had been very uneven, and they had been persuaded that extensive gigging was necessary, and its reintroduction had brought added strain on the membership. Nobody in the band seemed to like both recording and performing; they each had a preference of their own. A long time ago when they had become a four-piece after letting the original bassist go, and Brian had laid down the tambourine and picked up the bass, they had decided that all future decisions that came to a vote would have a built-in tie-breaker. Evan was the acknowledged leader of the band and as such got an extra vote. Ergo, he knew that he had only to get one other member on side for the band to move in any direction he wanted. It was a powerful tool but one he used carefully because he continued to espouse the group ethic, even when he was all too aware of contemporaries turning into tyrants while leading bands or else doing the obvious thing and breaking up the band to go solo. He much preferred to reach consensus and usually that came about eventually. Today was starting to prove to be an exception. He looked at Alex. Alex was standing, looking around and seemed not to even be dialled into the conversation. He was the least inclined towards hard work but loved hanging out in Millport where he had a favourite supplier and several other distractions that made his life worth living. He then looked at David. David was the most serious yet introverted musician in the band. He was subject to wild mood swings. He seemed to like the gist of the new song, even though he had contributed very little to its composition. He liked to work in the recording studio more than performing on the stage. But he was also appearing pretty cranky after a tour of night-after-night gigs throughout France, West Germany, Holland, Belgium, and Italy. Evan decided to take a chance.

'I am tired too, Brian, but a couple of days of recording and mixing gets us that bit closer to the new album. I am also tired of standing on this platform. It looks like we are at the point where we have to vote. I have not heard anything from either of you guys. What do you think?'

'Come on, you two. Support me on this. We can always go back in the studio later, or even use another studio and then we would not have to be stuck on that stupid island of Evan's,' Brian pleaded.

Evan looked to Alex first and deliberately. Then he looked to David. Then he looked back to Alex.

'Ok. Let's just get it done. We can lay down the track in one day, Brian, and then you and I can take off. The other two are the ones that like to live in the studio anyway.'

'Thanks, Alex. We have a decision. There, you did not even have to vote unless you want to, David.'

David said nothing.

'Come on, Wally, let's get us into taxis and over to the Glasgow Central for the train to Largs. Dubus is on the march. Confirm with Gus to make straight for Largs with the equipment, just as I told him to earlier. If you help me with the last verse of "Sailing into the Sunset", Brian, I will give you a composing credit.'

Brian had been outvoted yet again. He would have to make the best of it yet again.

'Ok. You are on.'

That evening, Robert 'Wally' Walker had shepherded the band into the Miller's Stone Hotel in Millport and had deposited the equipment, brought by Gus, at the band's own recording studio at Westview, an imposing Victorian mansion just outside town with incredible views of Wee Cumbrae, Arran, and Bute.

The Stone was the place the band almost always stayed when recording, even though the Westview had bedrooms. Evan felt it was important to be able to take a physical break from the rigours of recording. Many a wild night had been spent in the Stone, whose owners Bob and Cassie MacFarland were gracious and tolerant hosts. Alex had taken to referring to the hotel as the Stoned for that was often the way he was in one its comfortable bedrooms.

'Come away in, lads. How was Europe?' Bob MacFarland asked. Cassie produced the keys for their usual rooms. Luckily it was March and the holiday season had not yet got underway, so availability of rooms was not an issue.

'There is a message for you from Hughie. His wife is sick, and he will not be able to make it down until the day after tomorrow. He says just to carry on. You all know how to twiddle the knobs. He will fix things up once he gets here.'

Hughie McLean was the resident engineer at Westview, but he kept a home in Dumbarton and that was where he was presently located, apparently with an ailing wife.

'Great,' exclaimed Brian, 'just what we need.'

'Don't worry. We will be just fine. Let's go have a drink if Mr MacFarland would kindly open the bar. I need one of Cassie's specially mixed vodka martinis,' declared Evan.

After their debut album, Evan and David had taken over production of all subsequent Dubus' recordings and the latter could also turn his hand to the work of the engineer, so Hughie's absence would not be a fatal blow. The two liked to spend a fair bit of time mixing after getting the tracks down and for that they did like to involve Hughie. But that would come on the second day.

===000===

Next morning, a somewhat bleary-eyed foursome made their way around to Westview. The quarter-mile walk was not as pleasant as it might have been on account of a bitterly cold east wind. However, heads were a bit clearer by the time they arrived at their destination.

Wally and Gus were waiting in the foyer for them, having arrived two hours previously to set up all the equipment.

'Hey, Evan, there is another engineer here--says that Hughie wants him to fill in,' Wally announced

'Hmm. Hughie never said anything in his message or else Cassie forgot about it. No matter. Let's meet him then.'

'Make some coffee will you, Gus. Some of us need a pick-me-up.'

'Will do, Alex.'

'I will need some water too.'

'You got it, David. Brian, any requests?'

'Got any inspiration, Gus?'

The band made their way into the cavernous studio which was carved out of half of the ground floor of the old residential home. The bay window, with its impressive 180-degree vista, had been retained when the studio was created. Evan argued that it was a source of inspiration when required. Others argued it was a distraction and so, during recording sessions, the window was frequently blacked out by heavy drapes. They looked around for the newcomer, but he was nowhere to be seen. Then, David noticed movement in the producer's booth and pointed in that direction.

'Hello. We are Dubus. You possibly know that. And who are you?'

'I know who you are, Brian. I am Earl. Pleased to meet you all.'

'How did you get the gig, Earl?'

'Hughie wanted me to fill in. I am an experienced recording engineer.'

'Well I have never heard of you, Earl.'

'But I have heard of you, David, and we will get on just fine. I hope you are in the mood to do some keyboards as well as drumming.'

'When did you last work, Earl? You seem a bit older than our usual engineers,' said Brian, and then added sotto voce, 'Like a hundred years older.'

Alex laughed. Brian flicked his long hair back in gesture of the confrontation he so much enjoyed. Evan grimaced, and then glared at Brian. Earl said nothing, as if no question had been asked or no skewer had been thrust into him.

David shrugged. 'Let's get down to business. Why don't you explain your song to us again, Evan, and Earl can get an idea what we are trying to do with it.'

'Ok. Here is the scoop. The new album so far has taken us away from country music, which Alex and Brian were demanding. I would call it a little bit of country-rock and a big bit of straight rock. I think it is shaping up quite well, but it needs something that ties the album to our old sound and sensibilities. I would like this to be a sea shanty, folk-rock thing, that takes us somewhat in yet another direction but also gives a solid nod to the past.'

'It is called 'Sailing into the Sunset,' I understand. What do the lyrics convey?' Earl asked casually.

The band members looked at each other and wondered how he even knew the name. The song had been written on tour and no mention of it had been made to the press anywhere. Even Hughie would not have been expected to be familiar with it.

'The sailing into the sunset thing is a metaphor for getting tired of the music business and wandering off somewhere else.'

'Cynical bastard. Are you trying break up the band?' demanded Brian.

'That's funny. Ha ha! I am probably the only one not trying to break up the band. It is a metaphor, Brian. Look it up in the New Oxford Dictionary and you will get the idea.'

'As long as it is not bloody country and western.' Alex asserted.

'As our illustrious leader cannot read or write music, perhaps he would be good enough to run through the song for us so we can all play on the same page.'

'That approach has served us well so far, David. You can tabulate it later for your usual royalty.'

Earl clapped his hands. 'Is this how you guys practise teamwork? Let's just pull together and we will get something juicy down for Hughie, when he comes in tomorrow. Evan, if you please. I assume you will use your twelve-string.'

Evan proceeded to quietly strum the guitar for almost a minute and then a strident 2/4 pattern emerged from the ringing steel strings. The verses spoke of the strain of life and the need to get away from it all and the chorus sparkled with a nautical vista of handling a sailboat heading out on a silvery sea. Just as the others were beginning to warm to the sounds, he stopped abruptly.

'I need a new last verse. I don't want the song to end negatively. I want it to be a rejuvenating message.'

Earl said, 'Sing the last verse as you have it now and then we will all work on it.' The musicians looked around at each other and smirked. They were used to being masters of their own domain. Even Hughie knew his place and only followed directions. Yet this old, pale, slightly stooped guy with the shock of white hair, appeared to be taking over the session.

The interesting thing was nobody, not even the normally taciturn David or the belligerent Brian, resisted the direction the session was taking. An hour later, a final verse had been composed to everyone's satisfaction, including the original composer, and each member had a clear sense of what they would be contributing.

When Dubus had first recorded, most of the songs had been done live in one take with no overdubbing. Only a few had utilized the available second track. Then, as their musicianship improved and their songs took on more complex structures, they eagerly embraced the evolving technology. The Westview studio had 16-track equipment and multiple layers could be recorded using the full capacity, as well as bouncing tracks onto other tracks. Dubus' technique was to create a mosaic of pieces, then stitch the pieces together into a final song. That meant each member could play numerous instruments and still allow space for their trademark complicated vocals. Their sound from the very beginning had been two-part harmonies, doubled-up with all four singing, over ringing twelve-string guitars. Even though their musical journey had meandered through folk to folk-rock and on to a sideways trip into psychedelia and then off the deep end into straight country and back to a fusion of rock and country that the critics had called country-rock, the sound had remained recognizable and loved. That was even though their days at the top of the hit parade seemed to be over.

'Hell's bells. I don't believe it. This is going to be the very first song that all four of our names are on as composers. Talk about brotherly love!' Evan exclaimed as he finished another run through, this time with the group effort on the final verse lyrics.

'Maybe there should be five names. Earl here had as much input as I did,' David offered.

'No. No. Not at all. That was a group effort. I am just the knob twiddler.'

Evan looked pointedly at Earl and asked, 'Have you had a composing credit before? David is right. You deserve one on this.'

'Never had one. Never looked for one. I don't need one on this, thanks all the same.'

'Ok, man. Your choice.'

The rest of the morning and afternoon progressed in an interesting and unusual way. The band members, who were notorious for not getting along with one another in the studio, were on their best behaviour. Earl was positioned throughout in the producer's box but used the intercom frequently to make suggestions and offer encouragement. Hughie never used the intercom unless Evan or David signalled him to do so.

The band worked very well collectively and soon had laid down a basic track. Then, each member added individual instrumentation while the others remained in the studio giving support. This too was unusual. The members' escalating antipathy toward one another meant that usually, when the group work was completed, only the soloist remained behind to do his piece, while the others found things to do elsewhere in Westview or even headed out of the building altogether. It seemed to Evan as if each of them wanted to hear what Earl had to say to the soloist and wanted to see how the soloist reacted, and that was why nobody left the studio.

It was very noticeable that Earl understood each different personality and approached each musician differently. Alex was easy going but he often got bored, particularly when asked to do a piece over and over again. Earl patiently coaxed a fine performance out of him on take twenty of his twelve string work, a guitar he had largely given up from the early days when his love for the blues started to play a more prominent part in his thinking. Brian did not really like being in the studio at all. The thrill of posing on the live stage was what he was all about. His studio work was often spotty and tended not to improve as the day wore on. But this time, he nailed what was required early on and Earl quickly recognized that. Brian craved recognition and Earl not only poured it all over him but also managed to get the others to do likewise without actually asking.

David the introvert could make or break the session depending on his mood. This day, he appeared to be suspicious of Earl at first and was also taking a backseat in the production, leaving all the work to Evan. David's indifference did not impair his drumming, which was always of the highest calibre, and a jazz-tinged take was soon in the can that seemed to complement the entire feel of the song. But plaudits from Earl and then the others seemed to be falling on deaf ears. Then, Earl suggested that David try some keyboards, but the latter felt the song would not be enhanced if they went in that direction. Evan begged to differ and suggested if David did not want to play keyboards then Brian, who was still learning piano, should have a go. That set David off for a bit. He did not have a high regard for Brian's playing of any instrument, but particularly the piano. Earl rescued the day by suggesting Brian do some piano while David use the Hammond organ, which was kept in the studio for other artists and seldom ever appeared on Dubus' recordings.

'I don't know, man. I can play that thing, but I just don't know if it will fit into the song.'

'Trust me,' said Earl. 'I just have a feeling you might be able capture the sense of the water lapping against the sailboat.'

'Hmm. Fair enough. I will give it a try.'

'Good man,' said Earl. 'If we don't think the organ works, we can always mix it out later on.'

'Same goes for the piano,' said Evan. At that point, he knew David was won over. Amazing thought Evan. It took twenty minutes. Often it took several days to persuade David to shift his position and sometimes he stuck to it until Evan had to give up. David was listening to Earl, just like the others.

The band very rarely did more than a four-hour stint in the studio at any one time, but as this session rolled along positively and creatively, it was almost 7 pm before Brian and Alex started to get restless and mentioned galloping hunger. Evan looked up at the clock. They had been going hard at it for eight hours. He agreed that they should wind up for the day. All four members were happy with what they had got down on tape. They were at a point where the mixing could begin tomorrow, when Hughie was due to arrive.

As the others set out back to the Stone, Evan announced that he wanted to stay on for a bit and try some mandolin to complement the ringing twelve strings on the chorus. That was not unusual for Evan. He frequently stayed behind and not only added things but also fixed mistakes by the others. Each recording was his baby and needed lots of TLC.

Earl suggested he would stay too. He wasn't hungry and had no other plans.

The two sat in the producer's box and listened several times to the almost completed track, in particular noting where the fusion of strident twelve strings came to prominence in the chorus.

'I think it might work to have the mandolin fade in and out in the middle of the twelve string breaks.'

'I understand you. Give it a try. The timing will have to be just right.'

Earl was so correct when he mentioned the timing. It was on the fifteenth take that Evan managed to come in and go out exactly right. Then, the two worked on the fade in and fade out to fuse the mandolin seamlessly with the guitars. Almost two hours later, Evan expressed satisfaction and shook hands with the engineer.

'I think we have cracked it.'

'Sounds good to me, Evan.'

'Ok. I think we can call it a night. We will let the others hear it tomorrow. If they don't like it, we can always go with tape of guitars only. But I think they will like it.' Evan clapped his hands and thought mischievously that it only takes one of them to like it.

'Are you staying at the Miller's Stone, Earl?'

'No. I am in one of the cottages here, behind the Westview.'

'You have done a tremendous job. How come I have not heard much about you? Where have you been working?'

'Well I have not done much work at all for quite a while. In the 50s, I started off with the BBC, believe it or not, and then I freelanced around the London studios for a while. In the early '60s I moved up to Edinburgh and did some work at the Alpine Studios.'

'Alpine? They used to be our label. In fact, they still distribute our stuff even though it goes out on our own label Cumbrae Wrecks. You can't have been there for a while. I am as often in the Alpine Studios as I am here.'

'Not much lately.'

'Who have you worked with? Anybody big?'

'Not really. Joe Diamond in London and the Crestas in Edinburgh. Do you remember them? They were supposed to be the next big thing.'

'Sure, man. They broke up a long time ago, but I think their bassist still does sessions at Alpine.'

'Jim Frazier?'

'Yes. That's him.'

'Jim was a good bloke.'

'Look Earl, I am starving. Are you not hungry? Why not at least come around to the Stone for some supper?'

'No thanks. I can grab something here.'

'Alright. I want to say it has been a pleasure working with you. We will see you in the morning.'

'I don't know. That will depend on Hughie.'

'Hey. Hughie does not call the shots. I would like you to be here in the morning around 10 or 11.'

'That's nice of you. I think I will stay a bit and tidy up some of the tapes and leave some notes for Hughie, just in case.'

'Up to you. I thought I was anal about recording but you have me beaten. Goodnight.'

===000===

When Evan walked into the hotel bar, Alex and Brian were roistering mightily with a couple of locals and the owners. David had consumed a quick supper and had retired for the night, which was not unusual for him. Wally and Gus had disappeared into the town of Millport to visit the haunts they were familiar with. They might or might not be back that night. Cassie had prepared a cold plate in advance for Evan, which he ate heartily while trying valiantly to catch up with the others on the drinking side.

'Quite a day, lads; don't you think?'

'Alex was just saying to me that the whole strange day was down to Earl. He seemed to make us want to work on and on. I don't think any of us have ever heard of him. In fact, I don't think we even know his second name.'

Bob, who kept a pretty close watch on things that happened at Westview because most of the participants ended up lodging at the Stone, confessed that he had never heard of an Earl being involved at the studio or anywhere else on the island.

'Well, Hughie should be around tomorrow, and he will be able shed some light on Earl.'

'Do you fancy using him again?'

'I would not mind, Brian, now that you mention it. He has a good ear and good ideas. And, he made you clowns behave yourselves which is an achievement in itself.'

'That sounds like we need to offer a toast to Earl. Robert, fill up the glasses for all.'

Next morning, the four band members made short work of an artery-busting full Scottish breakfast, in spite of their exploits during the previous evening which had not ended until well after 1 am. They had been about to call it a day at midnight, the drinks license only being good until 10 pm, when the local policeman Constable Henri Jardin and the uncrowned king of Millport, Town Councillor Scottie Green, paid a call. Both these dignitaries were well known to the band and had made great efforts to protect them from the media, when they spent time on the island. The Westview studio was now two years old and had surreptitiously crept into the fabric of Cumbrae life. Further imbibing and sharing of tall tales had been inevitable.

David was considerably less hung over than the rest and consequently a little more talkative than usual. He confessed that last night, unable to get to sleep, he had slipped past the noisy party in the bar and wandered back around to Westview with the intention of tidying up the tape with the Hammond organ and wiping clean the tape with the piano. 'Just joking, just joking.' That was something of an event in itself and cut off Brian before he could explode into an expletive-replete diatribe.

'But you know what? It must have been almost one o'clock and Earl was still there. Just tidying up, he said.'

'Does he never eat or sleep?'

'Well, I will tell you what we did. We did not even touch the Hammond tape. Instead we bounced a copy of it, and then turned it way down low and I added some strange things using the Moog synthesizer. You remember the infamous Moog synthesizer, don't you, Evan? The contraption we just had to have, and which has never been touched in two years since we wasted a fortune on it. It was well and truly used last night. Earl and I spent four hours programming it and then I played some very weird things on it. I hope we can mix them into the final cut.'

'What kind of weird things?' asked Evan.

'Earl said to think of the lapping ocean and it all just came to me. It is quite an amazing instrument, or machine I probably should say.'

'So, Earl was familiar with the Moog? He gets more interesting by the minute.'

'Said he had never worked with one but took to it like a duck to water.'

'I would wager that Hughie wouldn't be so hot on a Moog synthesizer,' offered Alex.

Brian puffed, 'We don't want or need him to be. We will never be able to drag that contraption on to a stage so why should we have it on our records?'

'Thank you, Ned Ludd,' replied David.

'Now, now children. No bickering. We have lots of options to mix into the song. I suggest we get around to the studio, if you have all finished breakfast. Hughie should be there. And I am looking forward to seeing Earl again.'

'Alex and I were just going to bog off for the ferry with Wally. Gus has to stay to bring the equipment home. We never get a say in the final mix anyway. Are you still game, wee man?'

'No, Brian. I think it might be quite interesting in the studio today. I think I will stick around.'

'Bugger me. I guess I am going to have to stay too in the interests of solidarity.'

'Good show. Dubus is on the march again.'

It was almost eleven o'clock by the time the band reached the studio at Westview. Hughie had come over from the mainland on the first ferry and had already spent almost three hours reviewing the work that had been done the previous day.

'Ah, there you are at last. Boy, did you guys have a productive day yesterday. Who took the trouble to write up all the notes?'

Evan responded, 'That was Earl. Where is he, by the way?'

'Earl who?'

'Earl, the engineer you sent in to sub for you.'

'What are you talking about? I didn't arrange any sub. Who is Earl?'

David joined in. 'This is crazy. When we got here yesterday, there was an old guy called Earl waiting for us. He said you had arranged for him to take your place for the one day.'

'Well it wasn't me who arranged it. I don't think I even know any Earls in the business. Was he any good?'

Evan exclaimed, 'Good? He was damned good. He is a big reason why the tapes are so good.'

'This is really weird. We were just saying that we did not even know his second name, but he was a damned fine engineer. In fact, I would think he has produced records as well, based on the input he was giving us,' David continued.

'There has to be a rational reason as to how he came to be here. And if it was not Hughie, then somebody else must have set him up. Maybe the folks at Alpine? He could not just have shown up on the odd chance that we were going to record. We were not even booked in for the session. I just coerced the others on the way back from Europe. I phoned you, Hughie, from Calais, and left you a message because you were not answering your phone. You were the only one outside of the band to know our plans.'

'Is one of you playing games here? Was it you, Brian or.......?'

'Not me.'

'Nope'

'Nor me.'

'And it definitely wasn't me, so if it wasn't you Hughie, who knows?'

'Very strange. But the engineer must have been top notch if you were not doing it, David.'

'I never touched a knob. Earl did it all.'

'Who the hell is Earl?'

'We can't spend all day trying to solve that puzzle. We have a song to mix. Let's just get on with it and see if we can get it finished. Then, we can see if we can solve the mystery.'

'How is your wife by the way, Hughie?'

'She is out of bed and that is a good thing. She will probably come down here at the weekend.'

The band and their engineer ran through all the tapes and were amazed at the quality. They sounded as if extensive mixing and cleaning-up had already been done.

Hughie scratched his head. 'I don't how he managed it, but these recordings are mixed to perfection. I doubt that we can improve them.'

'When I left here at almost eleven last night, they were not as good as that then.'

'When I left here at 5 am this morning, they did not sound as good as that then either. Earl must have worked on after I left.'

'When did you get here, Hughie?'

'Must have been about 8:15, Evan.'

'Then Earl must have worked on until almost the time you arrived. He must be absolutely knackered. He has probably gone to the cottage where he is staying and crashed. Mystery solved!'

'Sort of. Still does not explain who he is. If we don't need to do any more cleaning-up, then the only thing left is to decide whether we mix in the Hammond, Moog, piano and mandolin. I would propose no, yes, no, yes.'

'I am sure you would, David, but let's have a listen to them all again and try permutations of them.'

'Have it your way, Brian. We have nothing else to do.'

So, they tried various combinations of the additional instruments. Perhaps, because the actual recordings were of such quality, there was none of the usual fractious squabbling over what should be included. Each of the band members was actually looking to the best interests of the band and its product rather than their own interests. However, it pretty soon became clear that there was consensus without any dramatic votes necessary. The instruments to be mixed in to the final version were exactly as David had proposed earlier.

The final mix was quickly accomplished by Evan, David, and Hughie and the finished version sounded just great to five sets of ears. The track was ready for inclusion on the album.

By the time the band left the studio at four o'clock, Earl still had not appeared. Evan had mentioned going around the dozen or so cottages clustered around Westview to see if they could find him. But in the desire to get off the island and on their way back to their respective homes, the idea was not followed-up. Hughie said he would look out for him because he was booked in to work over the next six weeks.

===oOo===

Some four weeks later, the band and both roadies were ensconced in Robertson's Bar in Rose Street, Edinburgh. The album was finished, and drinks were called for. The final track had turned out to be the old sea shanty "Heave Away (My Johnnies)", which was in the same vein as the track they had recently recorded in Millport. For this one, they had used the local Alpine Studios, where they were always welcome. Everyone was in agreement that a second song with a nautical theme nicely balanced out the album. In fact, there was a pervading atmosphere of agreement throughout the session, and each band member had performed at their best level to produce another top-quality track. Even Brian, who could usually be counted upon to grumble at the use of old folk songs in the public domain, was well pleased with the result. And he was especially pleased that his piano had been mixed well up front. The piano worked just as well as the Moog had done previously.

'It feels good to have the album completed. I think it is one of our best.'

'It is better than the last, Alex, for sure. But we have a lot of ground to catch up on in terms of sales. That last one could not draw flies.'

'That's country and western for you, Evan. This will put us back on the charts.'

'Maybe so, Alex, but we will have to promote it, when it is released. That means more touring as well as doing the interview circuit. Are you up for that, David?'

'Right now, I would say no but maybe I will get in the mood when it comes out. Did they say June first for release?'

'Yes. But we will have to start making arrangements for a promotional tour next week. And, we have to talk more about the idea of organizing a music festival, but that too is for another day. Today is about getting rat-arsed. Wally, get another round in sharpish.'

As the evening wore on, Evan pulled a note out of his inside pocket that the receptionist at the Alpine Studios had handed him as they left the building. The note was from the department handling the design of the album cover and reminded Evan that he had not told them who was involved in the recording of the second last track that was done at Westview. They needed to give credit if there was anyone involved that had not already been included in the album credits.

'Look at this, guys. A reminder about the credits for 'Sailing into the Sunset'. We have not acknowledged old Earl. Remember him?'

'Who could forget him? He was great. Did he ever get in touch?'

'No, David. I spoke to Hughie about him only this week. Earl never showed up again at the studio. Hughie asked around but nobody had met the guy or knew anything about him.'

'Weird. What do we do about crediting him as the engineer then?'

'Here's what I would suggest, Brian. We just say something like 'Special thanks to good old Earl' and leave it that. Kind of adds a bit of mystique to the album. I've seen partial names and even false names among credits when people have worked on an album, while legally contracted to another label or studio.'

Each of the band members nodded in agreement and the matter was settled. Evan wrote the decision on the piece of paper and popped it back in his pocket lest he forget about it now that they were entering the serious drinking phase of the celebration.

As May rolled around, the band looked forward to the release of the new album, now to be entitled 'Toward Tomorrow from Yesterday'. They all felt the somewhat whimsical title captured the mood of the work, with a heavy focus on new directions, while still giving recognition to where they had come from. An extensive promotional tour of the UK and Europe had been scheduled for the month of June and then the band would be returning to the USA and Canada in August. Sandwiched in between the two tours, they were at the advanced stages of planning a three-day festival on the Isle of Cumbrae. Word was coming through of a massive festival planned in upper New York State in August, at which Dubus were hoping to perform, and the band had decided to try to emulate that in Scotland on a much smaller scale, as a thank you and economic booster to their new-found friends in Millport. The only cloud on the horizon was Brian Rodgers was adamant that he did not want to play out of doors, although he was happy to do the continental tours of clubs and interviews. The others had tried to implore him. They had tried to taunt him, as in 'What's wrong Brian? Are you afraid the wind will blow your hair about?' Neither approach had thus far succeeded. The rest of the band was adamant they wanted to do the gig and were now talking about playing as a trio, if necessary. If the truth be known, Brian had recently taken up with a young singer,

Mary Fielding, and, in addition to having a passionate affair with her; he was determined to create an instant career for her by producing her debut album, which would feature several of his compositions. He would much rather spend the time with her than play in the cold and likely rain on "Evan Davis' bloody island".

The first single from the album had been selected and it was "Blue for You", written by Evan and David with "Sailing into the Sunset" credited to all four members as the B-side. Rush-released on both sides of the Atlantic, it was attracting good playtime response from radio stations. The B-side had brought back into their conversation the mysterious engineer, known only as Earl, and it was for that reason that Evan made a visit to the Alpine Studios in Edinburgh. The front office staff members were all pretty young and newly recruited, so the name meant nothing to them. It was only when one suggested looking in the record company's archives that Evan remembered Earl's reference to the Crestas.

'Yeah. You will find the Crestas in the archives. They were the label's Great White Hopes at one time in the early '60s. Unfortunately, they flamed out almost as quickly as they arrived but, for sure, there should be clippings of them. Maybe something on this Earl too.'

Evan was thumbing through dusty files of press clippings. Alpine Records had been the new kid on the block in the early '60s in Scotland, and had been determined to give local talent their opportunity, knowing how difficult it was for Scottish groups to attract interest from labels in the south, with the Liverpool sound exploding on the scene and Manchester and London following not far behind. He recognized the names of different bands as he read about their eagerly awaited debut singles. Alas, a good many of them never got beyond that first single. He had heard that Alpine would offer a deal to just about any band for one single. If it took off, they got a three single deal and if they were hits, they got an album deal. It was very difficult for Scottish bands to get on any one of the various UK charts back then because, although local sales could be quite impressive, charts were compiled from sales of selected record stores and virtually all such stores were located in England.

He came upon clips of the Crestas who looked a rough lot, modelling their image on the Stones and the Pretty Things. Evan thought The Crestas was a pretty naff name for a tough looking rhythm and blues outfit and would have been better suited for a showband. However, one clip from the Melody Maker, no less, talked up their debut single, which had just entered the MM Charts. It noted that the group was on the verge of signing a new deal with their record company and was promising that their next single, which they were currently recording, would break them into the big-time. He then came across an article in the Daily Record with the headline *Are The Crestas Ready to Unseat The Poets As Scotland's No.1 Band?* The article was accompanied by a grainy black and white photograph of the group, obviously in a recording studio. The five members, looking meaner than ever, were in the forefront, but standing behind was a suit, presumably their manager, and another dude, noticeably older than the others. Evan screwed up his eyes as he peered at the last character. It just might be. It was five years earlier and his hair was not as grey as it was now. But it definitely could be Earl. The elusive Earl.

The photograph caption included the names of the group but omitted the two names at the back. He scanned the names but only Jim Frazier the bassist meant anything to him. Evan had come across him at sessions in recent years. In fact, he had played on a couple of things with him. But he did not know him very well.

Having closed up the files and armed with the newspaper clip, Evan returned to the front office. Jim Frazier was obviously known as a current working musician and he was able to obtain a phone number in Dundee, where the bassist resided. He called the number and had to leave a message. As arranged, later in evening he called at exactly 9 pm and a husky voice announced himself as Jim Frazier.

'Hi, Jim. This is Evan Davis calling. I am the leader of Dubus. I hope you have heard of us.'

'I have. Are you calling to ask me to join the band?'

'No. Sorry. Nothing like that. Though if Brian Rodgers keeps playing up the way he has been, we might well be in the market for a new bass player. So, you never know. I was really looking for some old information from you.'

'Oh aye.'

'You were in the Crestas, weren't you?'

'Scotland's answer to the Rolling Stones you mean?'

'Something like that.'

'Aye, I was in the Crestas from '62 to '64. That was all we lasted. When we didn't get that second single out, it killed us.'

'I was reading in an old Daily Record that your first single had made the national charts, and Alpine had offered you their follow-up three record deal that they seemed to like doing in those days.'

'Aye. That's sort of the way it happened. We had gone into the studios at our own expense, to record a second single because we were confident that the first one would hit the charts and we would get the deal. Shows what confidence does for you. We were just mugs.'

'Did you work with a guy called Earl in the studios?'

'Earl Holliman you mean'?

'Older guy. I think he is in a photograph with the group in the Daily Record clipping I have.'

'The one taken in the studio? Aye, that would be him.'

'I want to ask you about Earl, Earl Holliman, if you have the time.'

'He was the bastard that killed us.'

'Really. Tell me about it all if you will.'

'I hope you are seated comfortably. It was a wild ride. The Crestas got together in Prestonpans in 1962. Just five lads with stars in their eyes. Mickey McAskill the singer, who was more like Mick Jagger than Mick Jagger is, was the only well-off one among us. His dad ran a few used car businesses and gave us a lock-up to practise in. I must admit we were not bad and hit it off right away, playing mostly R'n'B. You know stuff from Chess and Atlantic. Chicago stuff. Just like the Stones were doing down south.'

'When did you start to gig?'

'That was not until the winter of '63. I mind that because it was a hellish cold one. The brother of our drummer became our manager. Slimy little shit he was. Took to wearing suits like a big shot but it took him a long time to get us any bookings. We just kept on practising and practising. Most of us had day jobs too. I was an apprentice fitter. Finally, he got us a gig at the Top Storey opening for the Rollers. That was before they were the Rollers. The Saxons, I think they called themselves. We blew them off the stage. After that, we gigged all over Scotland.'

'When did Alpine come into the picture?'

'Summer of '64. They offered us the usual deal of one single to see if we could crack it. That was when we met Earl Holliman. He came with the deal. He was the in-house producer and engineer all in one.'

'That's funny. Dubus had just got going by 1964 and we visited the Alpine studio a couple of times because they were trying to sign us, but we were not interested in the usual one-single deal. I don't think we ever ran into Earl Holliman. What was your impression of him?'

'Nice enough guy. He had been around the houses a few times, down south. He was a good bit older than us, but he knew his stuff.'

'What was your single again?

'It was called 'Midnight Blues'. Mickey and I wrote it. We thought we would have to record a cover song but when Earl heard it, he encouraged us to record it.'

'And it was a hit, first time out of the gate! Wow. Dubus never managed that.'

'Aye. It hit the upper thirties in all the charts. Never quite made it into the top twenty but we were delighted. Earl said that, if they had taken into account sales in Scotland, it would have got into the top twenty. We were gigging like mad in the north of England to promote the single, but Earl persuaded us the moment it hit the NME chart that we should go back in the studio and work on the follow-up. He said that was the key to success, the follow-up. So even though Alpine had not yet offered another contract, we bought time in their studios. Mind you I don't think we ever paid for it. The slimy little manager bounced a cheque. And, by the time Alpine discovered it, we were going to get the new contract anyway.'

'What happened then? Did the second single ever come out?'

'Did it hell. It was called 'It's About Time' and me and Mickey wrote it again. We recorded it in Edinburgh during the day and got back to Newcastle to play a gig in the evening. Those were crazy times. It was good song. Better than the first one. Faster and bluesier. Earl played piano on it. None of us could play the piano. It really added to our sound. He was a funny guy. He insisted that he should not be credited. He wanted it just to be the Crestas. We did a blues instrumental as a knock-off for the B-side. I can't even remember what we called it. We just made it up the studio. That was where Earl was good. He really got us cooking. Sometimes it was hard to get everybody concentrating on the same thing, but he knew how to get us working. Then it all went pear shaped.'

'How do you mean?'

'We had to rush off back to Newcastle. Earl had the master tapes. Because we had not yet signed the new contract with Alpine for the record, he did not want to leave the tapes with them. So, we agreed that he would hang on to the masters. That was the dumbest thing we ever did.'

'What happened'? Did he steal them?'

'Nothing as simple as that. I am surprised you have never heard this story. It was in all the papers at the time. Apparently, he took off to the west coast the following week. His landlady said he told her he was having a little holiday and would be back in a few days. He went to Rothesay. He went out fishing with another guy and they never came back. The boat was found washed up on the Isle of Bute near Kilchattan Bay. The local guy's body was washed up nearby. But Earl's body was never found.'

'You mean he is dead?'

'That was what was assumed. There was never any trace of him or our tapes for that matter.'

'But he is officially dead?'

'That he is.'

Save the Last Dance
Pour Moi

Finally, the second of a double-period of Mathematics was done; it felt like Old Man MacKendrick was never going to finish. I thought to myself that if I rushed downstairs from the third floor to the ground floor, I might catch Calum at our very own radiator just outside the girls' toilets and adjacent to the science labs. The radiator was good place to hang out in Spring and Autumn, although it tended to get a bit overpowering in Winter when the ancient heating system was going full blast. Still, that could easily be tolerated because that was where Calum Davies seemed to park himself a lot of late, even though the radiator was at the foot of the girls' staircase, or maybe that was the reason why he chose it. In any case, more often than not, that was where he could be found.

I took the steps two at a time, in a not very ladylike fashion I must admit, because I knew I only had ten minutes before my next class, Latin, was due to commence. Last year, it would not have been a problem because Calum was in my 5th Year Latin class, but in this our final year in high school, he had dropped the subject in favour of Accounting. I ask you! There was a good chance he would be at the radiator because he always seemed to have time on his hands. While my timetable was as full as it could be, even though I had already gained more than enough credits for university entrance requirements, in Calum's case his timetable was the barest minimum now that he had announced university was not for him. He was going to join an accounting firm when we graduated in two months and train to be an accountant. I ask you, again!

'Miss Randall!!!' The voice, often likened to a full hand of sharpened finger nails being scratched mercilessly across a blackboard, exploded from behind me and echoed in the bustling but relatively quiet stairwell. Those students who were going up or down the stairs automatically came to a halt even though none bore the name Randall; that was exclusive to me. They knew the voice as well as I did. Miss Ferrer-Todd, Advisor to Girl Students. Miss Terror-Fodd was the name that Calum had put to her in 4th Year and it had stuck. The rumour going around was that the Terror had learned of this and its source and was now known to patrol the girls' staircase with even greater zeal than for the simple purpose of providing sage advice to the female students. She also hoped to catch Calum at the foot of the stair and take undisguised delight in moving him along.

'Miss Randall, why on Earth are you running down these stairs like one of the little hussies who attend junior high school? You are enrolled at Barrington Senior Secondary School where the lady students conduct themselves.......like.... ladies! I know you are due to go to Latin on the third floor. What can possibly be attracting you toward the ground floor? I trust it is not to begin another assignation with that simply dreadful individual by the name of Davies!'

I felt my face redden as I heard the muffled sniggers from students close to me, who had now resumed ascending or descending in the safe knowledge that they were not the object of the Terror's ire.

I tried for words; none came; I felt myself getting hotter. I tried again for words; any would do as long as they did not coincide with the truth.

'Just popping down to the toilets, Miss Ferrer-Todd,' finally emerged from my lips for no good reason.

'And the toilets on the third floor, or the second floor, or even the first floor are not adequate for your particular needs, Miss Randall, that you have to forsake all decorum and bound down to the ground floor. I remain suspicious.'

The hawk-like visage seemed to penetrate right through me when I suddenly came back with the perfect response. Brilliant, it might even be described as.

'Ahem, you see Miss Ferrer-Todd, I felt I might be in, ahem, need of the, ahem, machine in the ground floor toilets.'

The Terror nodded as all was revealed. Of course, the needs of her young ladies were foremost in her responsibilities and the need to visit the ground floor toilets was perfectly understandable in certain circumstances. Barrington had a dispenser for feminine products on the ground floor but not on any one of the other three floors. This was totally inadequate in her view, but things were unlikely to ever improve until a woman was appointed principal of the school.

'Proceed, but at ladylike pace, Miss Randall.' That said, the matter was at a close and the Terror swung around to climb the stairs in search of another victim. Her robes floated out behind her as if she might be about to take to flight. Flight in the opposite direction returned to my thoughts and I took the steps again, two at a time, in the induced safe assumption that I could not be busted a second time. Time was of the essence now that precious minutes had been lost in the interrogation.

As I reached the bottom, my descent was hastily aborted. I simply stood and gawped for a second, then spun around and commenced a sad and heavy ascent toward Latin.

Oh, Calum was there alright, standing slouched against our radiator and in full conversational flow. But, so too was my sometime best friend and sometime nemesis Katey Chegwin, all the way from Toronto, Ontario, Canada on a study exchange. Katey Chegwin of wild afro-hairstyle and impossibly short skirts, which seemed to escape the attention of the Terror. Katey Chegwin of impossibly long eyelashes, that false eyelashes would have been rendered totally superfluous. Katey Chegwin with the smile that I was later to learn could only emerge from dental surgeries in North America. Katey Chegwin who served as a magnet for every good-looking boy in the 5th and 6th Years. Now Calum seemed to have succumbed to the attraction!

===OOO===

I was finished for the day, having just endured a grinding Chemistry lab session. What had possessed me to choose more Chemistry when I already had all the requirements for university entrance, I did not know. The rotten eggs smell seemed to reside in my nostrils long after each session and I swore never to take another Chemistry class once I graduated. I was heading along the ground floor corridor toward the main exit of this imposing, gothic-like building that served as Barrington SSS. As an alternative, it would have served admirably as Barrington Penitentiary, had there been the need. It was that kind of edifice.

Who should I bump into heading with great purpose in the opposite direction? Calum Davies, no less. Here he was, late for the last class of the day, when he had probably done very little else throughout the day. Indeed, at this time, on most days, he could be found, not in the classroom at all, but on the rugby fields outside. For Calum, high school, especially 6th Year, should involve as few classes as possible, augmented by as much sport as possible. In addition to starring as the starting flyhalf of the first school XV (information provided in great detail by him at the slightest invitation), he had been engaged by the rugby coach to help out with the younger teams of the 1st Year. And yet having attained the A-Level in French last year, and with apparently nothing else to learn, he had signed up for special additional studies in French. Why? It might have been because he intended to pursue a rugby career in France and would need all the conversational skills he could muster. I rather thought it was due to the arrival of Mlle. Brigitte Pardoe, the visiting student teacher. Visitors from France were nothing unusual; Barrington attracted one each year but none in our six years' experience had ever resembled the beautiful, sultry mademoiselle. Inevitably, Calum had christened her Brigitte Bardot, although I professed to not being able to see any resemblance, and he seemed besotted with her. However, that was a condition he shared with every boy in the 6th Year, even those who had not learned a word of French.

'Où allez-vous, mon ami?' I ventured while shaking my head disapprovingly. I should have known better than to try to wind him up.

'Pas de où vas-tu? Je suis très déçu,' came his response. I wished he would not tease me so. If I had used the familiar form of you, he would have teased me about it. When I did not, he teased me about that instead. I quickly reverted to our mother tongue.

'Off to worship at the good mademoiselle's feet? You better hurry, you are late, and there may not be enough room.'

'Now, now. Do I hear the meowing of a kitty? What are you doing tonight? I thought I might attend the Literary Society debate.'

I normally went to the debates but had clean forgotten about tonight's event. I had never seen Calum at any of the previous debates. This was an opportunity too good to miss.

'Oh, I am intending to go too but I have forgotten what the motion is. I am surprised that a debate would interest you.'

'The motion is "This House believes wedlock to be synonymous with padlock."!'

'I might have guessed. Are you speaking in favour?'

'No, I am not speaking at all. I am just going along to watch with an open mind. Then I was planning to go for a pint afterwards. Do you fancy joining me?'

Calum, like most of our contemporaries, had long since discovered the joys of underage drinking. I had not really developed a liking for alcohol or breaking the law, the former would come later, and the latter never really ever came at all. But this was an opportunity too good to miss.

'Ok. That would be nice,' I replied, in a sort of off-hand yet sultry manner that I thought our Brigitte Bardot (or even the real one) might have exhibited.

'Great! Got to run. See you later.'

And thus, that was the reason that the two of us found ourselves later in the White Cockade pub in Rose Street. Not in the Powderhall Arms, the dingy pub closest to school suggested by Calum, where I feared we would meet other thirsty debaters. We had walked for more than thirty minutes to the Edinburgh city centre, or uptown as it is called because it is on a hill, and sought out a quiet, snug establishment, typically quiet during the midweek. From here, both of us could later catch a bus to our homes in the opposite ends of the city.

Calum had declared the debate to be indecisive, although the vote had clearly come out against the motion. He expressed more confusion now than before as to the merits of marriage. After all, this was the swinging '60s and there seemed to be endless alternatives. Lest the conversation should take an awkward turn, I steered it into less choppy waters.

'It is only two months until we graduate. Are you still looking forward to entering an accountancy apprenticeship?'

'The more I hear about it, yes I am. I think it will be interesting, if I must leave Old Barrington. My first choice would be to stay on in high school, of course! I am having a ball. I think these will prove to be the best years of my life. I think you should be allowed to stay on for a few years if you wish. I could see myself being ready to leave at about say, twenty-five. At seventeen, I am but a callow youth!'

'You are the weirdest, not-so-callow youth I have ever known. Most of our friends are desperate to get out of Barrington. Some did not even last the six years. And, you want to stay on. Why on earth would you think that? I am so looking forward to going to uni after the summer hols.'

He quickly reeled off the limited number of classes, the sporting opportunities, the social life, the fact that he did not have to

65

have a job, as sound reasons for his stance on staying in school. Lastly, he expressed particular delight in being a prefect, that odd institution of British schools where not all students are born equal, because a very few are granted great privilege and very little responsibility to act as a sort of liaison between teachers and the student population. Most were granted the status in recognition of academic achievement and a very few for sporting achievement. Both Calum and I were prefects, having arrived at the pinnacle by the probably obvious different routes.

Having expended a good deal of emotional energy on the merits of high school education, as he saw it, he suddenly downed the remainder of his beer in one swallow. I had taken no more than three small sips of my half-pint. Then he surprised me by adopting something of a maudlin tone.

'Yes, you are going off to uni, far far away. That can't be good.'

Hmm, I thought.

'Aberdeen is just over two hours away. I will be home to see my parents at end of terms and maybe even on long weekends.'

'Maybe. I suspect you will get caught up in university life and forget all about your school connections.'

Hmm, I thought.

'I don't think so but just in case, we should be making the most of the last two months. I hear there is a dance coming up in the gym. Did you hear that? I so wish there was a tradition, like there is Canada and the USA, of grand graduation balls with everybody done out in their formal finery. Katey was telling me all about it.'

I immediately regretted even mentioning the name of my Canadian rival, but Calum did not seem to notice. He immediately got all animated again and proceeded to tell me at great length about the recently announced dance in the school featuring Dubus. The oddly-named Dubus was arguably the best group in Scotland and had even featured several times on the UK charts. They had appeared on national radio and had even made an appearance on Top of the Pops on the BBC. They were predicted to take the US by storm, now that they had firmly established themselves in the UK. I thought Calum sounded a bit like their manager of public relations, but he did seem to know an awful lot about them I had to confess.

He went on to tell me, even though I already knew, that their leader Evan Davis was a former pupil of Barrington. Calum called him an 'alumni' in the American vernacular. I was tempted to correct him and call him an 'alumnus', but I resisted. He should have persisted with his Latin! Anyway, Evan had decided to give back to his old school, now that he was famous and presumably getting rich. The dance would be a fund-raiser in support of a campaign to sponsor exchange visits for students to and from Scotland and countries in Europe. Evan was in favour of this goal and so was I. I knew too that Calum had spoken highly of the idea.

'That sounds great. I am definitely going to go. When do tickets go on sale?'

'This weekend I think.'

'I assume you will be going too. You should be the emcee. You seem to know everything there is to know about them.'

'I don't think so. In fact, I am not so sure I will even go. I have seen them lots of times in clubs around the town. They just might come and play pop songs because they are in a school playing for kids!'

===OOO===

A week later, Katey and I were chatting at the radiator outside the girls' toilets on the ground floor. She was bubbling enthusiastically, as she frequently was, to tell me that she had just acquired two tickets for the dance. When I asked naively why two, she stated quite matter-of-factly that she was fed up waiting for Calum to ask to take her, that she had decided to take control of the situation and ask him. Apparently, that was quite common practice in Canada. I tried in vain to hide my feeling of appallment.

'That doesn't bother you, does it, Heather?'

'No, no. I am just not familiar with doing things that way. I have always believed that it is the boy's role to do the asking'

Katey shook her mane of golden curls and rolled her eyes.

'Hell yeah. If you stand around waiting for guys to make the first move, you will be left there, just standing around waiting. I am going to pounce on him the next time I see him. You weren't just standing there waiting by any chance, were you?'

'No! No! Not all.'

'Then you must have bought two tickets as well!'

'I am afraid I haven't bought any tickets......yet'

'Well, I think they are already sold out. At least, that is what I heard in the loo just now. I don't know who was talking in the next cubicle mind you, but that is what they said'

I pondered what I was hearing. I didn't think I was assuming that Calum would suddenly furnish two tickets and invite me. Well, maybe I was kind of hoping he might. I most certainly was not intending to buy two tickets and collar him. I had not even thought about that. I was not sure I could even summon up the courage to do it now that I heard of the practice. Canadians were obviously a whole lot different from Scottish girls. I think I had realized that when I first set eyes on Katey. I had not even got around to buying a single ticket, so at least I could get into the dance. That was how most girls would be doing it, I was sure. However, my hesitancy had now probably caused me to miss out on the event altogether. Unless, Calum came through……………..

Who should come through, or at least down the girls' staircase, which he should not have been using, even as a prefect…..the aforementioned Calum.

'Good morning, ladies.'

'Calummmm. I need to have a word with you.'

'Not right now, Katey. I am engaged on prefectly duties and I can't stop long. I have been sent out by the Terror to find one Angie MacTavish from 1st Year. I was even sanctioned to use the girls' stair. Young Angie must really be in trouble.'

'But Calummmmm. It is important.'

I decided to end my silence, feeling that I needed to stop looking from one of them to the other and back again with my mouth open and nothing coming out.

'Katey, let Calum do his assignment. Miss Ferrer-Todd will be all over him if she spots him standing here gossiping.'

'I could always say I was making enquiries in pursuit of the suspect,' replied Calum with a mock serious face, much in the same way as his brother might have said. I knew his brother to be a police constable.

'Heather, chill out. A gal has got to do what a gal has got to do around here'

Just as I turned to admonish Katey, two formidable-looking teachers stopped their conversation in mid-stride and joined our little group. The taller of the two was Mr Murray, Master of Picardie House to which Katey, Calum, and I belonged as well as our History teacher, and the other was Mr Hamilton, Head of the Physical Education Department. Calum, being closely associated with all matters PE, had often opined that he could call Mr Hamilton by his supposedly given-name 'Wally', but had never been known to have actually done so to his face. No such liberties could even be contemplated with the stern, scholarly, Mr Murray, whose only alternate moniker would be 'Sir'.

'And what do we have here?' intoned Mr Murray, in that resonate baritone voice that could make one feel guilty even if completely innocent.

Katey shrugged in an assumedly Canadian fashion. Calum replied, 'Er, nothing,' and I started to explain that we were trying to assist Calum in his search for the 1st Year student scheduled for an audience with Miss Ferrer-Todd.

'Sounds like much ado about nothing then. I am sure you all have classes to go to rather than cluttering up the corridor. I know for fact that you, Miss Chegwin, and you, Mr Davies, are due me a paper on the Second Punic War by Friday. If you have nothing better to do, you could always work on your papers. I trust Mr Davies that your references to Hannibal's ultimate failure to lead the Carthaginians to victory over the Romans will include more than attributing it to his elephants tripping over their trunks, like some other worthies you have come up with in your quest to put a humorous face on history!'

I waited with apprehension for Calum to come back with some smart-aleck comment like 'thank you for tip, Sir,' but he held his tongue for once.

Meanwhile, 'Wally', who had stood by while Mr Murray took command of the situation, must have felt that he was compelled to contribute something to this insightful piece of education that the masters were instilling in the pupils.

70

'If you are to spend most of your time with the fairer sex, Davies, perhaps you can ask the ladies to explain to you when you should attempt a drop-goal and when you should not, so you do not repeat your blatant error that might have cost us the game last Saturday.'

I was totally bewildered by the comment. Katey kind of shrugged again while looking vacant, and Mr Murray looked just as non-plussed as either of us. Mr Hamilton gave a little toothy grin in our direction and looked pleased with his witty but admonishing contribution. Calum looked like he at least understood what had been said, but did not particularly welcome it. Was a riposte coming? Fortunately, not.

Without further discussion, which I was not necessarily upset about, Katey, Calum and I went our separate ways.

===OOO===

As the days passed, my failure to get a ticket for the big dance and my lack of knowledge of how to attract a partner, bothered me. I had never been one who gossiped with the other girls about matters of the heart. I preferred just to listen to other tales of intent, conquest, and ultimate heartbreak, and was probably considered a bit stand-offish, or even snobbish, by the other girls. However, on this potentially important occasion, I stepped out of my comfort zone and seized every opportunity I could to chat one-on-one with others and even to join a few small groups.

I learned very early on that the tickets were indeed sold out. Even though the dance had been intended for Barrington students, word had soon got around the city that Dubus were playing. As a result, Barrington students had been buying up tickets for friends in other schools. There were even some rumours that Danny Bain, a 6th Year Mathematics genius but otherwise a character of highly dubious moral fibre, had bought up a load of tickets and sold them on at a profit. Now even our local tout had exhausted his supply and was bemoaning the shortage. He allegedly was now offering to buy tickets off students because he had a waiting list of students ready to buy.

My own moral compass directed me away from any notion of joining his list. However, that did not leave me any idea of how I was going to acquire a ticket. Calum had once told me about groupies who never bought tickets and always got into concerts and clubs as "guests of the band". I had dismissed his story at the time and was not prepared to revisit it by expressing an interest in pursuing that approach. I would not even have known where to begin in any case.

So, no ticket, but I was picking up a lot of information on how other girls were going to the dance. By far, the most popular approach was for them to individually buy tickets and then go in pairs or small groups, in the hope that they would encounter boys inside the gymnasium who had adopted the same approach. We always had some boys and girls who were already dating, and they had obviously bought two tickets and intended to go together. That just left Katey's strategy to be sounded out. Among the students I spoke with, I did not find a single other girl with the same intention. Several, however, were much enamoured with the idea and were left to rue that they had only bought a single ticket!

I was left to conclude that that Katey's devious plan was entirely down to her Canadian origin, but that did not make it any easier to acknowledge. My parents had always instilled in me the importance of embracing cultural difference, but I have to admit I awaited the outcome of this cultural difference with much trepidation. In fact, I pointedly did not raise the subject of the dance or any of its associated issues whenever I was with her. Alas, my luck ran out when Katey breezed into the library one afternoon and I could just tell by the smirk on her face that there was going to be an announcement!

'Well my dear friend Heather, I am just about there! I am so close to it I can almost taste it. Or maybe, I should say I can just about taste him!'

'What on earth are you talking about?' I asked, knowing it to sound like a feeble response.

'Calum, you nut. I have asked him.'

Just at that moment, the Terror, who happened to be doing a spell of library supervision that day, gave out a hiss and a glare to suggest in no uncertain manner that talking in the library was not acceptable. Katey looked like she was going to explode with exasperation but, nevertheless, flopped down beside me and pulled out a book from her bag. I suspect any book would have served the purpose. Meanwhile, I returned to my study of an information pamphlet on the Cumbraes Environmental Research Station, which I had been invited to visit as part of a school field studies trip.

After a few minutes when the appropriate level of silence had returned to the library and the Terror had returned to whatever she was reading, Katey felt empowered to resume our conversation in a serious of cautious whispers.

'Did you hear what I said?

'You said you had asked Calum, presumably about going to the dance with you.'

'Precisely,' she said, her voice rising a little and prompting a quick scan of the students from the library supervisor.

'And did he agree?' I asked unable to disguise the forlorn timbre in my voice.

'As good as.'

I turned to look her straight in the eye. That did not sound like a ringing confirmation. My look must have been interpreted by her because she continued.

'It's in the bag, I would say. He said he would give it consideration, no "serious consideration" were the exact words. Don't you think that is tantamount to a yes?'

Ever since our English teacher had introduced us to the word 'tantamount' last term, Katey seemed to have adopted it as her own personal word to be used on as many occasions as possible, and not always totally in context. I don't know about anybody else, but I had gone from being mildly amused by its incessant use to mildly irritated. Now, it stabbed me in the stomach as surely as any Shakespearean dagger might have.

'That might be a stretch. Consideration does not automatically mean agreement,'

'Sure it does. Anyway, you had to be there to hear how he said it. He just did not want to say yes outright so he kind of stalled a little. Calum would be good in a romantic Shakespearean play.'

'I have seen him in one and, believe me, he wasn't!'

'Well Heather, if I did not know any better, I would say I detect in a little jealousy in your lack of enthusiasm, tantamount to a little bitterness even. Am I correct in my assessment?'

Fortunately, I was spared the need to find an appropriate answer, as a voice boomed from the desk in the corner.

'Miss Chegwin, our practices here in Scotland call for absolute silence during library study. You seem incapable of keeping quiet, so I suggest you go find somewhere else in the school to do whatever reading you are pretending to do.'

'But Miss Ferrer-Todd!'

'Now! Begone!'

As Katey grabbed up her book, stuffed it into her bag and made to leave, she hissed sotto voce behind her to me, 'just wait and see, he will say yes.'

As all eyes including those of the Terror were focused on departing Katey, I was able to retort without being noticed.

'Perhaps so, but there's many a slip 'twixt the cup and the lip,' without knowing if Katey was even familiar with the saying, but feeling strangely satisfied with having said it.

===OOO===

One of my best subjects in high school was Biology; in fact, it was to have an impact on my future careers on three continents. By 6th Year at Barrington, I had done all the courses I could and had achieved the prerequisite A-level for university entrance. I had been such a keen student and I had established a great relationship with all four teachers in the department, but notably with the head of department Dr Livingston. I probably had a bit of a crush on him, because he was very good looking and had the nicest manner. In that I was not alone however, because just about every girl who did Biology felt the same way. However, given that one of the other three teachers was his very attractive wife, there was never any fear of hanky-panky. She took it in her stride that he constantly had a troupe of starry-eyed girls following him around the labs and hanging on his every word. I was part of that troupe and even in 6th Year I was able to find opportunities to visit the lab and keep connected with what was happening. For that reason, when Dr Livingston decided to take his 5th Year Class on a week-end field trip, he invited me along to help out with the logistics and do a little research myself in preparation for what I would be experiencing in university.

The Cumbraes Environmental Research Station is located on the Isle of Cumbrae in the Firth of Clyde, just outside the only town of Millport. As I sat in the special meeting for those going on the trip that weekend, I could see that I was one of the few students who knew anything about the station, and I was almost certainly the only one who knew about Millport and the Isle of Cumbrae. All the students were enthralled to hear everything Dr Livingston had to share with them about what they would be doing. I could not help drifting in thought because I heard about so much of it before.

In one of our very infrequent dates (sort of), which had entailed a long walk among the hills of Holyrood Park, Calum had somehow got onto where he had been on holiday the previous summer. In fact, it was where he had gone on holiday for just about every summer in his life. He was somewhat obsessed by Millport and the Isle of Cumbrae, had developed an encyclopaedic knowledge of the island, and was happy to talk about it at length. Though it pretty much dominated what I had in mind, as a walk where we might share some things and feelings about each other, I could not help getting engrossed in the subject. However, I never dreamt that it was the place I would visit just a few months later. As I sat, trying to remain focused in the briefing being provided, I realized I had not had the opportunity to tell Calum where I was going. I had not really had the opportunity to talk to him much about anything since the dance had been announced. Oh well, it would have to wait for now as I knew he was already off on a rugby tour of several towns in the Scottish Borders and would not be back until the same time I returned from Cumbrae. We would have interesting stories to share if only I could get him on his own. That meant without Katey, and I realized I had not heard any more recently from her either. In her case, no news probably meant good news.

The field trip was an outstanding success. Great Cumbrae, in common with its nearby sister island Little Cumbrae, is a geological and biological haven, which the students were quickly to learn and appreciate. The island offers some very unique rock formations that fan out from a bisecting fault line. There is an abundance of orchids and other wildflowers and ferns that are easily accessible on the small, ten-miles-around island. In addition, Cumbrae is home to a wide range of sea birds and waders, kittiwakes, kestrels, buzzards and other birds. Furthermore, the waters surrounding the island are populated with porpoises, dolphins, seals and occasionally sharks. In the two full days of research, the students were given the opportunity to discover, hands-on, numerous examples of what they had learned in theory in their school studies. Breaking into small groups, with me charged to lead one of them, we had spent long hours following the hints and directions that had been prepared in advance. All day, we heard whoops of delight after much sought-after evidence was located, observed, and written up in our log books. I could not help feeling some envy for the 5th Year students, who were getting this tremendous advantage of information prior to writing their A level examinations. However, I had not had the same opportunity, but had still been able to pass the examination with flying colours!

The evenings were a delight where we all met back at the research station to debrief on our day. Reports were delivered with much greater enthusiasm and no little professionalism compared to what I remembered in class and the teachers, notably Dr Livingston, seemed to be delighted with the outcomes. On the first night we ate in the station cafeteria, and although everyone was now in high spirits, it had to be said that the food was pretty plain. Perhaps we had been looking forward to some of that wonderful local seafood we had been learning about, but it was not on the menu. So, on the second night, Dr Livingston suggest after the debriefing that we conclude our successful field trip with a visit into the town of Millport for dinner. In spite of his impressive planning of the whole weekend, this was an impromptu suggestion and he was stumped as to where to actually go. I immediately piped up.

'I hear the Nixé is the best place to eat on the island and it is not too expensive!'

Heads turned toward me, including those of the teachers, and several enquiries were made as to my hitherto unrevealed source of local knowledge. I had to confess my source with a little pride and good deal of embarrassment. After I had passed on much of what I could remember Calum telling me about island life, including the wonders of the Nixé, Dr Livingston mentioned that he should have included him in the research group, although that might have incurred the wrath of Mr Hamilton, as it would have affected the rugby team. I could not help wishing, nevertheless, I had been able to tell Calum about the trip in advance.

Dinner was an outstanding success; just what the students wanted. And the teachers seemed to have a great time too, particularly Dr Livingston's wife, who displayed admirable knowledge of contemporary music in keeping the jukebox playing all the time we spent there. We had virtually taken over the Nixé on what was otherwise going to be a quiet Sunday evening, and the owners were delighted to have us, and wished us well at the end. I anticipated Dr Livingston would be adding a notation to his plans for next year's field study trip.

On the Monday of our return, I did not see Calum much at all, other than to run into him in the corridor as the thronging masses of students moved from one class to another. He seemed very upbeat and quickly, and a little loudly for my liking, suggested that we get together after school for a coffee on the way to catch our respective buses home. I, less loudly, but just as enthusiastically, agreed.

The Modern Café was anything but, however it was handy, and today it was deserted, which probably proved to be a good thing. Calum rushed up to order two coffees when we sat down. I could tell he was dying to talk. I had noted in my head I wanted to talk about Millport and Katey; those were my priorities. Once the coffees arrived, he took a quick gulp, uttered an expletive about how hot it

78

was, and began. I had some time ago noted the protocol that Calum went first when he was bursting to say something.

'What a trip! Four games in five days. We won three of them and really should have won the other one in Peebles. The referee did not show up and one of their teachers took over. Talk about biased! I almost got sent off for questioning one of his many bad decisions.'

'Which schools did you visit?

'Peebles, Galashiels, Melrose, and Hawick.'

'Those are nice towns; it must have been a great trip. What else did you do other than play rugby?

'We practised rugby of course. They also laid on some trips to historical places. That was ok.'

'Ok? The Borders is choc-a-bloc with history. It must have been fascinating.'

'Hmmm. Unfortunately, we were not allowed out on our own at night. The other teams all said they would meet up with us afterwards, but Wally Hamilton forbade any drinking or going out after supper. That was a bit of a bummer. That is what rugby is all about, the social life, otherwise it is just a game!'

I shook my head in mock sympathy with his plight. Was it coming to my turn to talk?

'I must tell you about the funniest thing of all. You know how Wally is always singling me out to make fun of me. He loves me really. He darned well should, I scored four tries and was top scorer overall on the tour. Anyway, back to the funny bit. In the last game against Hawick, they are always a powerhouse--they might be the best school team in Scotland--we were losing by only two points with a minute to go. Guess who had the courage, and dare I say the skill, to try a drop-goal from at least forty yards out from the posts?'

After what seemed like an eternal silence I offered 'You?'

'Absolutely. My longest kick ever. We win the match by a single point. Hawick loses at home for the first time all season. And get this, after the match Wally announces "I am pleased to commend Davies on his match-winning drop-goal. I can only think he has been taking the advice of his technical advisors that I saw him with the other day!" Nobody had a clue what he was on about, but everybody cheered. I was going to explain it but then I thought better of it. What a hoot, eh!'

'I am glad you kept it to yourself. But I am pleased to hear all about your glory.'

'I am not sure that is being said with the appropriate amount of sincerity, but I will take it. What did you get up to this weekend?'

I decided to leave Katey until later. After all, that might be a negative conversation. Talking about his beloved Millport could only be positive, couldn't it? I had only got a few words out about the late invitation to join the field trip, the location, and our journey to the island, when Calum almost exploded.

'I can't believe it. You go to my island without me!'

I thought at first he was joking and was about to make some witty response, when I noticed his eyes aflame.

'I didn't have control over who went; Dr Livingston did. Although when I told them how much you liked the place, he said he wished you could have joined us. He knew that your rugby took first priority, however.'

'Like heck it does. If I had known about the trip to Cumbrae, I would have pulled out of the rugby tour, just like that.'

'Oh Calum. You know you don't mean that. Rugby is important to you and look, you would have missed out on all your glory.'

'Don't you tell me what is important to me; I am really pissed off you kept your trip all to yourself.'

'I did not. I only learned about it a couple of days before it happened. I don't see you every day. I just did not have the chance to tell you.'

'You could have looked for me.'

'Well, I am sorry I didn't. But in any case, you would not have been able to go. You were already committed to the rugby.'

'I could have called off injured. The elbow I cracked in 1st Year always aches when the weather is wet.'

'Come on, you would not have wanted to call off. Mr Hamilton would have been angry to lose his star player.'

'I am not the star player really. I would much rather have gone to Cumbrae. I can't believe you kept it from me.'

'I did not keep it from you on purpose. Honestly. You dropped Biology after 3rd Year. You would not have enjoyed the research we were doing.'

'Don't tell me what I enjoy and what I don't enjoy. I know exactly what I don't enjoy, and I think I will just head off home right now!'

===OOO===

I spent a totally sleepless night and then had to battle through torrential Edinburgh rain to get from the bus stop to the school. My umbrella blew inside-out just as I was passing by the playing fields, so I turfed it over the railings onto the grass. Maybe you-know-who might trip over it at his next rugby practice. As I was battling up the stairs to the front door of the main building, by now thoroughly drenched, I heard the voice with the distinctive accent yelling at me from some yards behind.

'Heather, hold up. Heather, I need to talk to you.'

'Not now, Katey!' I positively spat out over my shoulder as I crashed through the doorway and into the corridor. I did not stop walking at great pace, and I did not stop dripping at even greater pace, until I reached the girls cloakroom on the third floor. I assumed Katey would be using the ground floor cloakroom as she usually did.

Later at lunch, even though I sat pointedly among some 1st Years at the long table farthest away from the kitchen and serving area, Katey found me. The 1st Years were already wondering why a 6th Year, and a prefect at that, was in their midst, when the brash Canadian forced herself onto the bench beside me in a space that did not exist.

'Hey, you kids, move along a bit. Jesus H. Christ, it won't kill you, will it?'

Amid much grumbling, and I could have sworn I heard a mumbled 'fecking Yank', Katey was able to establish a place beside me. The fact that she did not have any food meant she was primed and ready to get into full flow.

'That Goddam Calum!'

'Hush,' I said, and nodded toward the youngsters, now eyes agog and fully intent on witnessing the drama.

Katey took the hint and lowered her voice to an almost comic whisper.

'Can you believe it? Calum stood me up! What do you think about that, Heather?'

'Calum is not exactly in my good books right now, but no doubt his misdemeanour pales into insignificance in comparison to what he has done to you. Do tell me.'

'Misdemeanour? I consider it a federal offence, more like! I called him last night and...'

'You called him? How come you have his phone number?'

'I got it out of him when I provided him with mine. Fair's fair.'

'I see.'

'Anyway, I had not heard from him in a few days and I knew he was back from his rugby because I heard he had been seen in school yesterday. I figured he had had more than enough time to make the obvious decision.'

Somehow, I sensed a funny feeling of relief gently flowing over me. I don't think I smirked, but Katey's face took on an even more angry look.

'When I get to him, he is in an absolutely foul mood for some reason. I don't know what had happened to him, but he was in no mood to talk. That did not deter me, of course, and I hit him between the eyes, so to speak, with 'Well, Mr Davies, are we going to the Ball?''

'That was subtle. Did it bring him around?'

'Did it hell! He said, "You might be going to the dance, but I am not going with you; in fact, I am probably not going, full-stop." I just got out a "C'mon Caluuum, you virtually promised me," when he hung up on me. Hung up on me! And when I called back, he would not pick up.'

'I am sorry to hear that,' I said disingenuously.

'Not half as much as I am,' came the retort, as Katey caused another scatter of the 1st Years as she extricated herself from the packed bench and stormed off.

All I could do was sit with my head in my hands, not knowing whether I was sad or relieved. I could not help hearing the whispered comment among youthful giggles.

'I bet that was Calum Davies they were talking about. He is gorgeous!'

===OOO===

I spent almost the rest of week in bed with some kind of flu. Whether it was brought on by the Barrington drama, the weekend exposure to the bracing climate of Cumbrae, or was just common or garden flu, I don't know. But it laid me low. When I was able to return to school on the Friday, it was, of course, the eve of the big event, the Dubus Dance.

I had not heard a word from Calum and did not see him at all that day. The rumour was he had not shown up for classes. At the lunch break, I was again accosted by Katey, this time fortunately outwith the hearing range of the 1st Years.

'There you are! I heard you were back. How are you?'

'Hi Katey. I am still a little wobbly, but I had to get out of the house. My mother was killing me with her kindness. I said I had paper I had to hand in today.'

'Calum has been missing for most of the week too and he is out today as well. That might refute some of the rumours that you two had run away together!'

'You are kidding?'

'You know me, always kidding. But it might have been true; you can never tell these days.'

'That is nonsense. I was sick. What is the word on him?'

'I have not heard. Somebody said he was out on the streets of Edinburgh telling anybody who would listen about his match-winning score in the rugby. But I think they were just being unkind.'

'Are you going to the dance?'

'Are *you* going to the dance?'

'You are the one with a ticket. I haven't been able to get one.'

'I am the one with two tickets, remember? If you are fit enough, how about I give you one of them and we go together. We might strike it lucky. We have got as much of a chance as most of the girls; and, a better chance than a few I could name! How about it?'

'Only if I can pay you for the ticket.'

'Whatever! It is only money'

And that is how Katey and I found our way the following evening, into a scrum of rugby proportions that was trying to get through the doors into the school gymnasium. There seemed to be many more young people than the 200 limit that had been set by the Principal. Rumours were abounding that many more than 200 tickets were being proffered to the beleaguered teacher whose job it was to collect them. Even wilder rumours were starting to circulate that one Danny Bain had been seen in the Duplicating Room after hours and he might be the source of tickets even at this late stage. I thought I saw him hanging around in the shadows outside the building. He was a brilliant mathematician who would ultimately get a PhD at M.I.T in the US, but just as easily could have gone to jail.

We finally made it into the gym, except I hardly recognized it as our humble gym. There was a large stage at one end, which was loaded with huge amplifiers and framed by an incredible array of lights, which were projecting all sorts of psychedelic images around the walls and ceiling. The main lights were turned off and so the garish light beams were giving the place an unworldly feel. It even seemed to be a smoky atmosphere. Surely Barrington was not allowing smoking. Smoking was normally a capital offence. No, it was some sort of machine-produced smoke, I was sure, but it contributed effectively to the sense of a happening.

After another half-hour, the dance floor was so crowded that we could hardly move. Katey's eyes were aflame. This was her kind of scene. Straight out of downtown Toronto, without a doubt. I doubted it was my scene, but I could not help getting caught up in the atmosphere. I kept seeing girls in this totally different context from the normal school image. What an image it was too. The slightly wild students at the best of times, were now dressed totally outrageously. The more sedate students were now verging on the outrageous. Even a few students, notorious for their fuddy-duddy images, looked like I had never seen them before. I sincerely hoped I looked the part, and was thankful that Katey had offered some sage advice the previous day on how we should be attired.

In all my people-watching, I did not catch even a glimpse of Calum!

Finally, a roar of anticipation went up as someone walked on to the stage. It was quickly followed by audible groans. It was Mr Hamilton, who was to be our emcee. No Ed Sullivan was he! He spent the next five minutes laying out the rules of enjoyment. The dance was to be enjoyed as long as there was no smoking, no surreptitious drinking, no pass-outs, no close dancing, and most certainly no inappropriate behaviour of a sexual nature. Another roar went up. That only encouraged him to repeat all his rules with added emphasis.

When he was satisfied that the message had been delivered and received, he went on to announce the opening group, which was our very own Hoppies. The Hoppies were five boys and one girl from the 5th Year, who were starting to garner a reputation around the city. This was by far their biggest date thus far, and after a bit of a nervous start, they played a great set. Every song was well received, and they even felt comfortable enough to throw in a couple of their own songs toward the end. I loved them but alas, that night was probably the highlight of their short career, as they were to break up before they even made it to 6th Year.

At first, Katey and I danced together, but soon we were being asked to dance by boys we knew from Barrington and by boys we didn't know at all, all dressed up in their finery. I was amazed how the boys also took a totally different appearance once they were out of their school uniforms. The opening set passed by in a flash as we danced to every song that was played. There was no room to sit one out even if we had wanted to.

When the Hoppies finished their last song, the audience started up a chant for more, but on came Mr Hamilton to announce that was it. No encore. Instead there would be a short intermission before Dubus (his intonation sounded more like Dubus than the Doobus it should have been) would come on to play. There were even some screams at this, which seemed to quite unnerve him. He mumbled something about soft drinks being available at the other end of the gym, and warned students not to spill any on his prized floor.

At that point, the 300, if that, indeed, is what we now numbered, all attempted to head in the same direction at the same time. Chaos ensued. Needless to say, by the time the thronging mass had made its way toward the drinks' tables, we were stuck at the back, farthest from the drinks. I don't know what made me look around to the relatively empty dance area in front of the stage; I could only grab Katey's arm and nod with amazement.

In some sort of cosmic happenstance; the circulating light beams landed on a couple who appeared to be just arriving on the scene. There was Calum, dressed in a green velvet suit that I had certainly never seen before. And there, taking his arm and dressed in a short leather jacket, even shorter leather skirt, and long leather boots, was... Mlle Brigitte Pardoe.

She was looking almost serene, smiling to the right and then to the left, and totally cool. He had that silly mock serious look on, biting his lip as if he were concentrating on something. He was trying hard to be totally cool!

Within seconds, it appeared that more and more people at the drinks' congregation had turned around and seen the new arrivals. Suddenly the thronging mass was making its way back to the dance floor. The couple were quickly engulfed.

'What do you make of that?' I asked Katey, who was doing a lot of curly hair-shaking and muttering 'Jesus H. Christ!' to anyone who would listen.

'That French bitch. Who woulda thunk it? You can never trust the French. It is the same in Quebec.'

'You can't assume she asked him. He could have asked her.'

'Yeah, he probably did. The SOB!'

I was concerned that Katey was going to have a heart attack and I desperately wanted to get off the topic, for I could not help feeling something dramatic welling over me as well. Was it disappointment, anger or just shock?

Fortunately, we were sort of rescued from our trauma by the arrival again of Mr Hamilton on stage. He took way too long to introduce the four Edinburgh lads who had grown up together in the same street, all gone to different schools, but come together to form a group. That group had gone on to bigger and bigger things. He then went to sing the praises of the leader Evan Davis, former pupil of Barrington Senior Secondary School, as a musician, as a stellar flyhalf in the First XV of course, and now as something of a philanthropist, leading the fund-raising effort to develop a Study Abroad programme for his alma mater.

The crowd was getting restless. I happened to spot the Principal, who had paid a fleeting visit to the event, and he was motioning with hands in a circular motion for the emcee to get on with it. Mr Hamilton seemed to spot him as well. Stopping in mid-sentence, he announced with great drama;

'Ladies and Gentlemen, please welcome Dubus!'

The roof was almost blown off the gymnasium. I have been to many concerts in many places in the world since that night, but I do not think I have ever experienced anything quite like that. The boys bounded on to the stage, unlike their normal slow, deliberate, cool appearance, and they plugged in, waved to the crowd, thereby causing an even greater roar, and then started to play, which at first threatened to cause a full-scale riot.

I have to say they were amazing. I liked all their records but somehow, they made them sound even more magical when they played them live. And loud! It was said later that the music could be heard in Edinburgh city centre almost three miles away. When 'Illusions', their only number one record at that stage of their career, was played, I felt weak at the knees. The flu returning? I don't think so.

Now the demeanour of the crowd had changed. Many were happy just to stand and wonder, they had given up on dancing. Some were dancing on their own because it was nigh impossible to move around to find partners; and some, those farthest away from the stage, tried to carry on dancing as they had to the opening group. We were sort of caught in the middle of the masses.

I noticed Calum and Brigitte Bardot had eased into the latter group and were dancing up a storm. She had all the moves, even for a teacher. Huh, she was probably barely twenty-one!

However, the next time I looked; Calum was kind of standing on his own. The inevitable had happened. A line-up had formed of boys desperate to have the next dance with the mademoiselle. I tried to catch Calum's eye to signal goodness-knows-what to him, but he was focused on the stage. I hoped he was enjoying the band that he felt so strongly about. They were certainly doing their part to please him and everybody else.

Katey touched my arm and pointed toward Calum, but I had already been watching him for quite a while. For one horrible moment, I thought she was going to set off in one last attempt to snare him, but happily, screams erupted at the announcement of another song and she was distracted.

The set eventually drew to a close, but Dubus had obviously been watching what had happened with the Hoppies earlier. As they unplugged and moved to the side of the stage and the roars for more reached a crescendo, they suddenly about turned and prepared to play an encore before Mr Hamilton could get on the stage and shut things down. They played three more long songs. It could go not on forever, however. This time, Mr Hamilton was wise to their ploy and the moment the music went quiet, he made to walk out on the stage. The crowd went quiet except for some who booed.

Evan Davis took one look at the crowd then turned to the approaching teacher:

'C'mon Wally, Just one more. There has to be a last dance, surely.'

Mr Hamilton might have risked life and limb if he had done anything other than nod in acquiescence and with a dramatic flourish that he had now seemed to have acquired, he bowed to the band.

'We have had a great time tonight. Hope you have too. Good Old Barrington. I thought about closing the set with the School Song, but the others objected. Well, they would, wouldn't they? Instead, we are going to do something we have never done before.

90

This has been like a good old-fashioned school dance and it must have a last dance to bring things to a close. So, everyone, go grab somebody that is important to you. We are going to play this one real slow. Sorry Wally.'

The first two lines of 'Save the Last Dance for Me', made famous by the Drifters, had rung out, when a hand touched my arm and Calum stooped to whisper in my ear.

'Can I have this dance? I will understand if you say no.'

I did not answer. I just gently seized his arms, moved us a little way from Katey, and then buried my head in his chest and started to sway.

Long after the song was finished and the group was leaving the stage to incredible acclaim, we were still dancing to our own music.

'I am sorry, I acted like a prat. You did not deserve it.'

I looked up in his eyes and smiled a forgiveness.

'Which crime are you referring to—Cumbrae or Brigitte Bardot?

'Both'

'Ah'

'All I can say is that Cumbrae means an awful lot to me.'

'I know that.'

'And, I am going to make a pledge right here and now. Someday, it may be sooner, or it may be later, you and I are going to be together on that island.'

I remembered those words for a long time in my university and career life but eventually they dimmed in my memory. That was until the day that they finally came true.

A Breach of the "Piece"

Caleb Davies glanced around the kitchen one last time. Have I got everything? If I don't get going, he thought, I am going to be late and I don't want to miss that damned bus waiting at Gayfield Square.

'Caleb! Are you not on the road yet? You are going to be late. There is no point wishing you didn't have to go beat up the miners. It's just part of the job.' Caleb's wife Eileen's dulcet voice wafted through from the living room, where she had settled down to watch the evening film on television, while he set off for the night shift of an Edinburgh police constable.

It did not help his reluctance to go to work to be reminded so starkly of what the night held for him. Not the usual quiet beat patrol around the neighbourhood of the Gayfield Square Police Station. Not the usual midnight stop-off at Gardners the Bakers on Albert Street to enjoy freshly baked rolls straight out of the oven along with a big mug of steaming tea. No; tonight, like many days and nights recently, involved getting straight on to a special bus at the Police Station to be taken out to Bilston Glen Colliery, south of Edinburgh.

This was 1984. Not quite as George Orwell had predicted, but a physical and psychological war, nevertheless. The miners had gone on a national strike with the intention of blocking the closure of any mines and loss of jobs, irrespective of how uneconomic they were considered to be. And, if along the way they just happened to bring down the government of Margaret Thatcher like they had done to another Tory "bastard" Ted Heath in 1974, so much the better.

The UK coal mining industry had been in unstoppable decline for decades. Only taxpayer subsidies had slowed the decline. Now, Sir Ian McGregor, the newly appointed head of the National Coal Board, who was just fresh from dismantling the overfed and overweight UK steel industry, had announced sweeping plans to close twenty of the most inefficient pits with loss of 20,000 jobs. It appeared that Mrs Thatcher had reached the end of her tether of subsidising yet being held to ransom by many of the public sector trade unions; and most notably the National Union of Miners

(NUM). The NUM was more than happy to bite the hand that fed its members. Their sense of entitlement knew no bounds. After all, families were dependent on breadwinners and complete towns, full of families, were dependent on work at the local pit. In many instances, it was the only industry in the entire area. That translated in the NUM's mind into a need for absolute job security and good pay, in fact better pay was needed and right now. National and even global economic crises were the stuff of the media and nothing to do with the miners. Just pay them to do their work, regardless of productivity or any other governmental gobbledygook, and keep bread on the family tables, not to mention ale down their throats, was all they demanded.

Now, all that was under threat. Thatcher had defeated the outside enemy, the Argies, in the far-away Falklands War, all on her own it seemed, and now she was bent on defeating "the enemy within". And, she had come up with an "unscrupulous confederate" in McGregor who was half-Scottish, which made him a traitor, and half-American, which made him a "foreign bastard". The gloves were well and truly off!

Caleb grabbed his keys and was leaving when Eileen's voice boomed out again, 'Don't forget your piece. You've got some of that nice salmon that Calum brought over.'

Ah, thought Caleb; every cloud has a silver lining. His piece, his mid-shift meal, which usually consisted of egg sandwiches or potted meat sandwiches, would tonight feature a rare delicacy thanks to his little brother. No matter what the miners threw at him tonight, and they would for sure, he would at least enjoy fresh salmon sandwiches.

As Caleb drove the dark and largely deserted streets toward Gayfield Square, the driving rain probably had something to do with that, his thoughts turned to Calum. His little brother, seven years his junior and now in his early thirties, had turned up out of the blue at the house tonight, just before tea time. He was armed with a weighty salmon, the source of which was not revealed but probably came from one of his accounting clients in lieu of his fees, and an even weightier piece of news. After almost ten years of running his own little accounting practice in Galashiels, thirty miles south of Edinburgh, he was going to up sticks and emigrate to Canada. Just like that. No prior warning. Nothing. Apparently, his wife Susie and the kids had at least been consulted and were reported to be in favour. But, he, the big brother, who made it his role in life to look over the shoulder of his at-times wayward, at-times outright impulsive, junior sibling, had not even been informed until the airline tickets had been purchased and the house-cum-office put up for sale.

Bugger, he thought. It is always all about him. And now, he was left with the job of letting their widowed mother hear the news because Calum was going to be too busy in the next few weeks to visit her and she would not answer the phone they had newly installed for her. Of course, he would look in on her before they actually left the country; Calum had assured him amid a rare outbreak of feeling and compassion. Bugger, he thought again. Maybe I am just jealous. He gets to go off and try a new life in Canada while I get to deal with the miners. Well, at least I will have a cracking piece tonight, he mused, as he squinted through the fogged windscreen at a drunk making a precarious venture across Leith Walk. He just avoided him, wait a minute it was a her not a him, and turned into Gayfield Square.

9.59 pm

Caleb swerved into the last free parking space at the side of the Police Station, grabbed his priceless piece box off the seat beside

95

him, rolled out of the car in an ungainly, stumbling fashion, and ran up to the bus that was idling on the street in front of the only building with lights on in the Square.

'Ah. Good of you to join us. I was afraid Mr Scargill had got to you and you had lost your appetite for busting his miners' heads.'

Any hope that Caleb had entertained of getting on the bus without ceremony had been lost in the collision with the sarcastic Sergeant McClure, who was now trying to get off the bus.

'Raring to go, Sarge. Are you joining us for tonight's sport?' Caleb chanced his arm with a suitable riposte.

Laughter erupted throughout the bus.

'That will be right. Wullie has to look after the Station here in case the miners send a war party in this direction.'

'The Sarge had enough with the miners in 1974 and he has not been out on the beat since.'

'Now, now, lads. Show a bit of respect for your superior. Davies, get your arse into one of those seats and let's get this show on the road. I will be waiting for you when you get back at the end of the shift. Make sure you bring some scalps back. The usual rate will be paid. The rest of their dirty, unwashed bodies go to the Dalkeith Station cells, of course. Have a good night.'

He was gone and the door of the bus was closed before the repartee could be continued and the police officers settled down for the half hour drive out to Bilston Glen. Their assignment was to assist their comrades from Dalkeith in keeping the warring hordes of miners, otherwise known as flying pickets, from preventing those miners, who chose to ignore the strike and go to work, and the replacement workers who chose to do the same, from entering the pit. Both categories were despicable in the view of the Union and consequently called *scabs*. The pickets would try to block the scabs with lawful methods and unlawful methods, just as they had been doing for over four months.

While the bus made its way southward through a city dark and enveloped in that rainy mist so common on the east coast, individual conversations among the officers displayed the differing political views, united only in a firm resolve that they should not be doing this type of work. It was thankless, divisive, and downright dangerous. The opinions within the police force very closely mirrored those of the population at large with what seemed like almost half the people being sympathetic toward the miners and their goals, usually accompanied by a profound declaration that they would not want to do the kind of work required in the pits. In addition, there was a general desire to see the Conservative Government turned out after five years of austerity policy. Such views came from trade unionists and supporters of the Labour Party, of which there were many in the police. The opposing view was that the country was in dire financial straits and was again being held to ransom by the National Union of Miners. The Conservative Party and its leader Margaret Thatcher had been elected with the clear mandate to do something about it. That view was held by many in the police force, who were also sickened by the violence exhibited at the picket lines, putting them in a line of fire seldom ever seen in the UK, except perhaps in and around football grounds.

The bus had left the city boundaries and was closing in on Loanhead and the location of the pit, when it suddenly pulled to an abrupt stop. A dark saloon car had deliberately cut in front of it to bring it to a halt. Several officers were thrown from their seats into the aisle and others were drenched with tea and coffee that they had been drinking from thermos flasks intended for their piece later in the shift.

Yells and remonstrations with the civilian driver quickly dissipated when a stocky figure in a once white, now grubby, raincoat quickly boarded the bus. Most officers recognized Detective Chief Inspector Clancy of Central CID, who had the dubious honour of heading up the task force to deal with the Bilston Glen problem. Clancy held a reputation for enthusiastically giving out orders but seldom ever being seen in the thick of the action. There were theories as to how his raincoat had deteriorated over the years, but repelling the picket lines was not one of them.

'Sorry to barge in on you, lads, but I wanted to give you the latest intelligence from the battlefield, so to speak.' His attempted humour had zero impact on the officers who suspected that any news could only be bad news. It was.

'We have it from very reliable authority that tonight is going to be a bad one. Maybe the worst one yet. The Union has somehow got hold of news that the midnight shift is going to include a big batch of new replacement workers to add to those miners still working and the replacements already there. McGregor has decided that if Bilston really is the jewel in the crown of Scottish mining and is in no danger of closure, it jolly well ought to be increasing its production, even during a strike. The Union is, of course, dead set against that and intends to double the number of pickets, drawing more guys from other Scottish pits but also bringing in more of the fuckin' flying pickets from Durham and Yorkshire.'

'What does that mean for us? Are we going to get reinforcements? Maybe some English polis to crack the heads of their fellow countrymen?' A tentative question emerged from deep in the bus.

'We bloody well better be getting some relief. We only just stopped them breaking through our line last night. The workers going into the pit were shitting bricks.'

'Ah well, that is the thing. We are sending every available man from Lothian and Borders Police Stations and from all over Scotland, but we are maxed out. Crime doesn't just stop elsewhere because we have a job to do at Bilston. You know that as well as I do.'

'So, any more polis from last night's number?'

'Maybe two, if they came back in from sick leave. Otherwise, just like the fitba', it is an unchanged team for tonight's game.'

There was now silence on the bus as Clancy completed his pep talk and quickly turned to dismount and head for his car.

'You know you lads are trained for this sort of thing and have done a brilliant job to date. We will always be able to handle this riff-raff and come out ahead. Good luck.'

'Easy for that twit to say. He will be nowhere to be seen. Now we have got more of the English goons coming up. They are mental. Most of them are just professional thugs. They have probably never been down a coalmine in years.'

'Aye and they are still sore that we beat them at Hampden in April!'

12 Midnight

Caleb and his colleagues had been at the pithead for over an hour. The buses that had delivered them from all over had now backed out and returned to Loanhead. There was an uneasy stillness about the scene of previous battles. Police officers from various outlying stations had combined with the force from local Dalkeith Station to present a sturdy line-up on both sides of the roadway leading to the pit gates. But there was no sign of the pickets, who would be set on breaking through one or both of the lines to get at the buses bringing the workers through the gates. Surely, Clancy could not have got his so-called "intelligence" wrong and,

99

perchance, the pickets were taking a night off? They must surely be as exhausted as the police after four months of endless rioting.

'The buses will be here any minute now. Where the heck are the pickets?' Caleb asked to no-one in particular.

'Maybe we have finally scared the bastards off. There might be medals in this for us from Maggie.'

'Don't bank on that, pal. They will be here; just you wait'n'see. My brother telt me. He is on picket duty the nicht.'

'I didn't know your brother was a picket, Jimmy. How do you feel about that? Does it not split the family?'

'What do you think, Davies? It causes a hell of lot of tension. Our wives are no even talking to wan another. The daft thing about it all is I totally support the miners. It is ridiculous that we have to play Thatcher's hatchet men.'

Caleb started to say 'Thatcher's hatchet men! That is clever. You must have read that somewhere. I've got to say that I disagree.....' when shouts went up from officers furthest away from the gate.

'Here they come. The buses with the workers.'

'But, bugger it all, the miners are marching in front of the buses.'

'The buses cannae get past them. They are just creeping along.'

'What's that they have in front of the miners?'

Fully one hundred pickets, dressed for battle, were slowly making their way downhill on the narrow road leading to the gates. It resembled a funeral march and because they were spread across the entire road, the bus drivers had no choice other than to follow in a convoy at walking pace. As the procession got closer, the pennants and banners of the various mines and mining districts represented came into view and confirmed as much of an English presence as Scottish. It had almost the look of a medieval army striding on to the battlefield. But what was that being rolled along the road just behind the flag bearers? As the procession finally reached the police, who had immediately formed one single line in front of the gates, all was revealed.

Two giant lorry tyres, at least six feet in diameter, were being clumsily rolled along with great difficulty. No doubt they had been purloined from the heavy vehicle garage they had to pass half a mile back on the road. Suddenly, the procession stopped, the leaders disappeared behind the tyres, and tyres were made to roll on their own toward the police line. But that was not the most serious aspect. As the tyres rolled, they were seen to burst into flames. Obviously, they had been soaked with petrol in advance and, once ignited; represented a rapidly advancing threat on the police.

The officers scattered in both the directions open to them, lest they become the skittles to the giant bowling balls coming their way, to loud cheers from the pickets. That left the gates exposed to the imminent fiery assault. However, at the very last second, the two tyres collided with one another, rather than with the gates, and came to a stop in the semblance of a mighty funeral pyre. The toxic black smoke quickly enveloped everyone within thirty yards of the fire and caused police and pickets alike to scatter for safer ground.

Team leaders on the police side yelled out improvised orders, which at times were in contradiction, and the picket leaders did something similar. After fifteen minutes of confusion and occasional outbreaks of pushing, shoving, and fisticuffs, there emerged two distinct lines of the combatants, facing each other menacingly, while the tyres continued to burn furiously some distance behind the police line and just in front of the gates.

There was no meaningful communication between the two lines, just steely glares and a cacophony of threats and insults exchanged with increasing volume. Then, the pickets responded to the order to charge and headed directly for the police. Meanwhile the bus occupants, in the relative safety of their locked vehicles, could only look on with horror and dismay. Some of their friends and relatives were serving on both sides in the stramash unfolding in front of them. Such was the divisiveness of what the Guardian newspaper euphemistically referred to as 'industrial action'.

An ugly collision of bodies, with fists flying and swinging police truncheons countered by crude cudgels, took place, followed by an unordered break where both lines retreated a dozen paces to lick wounds and tend to the more seriously injured. Then they would launch into another charge, then another charge, and so on for the next thirty minutes. The audience in the buses could do nothing except watch. And the tyres continued to throw out noxious smoke, that every so often enveloped the combatants when the wind changed direction. Fortunately, the rain, which had begun the previous day and never let up since, actually served to help the situation by slowly damping down the fire, controlling somewhat the volatility of the smoke, and making the combatants thoroughly miserable to the point that an outbreak of peace, or at least a truce, might appear to be on the horizon.

During this time, there had been simply unbridled aggression by the two lines toward the other, but each had held their ground. The police had not let the pickets through to the gates, but nothing had been achieved toward the objective of clearing the way for buses to enter the gates. The officers had been so busy defending themselves, and frequently meting out cruel retaliatory punishment, that very few actual arrests had been made. That had been par for the course over the months of picket line violence. The only miners arrested tended to be the injured, ultimately left lying on the battlefield at the end of hostilities, or poor individuals who exhibited extreme bravery to break through the police line, only to find themselves isolated in no-man's land behind the police line and therefore easy candidates for arrest. The folly of their bravado never seemed to take root in the miners' minds, and such arrests were the only kind that had occurred on this night.

1 am

It seemed another charge was about to occur after a few minutes of separation for running repairs, when the unusual silence was shattered by the sound of sirens. A trio of fire engines came careening up the road and then screeched to a dramatic halt behind the buses. There was no way past the buses on either side because of the narrowness of the road and the drystane dykes on either side

'About bloody time,' a hatless Caleb muttered to a sidekick, who was taking the opportunity to remove his badly torn tunic in spite of the incessant rain. 'The tyres might be starting to burn themselves out anyway. They must have come in via the Borders.'

'Aye, the Welsh borders.'

'They might be here, but they are not going to be able to put out the fire from where they are parked right now. The fire engines are going to have to back up to the first crossroad, which is about a quarter of a mile back. Then the buses are going to have to back up. Then the fire engines can come down, run over the miners hopefully, scatter us, and see to the fire. Should be good for an hour or so!'

'Maybe we will get a break to eat our piece,' Caleb replied optimistically, thinking of that salmon in his piece box that sat in a pile safely behind the police line to the side of the gates with all the other piece boxes.

Several of the firemen walked past the buses and headed toward the two lines, now still formed and facing each other but clearly taking a break from the hostilities. The police might have been expecting their fellow emergency service colleagues to be headed to consult them about the logistics of getting the fire engines up to the gates. They were not. They stopped just behind the picket line and were seen to enter into huddled conversation with the union leaders.

After a full ten minutes of discussion, which quickly angered the majority of participants in the police line, the firemen eventually about-turned and headed back toward their vehicles. The pickets turned to watch the firemen walk. The occupants of the buses looked out the windows as the firemen passed without comment or indication of their intentions. The police watched and waited, unsure what was going to happen next. Once the firemen were back in their engines, one was left to return to the last bus and speak to the driver. Then, the engines fired up and started to back up at alarming pace. A roar went up from the pickets. They knew what was happening!

Along the police line, officers were heard to yell, mostly with anguish, but some with a few whoops of delight: 'Those bastards will not cross the picket line.'

Animated conversation then took place between the police team leaders, as the pickets celebrated with chants and even songs. They could sense a victory at last. Time passed with no action on either side. Then, the team leaders dispatched an officer to communicate with the bus occupants. The officer was a stalwart at stand-off for the Lothian and Borders Police Rugby Team and was lithe enough to leap over the dyke with the intention of getting to the buses without encountering the picket line stretched across the road. Alas, what he encountered instead was a quagmire of rain-sodden animal waste and mud. The momentum from his leap caused him to lose balance and disappear from view. Roars went up from the pickets again, and then the following silence was disturbed by a yell from behind the dyke: 'Aaaaagh. I've done in my back!' An even louder roar of triumph erupted.

More officers were dispatched to scale the dyke and tend to their fallen comrade. Mortified, and sensing a premature end to his rugby career, the officer insisted with some forcefulness that he not be moved until qualified medical personnel could be called to supervise the delicate action. Instead, his fallen cap was retrieved and placed under his head to prevent him drowning in the glaur, heaven forbid the thought, and there he remained.

The team leaders were stung into indignation by the failure of their sortie to connect with the buses. Probably that indignation prompted the next command to the police line, delivered with bravado, and some spluttering:

'This time, we do the charging!'

2 am

Another hour had passed, and several charges had been initiated by one line or the other. Exhaustion was setting in, not to mention the mounting numbers of casualties, and no breakthrough had been achieved by either side. The work shift in the pit, which was scheduled to last twelve hours, including nine hours underground, was already over two hours old and no progress had been made by the buses with their occupants toward the gates. Police team leaders were now discussing the prospect of giving up for the night and sending the buses back from whence they had come. It would mean no shift in the mine. That would surely be viewed as a victory for the pickets. A decision, as far-reaching as what was being considered, obviously was not going to be made quickly.

Discussions continued. The two lines stood and glared at each other in a somewhat bizarre fashion. The union leaders could even be seen to be in a huddle behind their line. Wonder what they were talking about? Maybe they too had reached the conclusion that the battle could not be won and were discussing how to pack it in for the night without appearing to have been rebuffed by the police once again, and this time with a larger force than they had ever had out before.

Police officers in the line started up little conversations with their nearest comrades, even though they might never have met them before. Such was the chaos of maintaining the police line to combat the picket line.

A voice from just outside Glasgow, which always seemed to mean anybody who did not actually come from Edinburgh, Aberdeen, or the Western Isles, opined: 'This is goin' naewhere, is it no? It's time I thought aboot hot-footin' it outa here.'

'Aye, gaun yersel, Jimmy,' came the response in a similar accent.

Caleb looked over to study the faces of the pedlars of such seditious talk. They had hard faces. They almost looked like miners with police uniforms on. No doubt, they were battle hardened from police work in the wild west of Scotland but here they were now contemplating desertion. Caleb looked the other way for signs of more familiar, and more loyal, colleagues.

Suddenly, the silence of the night was again shattered by sirens, this time police sirens, coming from a veritable flotilla of cars, vans, and buses. Reinforcements! Feelings like those felt at the Relief of Mafeking in 1900 swept through the police ranks. The miners glumly turned to view the prospect of being attacked from the front and rear.

Several new arrivals walked past the buses toward the pickets. No, walked does not do it justice, better to say strutted. And, strutting prominently among them was a once white, now grubby, raincoat. DCI Clancy, himself, had come to battle and it was he that addressed the assembled masses with a megaphone.

'Miners, your evening's activities are over. You will disperse now and let the workers' buses through. We outnumber you now by 5 to 1. We will take you from both sides if you don't leave immediately and we will arrest every last one of you. The Scots will go straight to prison in Edinburgh, not to the police cells, and we will hold you there for as long as we like, until we get around to charging you. The English will be taken to the border where our colleagues will be waiting to deal with you in any way they see fit. But rest assured, it will be in no more pleasant a way than what we will dole out in Edinburgh.' Clancy's voice had started off in a screeching manner that betrayed his nervousness, but had quickly softened and gained authority as he acquired confidence. 'I trust you all understand me. There is no further discussion. You have five minutes precisely to be on your way out of here. Or else, we advance from both sides.'

The sight of what seemed like hundreds of officers now assembled for combat, there surely had to be some military personnel amongst them, was enough for the miners. Well within the five-minute deadline, the vast majority had dropped their cudgels and other improvised weapons and were heading away from the pit. They even carried or helped the injured out, for fear they would be arrested if they remained. The new police line separated, with a mixture of pomp and triumph, to allow the miners to make their way past the scabs' buses and police vehicles and on their way back to their own buses up the road. Save for some surreptitious spitting in the direction of vehicles, there was no further action from the retreating army.

However, there remained a dozen or three diehards among the pickets, who continued to stand their ground daring the police to do their worst. They were firmly resolved to try to cause some more injuries before they were taken.

Clancy's screeching voice had returned.

'From both sides, advance!'

Perhaps, with more battle experience first-hand, the commanding officer might have deployed his men in waves, rather than all at once. What happened was that far too many officers rushed toward the pickets from front and rear and essentially collided in a flurry of confusion, swirling truncheons, and battle cries. More than a few officers actually inflicted injuries on their fellow officers. Eventually, arrests were made and a few telling blows were inflicted on the real enemy, but not before a number of the pickets managed to escape in the confusion over the dyke into the quagmire. They were able to make off in all directions in comical fashion as their feet were sucked into the squelching mud. One even had the temerity to aim a kick at the still prostrate rugby-playing constable lying awaiting medical assistance. Fortunately, it was ill-aimed and probably no worse than a normal Saturday retribution from an opposing prop forward.

After what seemed like a considerable period of time, that was punctuated by yelled commands from team leaders and the overwhelming screeches through the megaphone, officers managed to place each of the remaining pickets under arrest. Order gradually began to return, as more and more officers started to realise that it was more productive to actually get out of the way and leave the arrests to others. That would normally have been Caleb's inclination too, but for some reason he found himself, along with two unknown colleagues, making an actual arrest. This picket appeared to be different from the others, however. He was younger, probably in his early thirties; he was better dressed; and he was bleeding from a head wound. And he was terrified. It showed in his eyes, even though he mouthed some obscenities and invited the "pigs" to take him. While it was a popular epithet during Vietnam demonstrations and other confrontations in the last two decades, reference to the police as pigs was not that common among the miners and this too singled out the person now being arrested.

The sheer logistics of extinguishing the fire, getting the buses as close as possible to the mine property, getting the workers through the gates and onto a truncated shift, and managing the reversal of more than thirty vehicles, was to take over two hours. DCI Clancy had retired in triumph back to the city and left things to the team leaders, who were by now exhausted and more than a little bemused by the night's activities. Caleb had been left in charge of his arrestee, once handcuffs had been applied and tempers had calmed down. The prisoner would not volunteer any information other than the fact that his name was Colin Chisholm. Some thirty-two arrests had been made and it had been established that twelve were English. They were first to be marched off to a secure police vehicle, the so-called paddy wagon, with one officer escorting each prisoner and four officers on hand at the front and rear of the group in case they were needed. The transfer was accomplished without incident and the vehicle took off on its journey to the Scotland/England border.

The Scottish group, being larger, would take two vehicles and it was split into two. The first group was marched to its vehicle with minimum fuss, although there was still some confusion and jostling as the prisoner group encountered police officers moving in both directions. Some were on their way to buses and other vehicles to return to their stations; others were heading towards the gates to effect a clean-up of the area and to lend assistance to injured colleagues, who were now gradually being treated on the spot or transferred to the newly arrived ambulances. The stand-off was now actually on his feet and had safely renegotiated the climb back over the dyke. In all probability, his pride was hurting as much as his back, as a group of fellow officers surrounded him and replayed the drama of earlier in case he had forgotten.

Eventually, Caleb's group was given the order to proceed up to the waiting vehicle, which was still stuck behind several buses and could not be brought any closer to them. If anything, the coming and going of officers and now ambulance staff, was making progress up the hill even more difficult. The group, without specific orders, casually split into two on either side of the road to squeeze past one bus after another. Then, most of the group found its way onto one side of the roadway by the dyke. The small remainder, including Caleb and his charge, continued on the other side. As they neared the paddy wagon, Colin Chisholm stumbled and fell in a particularly muddy section between the road and the dyke. By the time Caleb had helped him to his feet; the others on their side of the road had squeezed between two vehicles and were now reunited with their colleagues on the other side of the road. Chisholm was making much of his tumble and was only able to limp slowly. Rather than try to squeeze between the two closely parked vehicles, Caleb chose to continue up the same side of the road as they came in sight of the paddy wagon. As they passed the paddy wagon with the intention of crossing over to the other side of the road at its rear, two things happened at exactly the same time. Chisholm again stumbled as his leg gave way and he ended up sitting in the muddy stretch between the vehicle and the dyke. And, an almighty ruckus broke out on the other side of the paddy wagon with yells, cries for help, and obvious collisions with the side panels of the vehicle.

'Sit there and don't move a muscle,' Caleb yelled at Chisholm as he sprinted off around the vehicle.

On the other side there was mayhem. Three of the prisoners, in spite of being handcuffed behind their backs, had suddenly attacked officers as they were being loaded into the vehicle. A prodigious *Glasgow Kiss* and several well-placed kicks had brought

110

down some of the officers. Just as two of the prisoners were about to hightail it up the road, they collided mightily with Caleb as he rounded the back of the vehicle. All three went down with a crunch, but Caleb ended up on top of the pile and hung on to the other two for grim life.

'Good man, Caleb. You nailed them,' exclaimed one of the officers who, after placing a well-aimed kick of his own in retaliation, gained control of one of the prisoners. Then the other prisoner was taken back under control and all three were bundled into the vehicle after several more blows from the now seriously irritated officers were inflicted.

'Ok, driver. Get these bastards off to Saughton Prison before we are tempted to finish them off here and now.'

The officers made their way back down the road to see to the replacement workers' buses as the paddy wagon commenced its backing up exercise at some speed. Caleb was last to follow the officers down the hill. It was only when the paddy wagon had moved some distance that he was able glance over the roadway and spy Colin Chisholm sitting rather glumly in the mud.

Jesus Christ, what do I do now, thought Caleb. He quickly crossed the road.

'This is your lucky day Colin,' he said, removing the handcuffs and helping the prisoner to his feet.

'Get the hell out of here before I change my mind.'

'Not at all! I've been lifted. I don't want to get out of here. I am bound for Saughton.'

'No, you are not. Beat it! Vamoose!'

With a firm shove in the back of the reluctant arrestee, Caleb issued a final threat: 'If you are not out of my sight in one-minute flat, I will bring back some of my buddies and they will beat the crap

111

out of you. Now hop it!' An unhappy Chisholm limped away without looking back

5:45 am

Once most of the battlefield had been cleaned up and the police presence had all but disappeared, the rain decided it had not had a sufficient impact and transformed itself into the torrential variety. The last of the officers, including Caleb, climbed on to the last bus due to make the precarious back-up to the nearest crossroads. Technically it was sunrise according to the almanac, but the rain was making the visibility worse than it had been throughout the night. The thoroughly drenched officers sat in their seats, not caring that condensation precluded any view out of the windows and just hoping that they would be safely returned to Gayfield Square Station in time for the end of their shifts. One or two of them finally broke open their piece boxes and quietly nibbled. Others, including Caleb, were so exhausted and miserable that they could not even summon up the energy or desire to eat. All of them had been through bad shifts at Bilston Glen. This had been the worst by far.

When the bus reached the Gayfield Police Station, they were met by the normally affable Sergeant McClure, who was wearing a glum look on his face.

'Sorry to do this to you, lads. There is another revolt afoot in our fair city. Why is everybody so revolting right now? Those of you who can read and do read the Scotsman will know that Edward Montgomery, the Minister for Science and Technology, is due to visit St. Andrews House this morning. He is set to announce a reduction in student grants for all universities in the country.

Needless to say, the students are not best pleased that their handouts will be getting cut and plan to give him a hot reception. They are already assembling outside St. Andrews House and getting a bit rowdy.'

'Why us, Sarge? We are *cream crackered.*'

'I know. I know. But we need extra men. We don't know how many students will turn up. It is easier to get you guys to put in a few extra hours than it is to call in other extras for a special shift. Will mean a wee bit more money for you all in your next pay packet. Think of it that way?

'We are drookit. Can we no even change wir uniforms?'

'No time for that, lads. And, what would be the point? You are only going to get wet again. This rain is on for the day.'

'Just as well it is July then and not December. Might have been snow,' offered some positive thinker's voice from the back of the bus.

'That's the spirit,' replied the Sergeant as he hopped off the bus: 'See you when you get back.'

'No, he'll not. He is off duty in five minutes,' grumbled his partner to Caleb. Caleb didn't reply. He was beginning to wish he had eaten his piece now. The salmon was getting more attractive again.

St. Andrews House was bit confusing even for Edinburgh residents. It was the home of the Scottish Office of the UK Government. That bit was relatively clear assuming you understood how government was minimally devolved from its base in London. However, there were two St. Andrews Houses. Old St. Andrews House was not that old. It was built in 1939 in an aesthetically pleasing Art-Deco style on the site, ironically, of the former Calton Gaol. New St. Andrews House, completed in 1969 to accommodate the burgeoning growth in government, was located atop the St.

James Shopping Centre and was designed in the Brutalist style of architecture. Brutal by name and brutal by nature, it was perhaps the most loathed building in the capital city.

It was to Old St. Andrews House that the Gayfield police were bound. Technically, it was within their jurisdiction, so providing the first response was appropriate.

More than a hundred students, armed with placards and banners, were already clogging the crescent-shaped car park in front of the building and not allowing access or egress for any vehicles. The bus driver decided to be diplomatic and not try to scatter the students. He parked further down Regent Road to let his group of unhappy officers alight.

The arrival of the police certainly stimulated the students. Boos mixed with cheers and laughs rang out. Then, a surprisingly tuneful rendering, beginning 'Have you seen the Little Piggies......' struck up, and the students began to sway in time. This was not the first protest for many of them.

That George Harrison has a lot to answer for, more than a few police officers thought, as they gradually eased their way through the mass of bodies to take up position outside the imposing, and currently locked, main doors of the building. Once the police had assembled in something of a line facing the students, it was immediately obvious that the former were significantly outnumbered. However, it was to be assumed that their adversaries were highly educated and much different from the miners they had faced earlier in the night. At least, that was the theory. There were probably as many members of the Communist Party of the UK who were also members of the National Union of Students as there were also members of the National Union of Mineworkers.

Sergeant MacCaskell, who had arrived separately by car, stepped forward to address the crowd as commanding officer. He was armed with a megaphone, but it did not project his voice particularly well. Angus Hamish MacCaskell was from the Western

Isles and spoke with that quiet, almost haunting, lilt, so common among his kin folk.

'Ach well now. It is a cood morning to you all, sure it is. A fine turnout I must say. Chust a wee pity the weather was not better for you.'

'That's all we need. A tcheuchter piggy,' brought a roar from the students, followed by massed snorting interspersed with shouts of 'where's your kilt?' and 'up your kilt'.

'Now. Now. Cood to see you are all in fine spirits. We are not here to spoil your fun, but you have to be aware of a few cround rules. After that, we will get along just famously'

'Pigs out. Pigs out. Deport the tcheuchtar,' rang out.

'Chust a wee minute. Let me tell you all what is on my mind then you can sing all the wee songs you like.'

Gradually, MacCaskell's persistence won through and the crowd quietened down to listen to what he had to say.

'The Minister will be arriving at 9:00 am and going into the building through the doors behind me. You will be allowed to stand in the car park and present your demonstration at his arrival and during his presence in the building. He will be meeting with Scottish Office staff and then holding a press conference at approximately 10:30. He is expected to leave the building by not later than 11:00.'

The chants began, this time not directed at the police but at the Government that had the temerity to reduce the already small grants that students received to go to university. MacCaskell raised his hand to indicate he had more to say.

'This is the important bit that you should pay particular attention to. I have told you that you will be permitted to demonstrate. You can make as much noise as you like but you must remain in the car park. If anyone steps on to this road in front of me and tries to interfere with the Minister's arrival, or even once he is inside the building, they will be arrested. There will be no forgiveness; no exceptions. Some of these officers here have spent all of last night at Bilston Glen and they are not likely to be in the best of moods. They will arrest you if you step out of the car park and you will be charged with a breach of the peace.'

Mention of Bilston Glen had prompted a huge roar of solidarity for the students' mining brothers. The Sergeant's almost kindly words of advice were, of course, largely ignored, and even though there was more than two hours to go until the big event, it was almost inevitable that some student would put the warning to the test. Sure enough, almost immediately, a tall gangly youth with long lank hair and brandishing a sign demanding an end to the budget cuts ,stepped on to the road and cried:

'Take me, Pigs.'

They did and rather roughly at that.

One or two others tried the same and ended up with the same result. Gradually, the crowd settled down as they realized MacCaskell's warning was not in jest.

For the next two hours, the students amused themselves with all sorts of chants and song parodies directed at the Tories and the police. The police line, containing many now very hungry, tired, and wet officers, stood its ground. The officers tried to maintain their stern faces, although it was difficult at times not to laugh at some of the songs.

9:10 am

Caleb was standing next to his best friend and fellow officer Rab Taylor. Rab was on the day shift this week but the friends were thrust together in the common cause of managing the student protest.

Caleb had told Rab all about his brother Calum's news of impending emigration and the gift of the mighty salmon, part of which was now in his piece, currently sitting in the bus down the road.

'Lucky bugger,' Rab responded. Caleb was not sure whether Rab was referring to Calum or himself and was about to clarify the statement when the lilting voice of Sgt. MacCaskell filtered out over the assembled line:

'This will be it now, laddies. Chust pay attention to what is happening around you and listen for my commands.'

When the Minister's car pulled up outside St. Andrews House some ten minutes late due to the late arrival of his flight from London, the student group increased the intensity of their protests but initially held their ground in the car park. They had been largely well behaved over last two hours but now that the focus of their ire had appeared, that record would be put to the test.

The police were poised in a curved line that quickly took in the car and the now-opened doors to the building. A senior Scottish civil servant was on hand to welcome the Minister, help him out of the car, and quickly usher him inside. Still the students remained on their side of driveway. Perhaps, everybody was going to get what they wanted on this occasion.

Alas, as is often the case in sporting disturbances, it only took one, then a couple, then a few, then a mass charge occurred. The first to break the line on this occasion was in fact a chunky young woman clad in battle fatigues. The clothing might have signalled the intent in advance. Waving her placard espousing her belief that education is a right, not a privilege, she stepped forward and slowly headed toward the police. By the time she had reached the line and was standing with her face thrust into the not inconsiderable chest of a PC Turnbull, another stalwart of the rugby team, she had been joined by a slowly growing number of protesters.

MacCaskell tried reason.

'Now. Now. Now! Have you forgotten what I was after saying to you chust a wee while ago? There is no value, no value at all, in encroaching now especially as the Minister is safely inside. Why don't you chust back up to your side of the road and I will just pretend this neffer happened. How about that?'

There was a pause and then some of the students started to retreat from the forbidden area. More started in the same direction. It might very well have been that a complete retreat would have happened had not the leader, who had not moved an inch and had not even looked up at PC Turnbull's face, chosen that point in time to add her own personal contribution to the situation balanced on a knife-edge.

'Fuck you, Pig'

With that challenge thrown down, students on the retreat turned again and charged forward and were joined by others from the car park.

Just as at Bilston Glen, the two groups clashed with similar intensity but thankfully lacking some of the extreme violence. Nonetheless, police hats were knocked off, punches were thrown, some but not all truncheons were drawn and deployed, and a lot of mean-spirited words were exchanged.

Sgt. MacCaskell, not accustomed to such behaviour in the Western Isles, but now seasoned in the ways of the Lowlands, appraised the situation and quickly made the order to begin arrests. Several officers got in each other's way in their zeal to arrest the leader but eventually she was subdued and handcuffed. Not before she had meted out a few telling blows of her own on the officers, whose zeal quickly abated.

Caleb and Rab apprehended another student, who initially put up quite a struggle before sinking to his knees in submission. A girl casually walked up to them and offered her hands: 'You might as well arrest me too. That's my boyfriend and he's got the keys to our flat!'

Some fifteen minutes after the first incursion into the no-go zone, about a dozen arrests had been made and the impact had had a salutary effect on the remaining protesters causing them to retreat to the car park.

Sgt. MacCaskell directed that the arrestees be put into a paddy wagon that had materialized out of thin air, and be taken to Gayfield Square Police Station under minimal officer supervision. He then surprised some of the other officers by directing those, who had been on duty all night, to return to their bus and go back to Gayfield. Reinforcements were just arriving from other stations in case the students blew up again while the Minister was still in the building and Caleb and others could now be stood down.

'That's a nice surprise. I am starving,' said Caleb.

'Don't go thinking MacCaskell has gone soft. It's the prospect of double overtime pay looming that is prompting you being sent back. You remember that after five hours of a double shift, all the overtime is at double-rate.'

Caleb smiled and headed off to the bus.

When bus and paddy wagon arrived at the police station, the day sergeant was quick to direct that the prisoners be sent downstairs.

'A little while in our cells should teach these overly-privileged rioters a little humility.'

After the thirteen students had been locked up in several cells, a little of the cockiness having drained from most of them, the officers were told they could go to the canteen and eat their pieces. Few officers ever actually ate the food on offer in the canteen, but it was used to consume the food and drinks brought from home.

With much anticipation, Caleb sat down with others to finally eat something after more than twelve hours. He had just started to open his piece box as several other officers, who were now in on his story, stared on with interest, when the seemingly inevitable happened. In rushed the day sergeant.

'No time to eat, lads, just yet. I have just got the order from on high. Some reporters apparently followed the paddy wagon here and want to see the prisoners and interview them. We are to formally caution them as quickly as possible, then let them go pending a future court appearance. If they want to blab to the press, they can do it outside and not on our premises.'

'Aw, Sarge, c'mon.'

'Never mind c'mon. Just do it. You know the drill. Each of you go down, caution the prisoner you arrested, and let them go. Toot sweet. I want it done before 10:30.'

'That figures,' said someone who knew the police constable contract provisions.

10:23 am

The day sergeant and an inspector, who had now taken an interest in proceedings, watched as the students and officers traipsed up the steps to the main public concourse, whereupon the students turned left and exited; and the officers turned right toward the canteen. The fatigues-clad leader let go with a colourful diatribe before being dragged out by her colleagues.

Caleb was at the back because he had had to process two cautions, one each to the couple he had arrested in the first place. They were really pretty decent kids, who had just got caught up in the excitement of mass hysteria. Both were now quite contrite and worried about what their parents would have to say. Caleb had taken pity on them and as they had left the cell; he whispered that in all probability they would never get into the congested court system and would likely receive a stiff written warning as to their future conduct. As he turned to follow the others back to the canteen, Caleb could not help smiling to himself over his second act of compassion of the young day. He was getting to be more like a social worker than a cop. Those officers from the west of Scotland would never have approved.

'Davies, before you disappear, just go back down and check that the cells are empty, and all the students have been processed.'

Had the inspector not been present, he would have mounted a protest, but in the circumstances, Caleb just nodded glumly to the sergeant.

He checked that three cells were empty as anticipated and walked along to the one furthest down the bleak corridor. A cursory glance was about to confirm the obvious when he did a double take. There in corner of the cell, almost out of view, sat a lone male with his head drooping, but not enough to conceal a recently sustained wound on the forehead. Colin Chisholm! He looked up when Caleb stormed in.

'Oh, you again.'

'Chisholm, what on earth are you doing here?'

'Busted, I'm afraid. That is the price of civil disobedience.'

'I don't remember seeing you arrested.'

'Aye well.'

'Who arrested you?'

'We were not introduced.'

Caleb's mind swirled as he thought what his next move was to be. He did not necessarily want to be parading Chisholm about upstairs in case the episode of earlier in the morning came out. Eventually, he walked out, slammed the cell door shut, and said with some conviction: 'You stay here and don't move while I get this sorted out!'

The irony of the order did not seem to register with either of them.

Caleb raced up to the canteen and to the table of his colleagues. He was relieved to see his piece box sitting unopened. Grand larceny of pieces was an endemic problem in the police force.

'There's somebody still left in the cells. Guy with a cut on his forehead. Who arrested him? You need to go down and process him.'

Officers looked blankly at one another. Not one owned up to the capture. Caleb turned on his heels and stormed off to consult the day sergeant.

'I sure as hell did not arrest him. If you can't find who did, then use your initiative and caution him yourself. You don't get into that canteen until you do it,' came the response from the unmoved senior officer, and that is why Caleb found himself back down in the cell posing questions to Colin Chisholm.

Chisholm was reluctant to give much information other than the fact that he had been lifted during the fracas at St. Andrews House, having driven in from Bilston without even going home. He was unable to describe his arresting officer but insisted it was obvious he had suffered the same fate as his fellow students. He gradually revealed that he attended Heriot Watt University, lived in his own apartment in the swanky Warrender district, and his father was in fact the Bursar of the same university.

Caleb removed his tunic as the temperature in the cell seemed to soar, and started to fill out the caution sheet when Chisholm remarked on the name tag on his shirt.

'C. Davies. I used to know a C Davies.'

'Oh yes.'

'Calum Davies. What is your first name?

'My name is Caleb Davies. Calum is my brother. How do you know him?'

'I knew him first in high school and then I saw him at uni when he was doing an accounting course. That was my first spell at Edinburgh. Then I went to Glasgow before Heriot Watt. Calum was off to become an accountant after graduation. I have never been with him since, other than nodding to him in the street.'

'He still is an accountant, in Galashiels. At least for next few weeks and then he is off to Canada.'

'Lucky bugger'

'You are not the first person to say that. Listen, I am going to lock you up again for a few minutes. I have something to do. I will be back to finish your processing.'

Caleb sat down at the vacant desk of the supervisor of cells, picked up the phone, and asked for an outside line.

'Calum! Amazing. I never get through to you normally.'

'How do, Caleb. My assistant is out at the bank, so I am answering the phone. What is up? Have you been enjoying that salmon?'

'Don't talk to me about salmon. I have been trying to catch it for twelve hours. Do you know a Colin Chisholm?'

'Colin Chisholm, I don't think so. Oh, wait a minute. A well-dressed little runt with a hoity-toity accent?'

'Sounds like him.'

'I knew him in school. Then he went to university at the same time my firm sent me on a course. We were in a couple of classes together although it was never clear what degree he was actually pursuing. I am not even sure he ever graduated. His parents were well off. His old man was something big at Heriot Watt.'

'That is him.'

'How do you know him?'

'I have been involved in his arrest. Twice as a matter of fact. Twice in the same night.'

'PC Plod always gets his man. Well done.'

'That would be the Canadian Mountie, not PC Plod, who always gets his man. You will need to learn that.'

'Mmm. What did you get him on? Wait a minute. It is all coming back to me. Colin always had an insatiable desire to get himself arrested. Even at school. He got kicked out of an Edinburgh Waverley game against Glasgow Erin. He was done for taunting the great unwashed after we scored. However, he was really pissed because the cops just let him go once he was outside the stadium. He wanted to be charged.'

'Why on earth would he want that to happen?'

'I think he couldn't stand his old man, who was always on at him to become an academic or something in the City. Colin would rather just bum around and acquire a bad reputation. When we were at uni, a bunch of us went to Murrayfield for the Welsh game. Colin managed to get himself arrested for arguing with the Welsh supporters. Annoying as they were, and still are, it is pretty hard to get yourself arrested for tangling with the overbearingly friendly Welsh rugby fans. He got fined that time, but only a fiver. He was irate and was looking for jail time. Strange bird. You didn't say what you lifted him for?'

'On the picket line riot with the miners and part of the student demo at St. Andrews House, although the funny thing is, I can't confirm that he was actually arrested the second time. The first time, I let him go.'

'Bloody hell. That sounds just like Colin. He must have been disappointed when you let him go and decided to try again with the students. He might even still be a student for all I know. I have never heard of him having an actual job.'

'Do you think it conceivable that he might just have jumped into the paddy wagon when nobody was looking?'

'Ha ha! I would think that quite likely. Was he handcuffed?'

'Good question. I have no idea. All I know is I have him in a cell along the corridor dying to finish his caution and become officially busted.'

'Yup. Success at last.'

'I better go. You have actually been of some assistance for once.'

'My pleasure to be of service to the constabulary.'

'I want to hear more about this Canada jaunt.'

'Why not come out to Gala on Saturday night? Or, are you working?'

'I am on early shift Saturday and off Sunday so that will work out well. Cheers'

Caleb unlocked the cell door and Chisholm looked up in fervent expectation.

'Well? Been checking up on me, have you?'

'Don't consider yourself that important. I had to call my bookie actually. Now let's get down to business and finish this caution. This is a very serious matter and you can expect very little sympathy in the court. The public views you students as just as bad as the miners and wants the book thrown at you.'

Chisholm nodded seriously and replied, 'I understand.'

Once the paperwork was complete, Caleb had Chisholm read it through and then sign.

'You are now cautioned. Get out of here.'

As Chisholm was jauntily walking out the station seemingly cured of his earlier limp, Caleb ran into the day sergeant.

'All done, Davies?'

'Yes, Sarge'

'Well don't bother going to eat your piece now. Just knock off. Your shift is over. Get on home and have some sleep.'

Caleb looked up surreptitiously at the concourse clock. One minute to eleven o'clock. A thirteen-hour shift, and no more. He nodded and went to fetch his piece box.

Caleb left through the side door of the station and spotted his car, now all on its own. He looked up. It was still raining but there was a hint of a break in the clouds. He pondered whether he should get right into his piece in the car or wait until he got home to eat it there. Hunger answered the question for him. He finally opened his box and peered in with a great deal of anticipation.

The box was two thirds full of water, rain water! A quick inspection confirmed that no fresh-salmon sandwiches would be enjoyed today. It kind of summed up what the last thirteen hours had amounted to.

Shaking his head, he proceeded to empty his precious piece into the waste bin by the door. He stood for a moment staring into the bin, an action that attracted some attention from a fellow officer exiting the station. Once he had passed by, Caleb went into the inside pocket of his tunic and pulled out the Crown copy of the caution sheet he had omitted to file inside the station. He rolled it up into a ball and fired it into the bin after the sandwiches.

Of Streakers
and Sneakers

Calum Davies and Nerys Jones were seated in a busy boardwalk café in Venice Beach, California. The beach and boardwalk were teeming with summer crowds, which presented a colourful and vibrant vista. But, Calum and Nerys were barely aware of what was going on around them. They were now into the third month of their relationship, having met by chance at a garden party at the University of California, Riverside (UCR).

Nerys was completing her third year at the University as an adjunct faculty member in the department of Political Science. But exciting things were ahead in addition to her new relationship. In September, she would begin the doctoral programme at the University of California, Santa Barbara and, upon completion; she had her sights set on a regular teaching and research position at one of the public or larger private universities in California.

Calum too was undertaking change. A year previous, on the back of a difficult divorce in British Columbia, Canada, he had uprooted and taken an adjunct teaching position at UCR, hence, their unplanned meeting at the garden party. Neither had set eyes on the other during the entire year on campus. Calum had now just been hired to a non-tenure-track position by the California University and would be part of the small teaching cadre at its new campus in Temecula, which would be opening for business next month.

The last three months had been an initially tentative, but ultimately intensive, time together for two somewhat shattered souls; coming off long, but now dissolved, relationships. Their careers had been stagnating somewhat and both had chosen dramatic changes in direction. Those facts alone might have been enough to make them kindred spirits; but they were also finding that in spite of the ten years and vastly different previous lives between them, they were developing common values and interests and the idea of a shared future. Nerys could not hear enough about the California University, the largest private university in the state with seven campuses already established and the new Temecula site about to open. She was not only delighted for Calum, who had way too much teaching and research experience, as well as extensive professional experience as an accountant, to be languishing as an adjunct at UCR. She was also very impressed by what the California University was offering new PhDs. She could definitely see herself ending up there after graduation. It was fair to say the California University was shaking up the university environment in California and causing the firmly established University of California (UC) and California State University (CSU) to look over their shoulders. It was not just the irritation of its much-too-similar name. The new university was the real deal.

Calum ordered another beer and chardonnay and finally took time to look out over the mass of tanned and oiled bodies, thronging in front of them.

'You know, this is not a bad place. After the bleakness of Scotland and the uncertainty of Canada, this is exactly what I would imagine a summer in California was meant to be like. All those beautiful blonde bodies.'

'Yes. And, that is only the guys.'

'What? I never noticed them. I should imagine Santa Barbara is just the same. I wonder if you will get any work done there, especially living on campus.'

'I am not going there to fool around. I am too old for that. I am going to complete my PhD in record time and then get a regular position somewhere. No more slave-labouring as an adjunct. I really like what I hear about your place. You never know. We might end up teaching together.'

'The accountant and the political scientist? Sounds like the start of a joke as in there was an Englishman, a Scotsman, and an Irishman........ I will, however, keep my ear to the ground on how the Temecula campus is going to develop. It is pretty small right now for its first semester; but it will grow, I am sure. The demand is there. A lot of students are finding that the UC and CSU are all about lots of things; but being student-friendly is not necessarily one of them. The California University is fast becoming a viable alternative.'

'Have you decided whether you will commute from Riverside or get something a bit closer? The I-15 is no fun drive.'

'Mmm. I have been looking at some patio homes in Irvine. It is not exactly on the doorstep of Temecula, but it is really central for all things in Southern California. I reckon I might just be able afford something with what my ex-wife graciously left me.'

'Patio home? Do you mean in one of over-55 communities? You don't qualify.'

'No. But I am getting closer by the day. There are actually some that are only over-50s and I definitely qualify for them. I can sneak you in over the wall, if you like.'

'As if I would be seen dead in an old age community!'

'Comes to us all, I am afraid. And, they don't allow children, which is a definite plus. I was thinking that, if your schedule allowed for it, you could spend a day or so a week in Irvine and maybe pick up a class to teach in Temecula.'

'I never thought about that.'

'I remember when I was doing my doctorate that, if you organize yourself as far as classes and dissertation work is concerned, you can have bags of spare time. Of course, I wasted it on wine, women, and song. You could teach a class and get a foot in the door, so to speak.'

'Mmm. You seem to have been doing a lot of thinking. And, not just about yourself. Does that mean you see a future for us?'

'I do, if you do. The last three months have been the best for me in an awful long time. But there is a test that you will have to face if we are going to be a permanent thing.'

'I am a cordon bleu cook; I will have you know.'

'That is not what I mean. You will find out later. One thing I did want to ask you. Do you fancy dropping everything and going over to London and beyond next week, before the semesters start? My dean has given the ok for me to attend the annual conference of my British accountancy body. And, it is in London next week.'

'Wow! Sure. What do you mean by beyond? Maybe Paris?'

'Something like that. That is where the test comes in.'

'Going to Paris would be no test.'

'I did not say it would be Paris. Maybe somewhere similar.'

'Alright, count me in. I am game for a gamble.'

'Would that be a Vegas gamble or a lamb's gambol?'

Nerys smiled and realized she was still trying to get to grips with Calum's humour. But that was the least of her worries.

===000===

London, in August, was sweltering hot and packed to overcrowding with tourists, while locals tried stoutly to go about their business. The accountancy conference was taking place in a large hotel close to Lincoln's Inn Fields and would run from the Wednesday to the Friday. Thereafter, the weekend would switch to the mystery location, which Calum had not revealed while he was making all the travel arrangements. Nerys still had high hopes for Paris. She had not been there since her honeymoon. Perhaps, that was a harbinger of something similar yet more lasting on the way.

On the Tuesday evening, Nerys joined Calum for the opening social event. She entered the function suite with some trepidation, having little idea what two hundred accountants looked like, off-duty, but imagining them to look pretty much like what they did, on-duty. Instead, she was amused to see an overwhelmingly male company decked out in the latest and most expensive business-casual attire. Yet the faces, and perhaps the waist lines, revealed them to be accountants, nonetheless. She could not help comparing them to Calum. He was an accountant, but he did not look like an accountant, and he most certainly did not act like an accountant. After a couple of overpriced drinks and a couple of mind-numbing conversations with strangers on the European financial market meltdown and, worse still, the upcoming release of a new recommended auditing practice on inventory valuation and write-down, Calum whispered in Nerys' ear.

'Let's get out of here before we catch whatever it is that they are all suffering from. I would love accountancy if it were not for all the accountants and what they find to talk about.'

'If you are sure you have paid your dues. Where do you want to……..?'

'Calum Davies. You old reprobate. How did Customs and Immigration let you back in again?'

They turned to find the source of the overly-loud question that had transcended the conversational hum. It came from some way across the room and had attracted more than its fair share of interest from the assembled company. Archie Young, resplendent in a three-piece pin-stripe suit, white shirt, and club tie, strode across toward them as the crowd seemed to part like the Red Sea.

'Christ, Archie. It is supposed to be business-casual.'

'I am casual. Look, my tie is the Edinburgh Waverley FC tie. Not my usual, prized White's Club tie.'

Calum and Archie had trained together as accountants in Edinburgh from 1969 through 1974 at the old and established firm of Brookes. After graduating joint top of their class, they had gone their separate ways. Calum immediately left the stuffy old firm and went on to an eclectic career in accountancy and higher education in Scotland, Canada, and now the USA. Archie had remained a Brookes' man to this day and had worked his way up the oh-so traditional ladder to now be a partner in the Edinburgh office. The two men were so different in every way, except their professional designation and, perhaps, their love of Edinburgh Waverley FC; but had maintained a strong, if distant, relationship over the years, first with the occasional letter, now email, and the very occasional face-to-face meeting, usually at an event like this.

Things looked up for Nerys. In spite of his ultra-conservative appearance, Archie Young was extremely funny, if not downright eccentric. The threesome, for Archie was a confirmed bachelor for life, found a quiet table outside the function room and proceeded to regale each other with reminiscences and topical adventures, while consuming large amounts of champagne, which Archie insisted on providing for the auspicious occasion. Although Nerys had little knowledge of the old stories and little idea about the contemporary events, she could not help but join in the mirth as the obvious enjoyment of the two friends got louder and louder and even attracted the attention of other accountants on their way to the Gents, no doubt wondering what accountancy trend could be worthy of such merriment. At the climax of the little party shenanigans, Archie performed the ultimate wardrobe adjustment for him and loosened his tie. The threesome was among the last to vacate the event and as they took their leave in the hotel elevator, Archie, in a somewhat slurred sotto voce, opined to Calum:

'You have a good one there, old boy. Would make a damned fine accountant.'

Nerys eventually realized he was referring to her and smiled her way along the corridor to their room.

For the next three days, Calum dutifully attended the conference while Nerys enjoyed the thrills of London sightseeing, shopping, theatre matinees, and bistro lunches. At least Calum was present at the conference; he did not however take in many of the presentations and lectures. He preferred to spend his time in the hotel lobby seeking out acquaintances from around the accounting globe. Over the course of the three days, he managed to encounter people he had trained with or worked with from more than a dozen countries. Each person did not fit the typical profile of the accountant. Rather, each had that quirky personality and sense of humour that Calum liked to relate to. They resembled a small non-conformist group in the accounting world but were no less dedicated to their profession.

In the evenings, Calum and Nerys enjoyed dining in those small ethnic restaurants that abound in London. Though the reputation of English food has improved in the last thirty years, they were proud to note that not a single drop had touched their lips; unless a good chicken tikka masala is now considered English, having surpassed fish and chips in popularity. Those intimate dinners seemed to put the development of their relationship onto fast-forward and discussion now centred clearly around future plans together. Nerys had suggested that they invite Archie Young on the last night because of his kindness and general bonhomie at the start of the week; but Calum confessed he had not seen Archie since and lied that he had no way of contacting him; Archie would be doing his own thing. In an abstract reference to the Byrds' song, he stated there was a time for fraternizing and a time for staying alone. This was a time for their own thing. Nerys wanted so much to know what was happening at the weekend, as stronger and stronger thoughts of Paris built up within her, but she played Calum at his own game by making no reference to it.

On the Friday evening at the conclusion of the conference, Calum announced that they should eat early and get a good night's sleep because they had an early start in the morning. They were headed to Scotland, first to Glasgow, then Largs, then to the island of Greater Cumbrae and the town of Millport. Nerys exhibited a hitherto unacknowledged skill in masking surprise, then disappointment, followed by signs of enthusiasm, capped by overt pleasure. And, she did it all in the short time Calum explained what Millport was all about. Euston Station beckoned at 6:30am.

When Nerys set foot on the Largs to Cumbrae ferry after two interesting train rides, she realized she had no idea where she was going. Calum had never spoken of Millport and, since he had dropped the bombshell of their impending visit, he had been reluctant to say much more.

'Wait and see. You will love it. It is my spiritual home. But there is room for you too.'

Nerys' parents had come originally from Wales and she had relatives dotted around the UK, but she had never heard of this island. She decided to view it as an adventure and put thoughts of Paris out of her mind.

Calum had had difficulty in finding accommodation at this time, the peak tourist season, although the town did not seem overly busy to Nerys. Probably, it was more a case of there not being much accommodation to start with. They would spend their first night at the Miller's Stone Hotel, which was a place Calum had stayed many times on his now revealed frequent sojourns to the island; and their second night at the Westview Hotel because the Miller's Stone was by then full up. Calum had never stayed at the Westview but knew it to be a hotel that had opened in the last few years. Before that, it had been slightly famous as the headquarters and recording studio of the Scottish rock band Dubus. Nerys was not sure she had heard of Dubus, but she confessed to having been keen on the Bay City Rollers in her formative years. Apparently, the tartan clad popsters had quite a following in the Los Angeles area to Calum's surprise and undisguised disgust.

'Dubus were great. Could have been a whole lot bigger than they were. I have all their stuff. I will play it for you when we get back.'

Calum announced that they would be busy outdoors for the next two days and she should dress accordingly. Nerys confessed that she had not packed sneakers. Sneakers were not exactly Parisian attire, after all. But that was soon righted when the local shop, that seemed to sell just about everything, came up with a pair, one size too large, and of a design that might have been in fashion in the 1950s.

Over the next two days, Calum and Nerys did what all visitors to Cumbrae did. They walked endlessly; the island was only ten miles around. They cycled on regular bikes, and then experimented on a tandem. They ate ice cream at the Ritz Café and fish and chips from the Deep Sea Restaurant, the latter consumed while sitting on the Old Pier with legs dangling over the edge. They walked the many sandy beaches and even waded in the frigid waters of the Clyde, prompting sharp intakes of breath.

'It used to feel a whole lot warmer when I came here as a child.'

'You have been coming here all your life?'

'Indeed, I have. I told you, it is my spiritual home, just as it was my dad's before me.'

Nerys looked closely at Calum. He seemed different. He looked different. He was acting differently. He looked like he did not have a care in the world. All traces of divorce, flight from Canada to the US, the strain of finding a decent job, and even the stress that might go with facing the start of a new job in an entirely new university campus, had disappeared, to be replaced by an aura of almost comical serenity. I thought only drugs could induce this kind of state, thought Nerys.

The local business owners were well versed in looking after the tourists and in particular went out of their way to make the American visitors welcome. The island attracted a steady stream of visitors each year, but most were like Calum and had been coming since their childhood. Americans, new to the island, were rarely seen. Calum, who was not overly chatty as a rule, seemed to thrive on engaging the locals and Nerys, who was quite gregarious by nature, found it very easy to get into interesting and often amusing conversations on subject matters of which she had little knowledge. In particular, they had lots of fun chatting with the two hotel owners, who could not have been more unalike. On the first night, they playfully persisted with a dour, taciturn, perhaps not atypical Scot for whom words were on strict rationing. But, persist they did and the owner's sense of obligation to, as a minimum, acknowledge his guests, eventually led him into a somnolent conversation with, invariably, a negative or pessimistic slant to each of his observations. On the second night, they came face-to-face with Sandy Green, mine host, raconteur, and self-appointed ambassador to the island. Over dinner, they enjoyed his undivided attention even though the dining room was almost full and, by the end of the evening, they would have willingly signed up if Sandy had been representing a time-share opportunity.

On the train back south to Heathrow, Nerys confessed to Calum that she now understood the importance to him of the spiritual home. And, she hoped that there would be room for her in future visits.

'You have passed the test. Congratulations. Let's plan to get married,' was the gleeful response.

===000===

Back in California, the semester for both Calum and Nerys was due to begin on the Tuesday after Labour Day, which fell on the first Monday of September. They had spent the time, since they got back, making plans for his teaching and her learning activities and for their life together. They were living in his apartment in Riverside but had agreed that they would look for a patio home in Irvine. On the Saturday prior to start of classes, there was to be an official opening of the California University, Temecula campus, which both planned to attend, but, at the last moment, Nerys decided her time would be better spent going to Santa Barbara to get her accommodation organized in the halls of residence. Consequently, it was Calum who set out for Temecula with his full regalia, to participate in the opening ceremony.

The campus was opening with only four buildings out of the twelve, planned in phase one, completed. However, the two classroom buildings, student commons, and administration building, would be sufficient to house the modest number of classes being offered in the inaugural semester.

A typical bright and sunny Southern California day had arrived to usher in the new campus. The opening was as much a media event as anything else and reporters and television crews almost outnumbered the crowd, which consisted only of a few curious locals. There had been some controversy over the desire to hold the opening before the start of classes and thereby deny students the opportunity to play a part in the proceedings. However, the Board of Governors and the Campus President saw the event as more corporate in nature than academic. As a result, a hastily constructed stage in the courtyard in front of the student commons was intended to accommodate governors, administrators, faculty and staff, as well as foundation members and donors and corporate sponsors. All told, the numbers on stage far exceeded the numbers in the media and crowd combined. It took a while for all the stage guests to be introduced as they marched into the courtyard, up onto the stage,

138

and took their allotted seats, arranged according to relative importance.

Among the general faculty, Calum had the dubious distinction of being last to be introduced and to take his seat on the very edge of the stage, albeit in the front row. He sat down gingerly, lest he should cause his chair to move and he disappear ignominiously through the side curtains and onto the courtyard floor.

The speeches from the Chair of the Board, local Mayor, State Governor's representative and finally Campus President, seemed to go on interminably. Calum sat baking in the hot sun, thinking that, at best, the event would capture thirty seconds on the evening news. He might even have been falling asleep as the monotone voice droned on; not the best thing to do when in the front row, but understandable in the circumstances. Just when President Jerome Dale Eisenhower PhD appeared to be reaching a conclusion by inviting the other speakers to join him in the ceremonial ribbon cutting, a totally unexpected thing happened.

A vision shot out of the student commons and mounted the stage by the stairs to the right. The vision was a woman, of that there could be absolutely no doubt. She was clad in the brightest yellow sneakers and an almost matching yellow mask, favoured by some wrestlers. And, absolutely nothing else. We had a streaker! But no ordinary streaker was she. This one had a body of Amazonian proportions and, instead of the historically rumoured one breast, had two very large and round ones.

As if time had decided to suspend itself, nothing moved, nobody said a word, all eyes followed the vision as she dashed across the stage, arms outstretched above her head as if those breasts needed any help in accentuation, and leapt off at the left side without even bothering with the stairs. She glided behind the side curtains and disappeared from view.

President Eisenhower stood with a stunned look on his face and uttered not a word. A cheer went up from somewhere in the small crowd. Gradually, a hum of conversation was struck up between pairs of participants with a great many only able to say, 'Did you see that?'

Still President Eisenhower stood, looking straight forward, and mute. Heads from all angles turned toward him. Quickly, not a single pair of eyes was focused on anything except on the President and still he remained almost comatose.

The silence was finally broken when he uttered, with persisting glassy eyes, but sufficient pomp and circumstance in his voice.

'We will now proceed with the ribbon cutting.'

The grand reception afterward, in the student commons, featured a sumptuous buffet and lashings of local Temecula wine. This had been the real purpose of the event, the opportunity for the university bigwigs to rub shoulders with donors and corporate sponsors. However, it was fair to say that each little huddle of conversation, which might have contributed to the future advantage of the new campus, was instead a-buzz with reflections of the interruption to the ceremony. The yellow vision had captured the day. As the reception started to wind up quicker than had been planned, Calum and some of the other faculty grabbed a couple of bottles of wine and made their way to the faculty club, a small and modest room in the Administration building, which would serve in the short term as the faculty domain.

President Eisenhower was still feeling shell-shocked that such an outrage should have occurred on this, his big event, at his brand-new campus. He thought that, if the perpetrator was a student, she would be summarily expelled. He did his best to oversee the wind down of the reception and to make sure that the more important guests were appropriately looked after. He was well aware that his job had little to do with academia and a lot to do with raising funds. There was no generous state funding here.

On looking around and noticing the absence of most of his faculty at the end, he assumed that they had retired to their faculty club. Schmoozing with suits was not generally an activity that many faculty members liked to engage in. In the interests of trying to ensure no loss of face for himself over the streaker, he decided to drop in on the faculty and have a last glass of wine with his boys, so to speak.

'Christ Almighty. They were like bloody melons, were they not....................?'

Eisenhower glared at the commentator, one Dr Seamus O'Flaherty, a giant Irishman and doyen of English Literature, who happened to be in a small group which included Calum. A total silence ensued.

Eisenhower had intended to try to put a positive spin on things but could only lapse into a melancholic repost.

'An unmitigated disaster. How could one individual ruin such an important event? I want her found. If she is a student, she is toast.'

The silence ensued until Calum felt moved to try to lighten the atmosphere.

'Never mind sir. Look on the bright side. At least we will get more than thirty seconds on the evening news.'

The room quickly exploded into laughter then just as quickly into silence as President Eisenhower's face transformed from melancholy to fury.

'You, Davies! You were seated at the edge of the stage. You could easily have apprehended her. You have let me down badly.'

'And, what was I supposed to hold onto, without being up on a charge myself?'

The room again exploded into laughter and, this time, Eisenhower turned on his heels and walked out.

If Calum had been intent on creating a good impression, and he probably wasn't, then he hadn't. That was the general consensus; but at least the rest of the faculty felt better as they emptied out of the faculty club.

The first week of classes on the brand-new campus went mostly the way that first weeks on campus do; but with added element of

141

the streaker and the desire to uncover her identity. However, as she seemed to have covered herself up quite well, the topic soon evaporated, and students and faculty alike got down to what they were there to do. The Board of Governors had arrived at the conclusion that no harm had been done and the incident had certainly aided their relationship with the media. President Eisenhower chose to stew privately. The semester unfolded.

Calum was assigned to teach two sections of Accounting 100, which meant four classes a week. His first section was uneventful and was filled with freshman students, attending university for the first time and looking like a herd of deer caught in the headlights. On top of that, a good many of them had that common faceless look of accounting students. Why did so many accountants, even accountants-to-be, look like accountants?

His second section was slightly different. It was a small group, less homogenous than the first, with some older students who had transferred in from other campuses and universities. They were mostly taking accounting as an elective subject and looked less likely to be on the inevitable road to becoming accountants. Just as Calum was about to begin the first lecture, the class was augmented by the arrival, technically the late arrival, of two of the most unlikely accounting students. She was Erica Rowlands he found out later, standing a statuesque six feet or more and dressed in a flamboyant kaftan-type gown with a long brightly-coloured silk scarf wrapped many times around her neck. Her wild curly hair, in a version of a Caucasian-Afro, completed the image. He was Carlton Webster, had long straight hair and was decked out in a black pin-striped three-piece suit with a black tee shirt, where a white shirt and tie might have been. And, he wore the brightest yellow sneakers.

'Sorry we are late, man,' he muttered, as they made their way to the very front of the class. No quiet entrance by slipping in to the back of the class for this pair. It took Calum several minutes before he felt that the class was ready to recommence. This was going to be interesting.

===000===

Nerys was now deeply engaged in her studies in Santa Barbara. She had not been kidding when she had said she was not there to fool around. Faculty had already noticed her voracious appetite for learning in their classes, and a clear idea of what her dissertation would look like and how the research necessary would be carried out. This was all evident in the first few weeks.

She called Calum every night to enthuse about what she had learned that day. In turn, he gave her a slightly less enthusiastic report of how the new campus was faring and how his classes were going. Although she had not been able to pick up an adjunct teaching appointment in the first semester, prospects were looking good for the second. On a personal level, they were now pursuing with vigour a patio home, which had just come on the market in Irvine. Both had been to see it and declared it ideal. Finally, over wine and delicious tapas in a Riverside restaurant, they had decided to get married in Palm Springs over the Christmas break.

As the semester proceeded, Calum's two sections were getting through the curriculum in pretty much the same way he had experienced at UCR and previously in Canada. Accounting is an acquired taste. One either likes it or one does not. The curriculum is full of rules and techniques. These are not difficult. But, if one does not relate in general to the subject matter, one might as well be attempting to learn Advanced Sanskrit. As usual, the sections had already divided into those who got it and were moving quickly along, and those who did not and were either cutting classes as much as they could or were sitting in class simply wishing they were somewhere else. Some even scheduled dental appointments to clash with class times. It always amazed Calum how toothaches and struggling with principles of accounting have a strong correlation.

Erica Rowlands and Carlton Webster, however, did not quite fit the pattern. They grasped the principles of accounting quite easily; but they clearly did not enjoy the classes and were a persistently disruptive influence. Smart-ass comments and obtuse questions were commonplace. Other students did not quite know what to make of them and, consequently, the two almost always remained as an isolated couple, seldom interacting with any of their fellow students. Their papers were dutifully submitted, not always on time, and were clearly the product of joint work, but Calum did not have a problem with that. He would rather students learned to work together from the very beginning, as long as they were capable of individually writing the necessary exams at the end of semester.

One day after class, Calum could not face the drive back immediately to Riverside on a particularly hot afternoon, so he decided he would pop into the student pub, which operated in the commons at certain times when there were no other activities scheduled. He was not surprised to spy, through the heaving mass of students and some faculty members standing around the makeshift bar, Erica and Carlton sitting on their own at one of the very few tables provided.

'Do you mind if I join you? I might be persuaded to refill your glasses.'

'We were just going actually.'

'Oh, come on, Erica. Let the man buy us a drink. He must be helluva dry after that lecture today.' Carlton's omnipresent cutting wit changed their response; and Calum was invited to join them.

'As two of the students doing quite well this semester, I would normally ask you simply if you were enjoying the class. However, I suspect from your faces each week that you are not. Is that the case?'

'It is just a class. Both Carlton and I need to catch up on some electives and we chose accounting.'

'First on the catalogue list?'

'Right. We would be in Zoology if we had started at the other end.'

'Accounting is normally not for the uncommitted, as you can see by the struggles some of your colleagues are having. I am surprised you are doing so well. It is nothing to do with your intelligence, which is obviously high. It is to do with the necessary commitment. You are showing up well in spite of your apparent indifference.'

'Don't bank on it, man. We might still drop out.'

'C'mon Carlton. You are more than halfway through. You should ace the term exam and, there, you will have three more credits toward your degree.'

'Some days, the degree does not seem very important to either of us.'

'Hey, that is serious talk. I don't know what your future plans are but, if you are going to get anywhere in life, you need to complete that degree. What are your plans?'

'I have none yet.'

'My only plan is to live off her body. Hollywood must be able to put those melons to work somewhere.'

Calum winced and looked from Carlton to Erica. He had obviously taken a step too far on his road to cynicism.

'Fuck you,' she mouthed at him and then asked, clearly intending to change the subject, 'Do you like teaching here, Professor Davies?'

'This is just the first semester, but so far so good. It is better than UCR, where I was one of the slave-labour adjunct faculty earning less per hour than that bartender over there. I spent a lot of years in the rat-race as a professional accountant. I decide to switch to teaching to maintain my sanity. On good days, I feel like I have succeeded.'

'You were a real accountant?'

'I was an accountant. How real I was, is open to debate. I never had the courage to wear an outrageous suit like Carlton's though.'

Erica giggled. She was about to ask another question when Carlton brusquely got up, took her arm and pulled her with him.

'We gotta go, man. Can't be seen sitting with faculty for too long. It is bad for the image.'

Erica looked back over her shoulder as they pushed their way through the crowd and mouthed, 'Bye.'

The semester eased into December. Nerys was still thoroughly enjoying her programme. She had breezed through her course work, proposed and obtained approval of her dissertation topic, and was now beginning her extensive literature search; in effect to identify the established body of knowledge related to her topic before she sought to add to that body of knowledge. She had no term exams and was essentially finished for the holidays. On Saturday she would return to Riverside and, on Monday, she and Calum would take possession of their new patio home in Irvine. Then on Christmas Eve, some of her more distant family and a few close friends would join them in Palm Springs for their wedding at a trendy country club. They had thought about a hippy wedding in Joshua Tree National Park but had ultimately eschewed the whimsical in favour of the conservative. Calum was an accountant after all. Nerys felt very good about life in general. Calum had just to get through supervision of his term exam on the Friday afternoon and then they would be together in Riverside.

The California University at Temecula would close for the holidays on the Friday. Exams taking place in the student commons were scheduled right up to the Friday afternoon. This was somewhat unusual because most universities allowed a day or two between the last exam and close of the campus, in case an exam had to be rescheduled. However, President Eisenhower was of the view that it served students better to maximize the time between the last class and the start of exams, to allow them to cram as much as possible. Hence, exams were running right up to the campus closure. Many faculty members, including Calum, believed that if students did not know the material by the end of classes, no amount of cramming was going to prepare them for the exam. But, the Faculty Senate, which normally made decisions on the exam schedule, was not really functioning yet at the campus in its first semester and the decision had been left to Eisenhower. As Calum faced the prospect of his exam taking place on the very last afternoon, he could not help thinking that the President might be getting his revenge for Calum's trivializing the once famous streaker, who was now all but forgotten by most.

It was not strictly necessary for Calum to even be there to supervise the exam. There were proctors for that purpose. Many faculty members left it to them and were already on the road to Big Bear Ski Resort or Hawaii. But, Calum had always believed that it was the right thing to do to show up for the exam, if only to offer some moral support, although those who were going to pass it did not need him and those who were not were beyond help of any kind, short of divine intervention, and Calum did not possess those powers.

When Calum stepped onto campus after grabbing a quick sandwich at a nearby café, he expected the morning exams to be finished and the candidates for the afternoon exams not yet to be assembled in the commons. Instead, he found a large group of people milling around the courtyard outside the commons in the full glare of the sun, hot even for December. There were students, faculty, administrators, staff and both the campus police and the county police present. Various conversations were going on, but it was not clear what was being discussed.

'What is going on?' Calum asked of the Vice-President of Business Affairs, whom he had got to know reasonably well over the semester.

'A bomb warning has been called in.'

'What? Who received it? What did it say?'

'The head of my campus police got it. Just said a bomb had been placed in the student commons; and the afternoon exams had better be cancelled.'

'Shit. That is my exam. You are not going to believe it are you?'

'I am not going to disbelieve it. We have handed everything over to the county police.'

At that point, a county police officer called for quiet and addressed the crowd.

'From what your Sgt. Rodriguez has to say about the call, I think it should be taken seriously. Unfortunately, our sniffer dog, who handles these sorts of things, is currently in Blyth, California and cannot be back here in time for a search before the exams are due to begin. I cannot tell you to cancel the exams, but I would suggest it.'

'Who can make that decision?' someone shouted.

'Eisenhower,' another responded.

'President Eisenhower and Provost Campbell are in Sacramento for meetings. I don't know if they can be reached in time,' replied the Vice-President for Student Affairs.

'Surely someone must be temporarily in charge during their absence?' Calum asked, and looked pointedly at the previous speaker.

'Well, I guess Donald and I sort of are,' replied the Vice-President for Student Affairs and pointed at Donald MacDonald the Vice-President for Business Affairs.

'So, can you two authorize the cancellation of the exams?' the county police officer asked.

'It is not as easy as that. The campus closes today for the holidays. There is no time to reschedule the exam this semester. That means that students, who need a pass to get into courses next semester, will not be able to register. This is an academic nightmare. I think we are going to have to go ahead with the exams. What do you think Donald?'

'Easy for you to say, Margarita. In order for the exams to go ahead, somebody is going to have to check out the commons for the bomb. It does not sound like the police are keen to do it without their dog. I do not want my staff doing it. And, I sure as heck do not intend to do it myself. I say cancel the exams.'

148

Margarita Delgado felt like the bomb had been tossed back to her....literally. As Vice-President for Student Affairs, she was intended to be the champion for students, to look after them and keep their best interests at heart. She regretted now not making more of opposing President Eisenhower's decision to schedule the exams as late as possible. She could now see that any cancellation that would lead to students not being able to register for some courses in the spring semester, would come back to haunt her, not the President and, not the Provost, who never took responsibility for anything and had even managed to sneak away to Sacramento today of all days, with the President. She felt compelled to repeat that she felt the exams had to go on; but she could not agree to any of her staff carrying out the search that could clear the bomb threat. In desperation, she suggested that she and MacDonald retire to her office to discuss the matter further. The two of them departed the scene with almost indecent haste, amid the growing disquiet among the rest of the assembled crowd.

The police officer tried to make a suggestion. 'Our sniffer dog, which happens to be called Sniffer, could maybe make it here by five o'clock. Could you not delay the exams until the evening?' He looked around for reaction, suspecting that he had done what the high-priced academics had failed to do, and that was find a solution.

The overwhelming response from students was no. Many had travel plans for the evening in order to get a vacation location or just home for the holidays.

'Send in the VPs to check it out. They are expendable,' some wag offered, and widespread cheering and applause broke out.

The Vice-Presidents, meanwhile, could hear the noise in the courtyard and, while tempted to believe that a viable solution had been found in their absence, resolved that they should huddle for a while longer to demonstrate that they had given the matter the greatest consideration.

The crowd had now grown considerably as the time came within forty-five minutes of the scheduled beginning of the exams. As word passed from those who knew what was going on to the newcomers, the mood started to get a little uglier. Most of the students were insistent that the exams should go ahead because the alternatives were not attractive. But who wanted to play Sniffer?

Calum noticed that Erica and Carlton had arrived on the scene. Instead of their usual clothing, kaftan and suit, which they always wore, both were garbed in what might be termed trendy après-ski outfits.

'Hello, you two. You look like you are bound for the slopes after the exam. Where are you off to?'

'We were supposed to be going to Lake Tahoe if we can ever get a flight now,' answered Erica.

'Can't someone around here make the obvious decision to cancel the exams?' asked Carlton.

'It is not as easy as that. There are ramifications for a lot of students. If they don't write this exam, they can't register for Accounting 101 next semester. It doesn't matter for you two because you are just taking accounting as an elective, but it could mess up some students' total programme plans.'

'Big deal,' was Carlton's response, just as the two vice presidents reappeared in the courtyard.

'Well?' someone from the crowd demanded.

'Ahem, the Vice-President for Business Affairs and I have given this matter very careful consideration. Cancelling the exams is not a decision to be taken lightly. We are of the opinion that we should delay any decision and continue to try to reach President Eisenhower.'

Margarita Delgado's announcement was met with a mixture of howls of protest and hoots of derision.

'Does anybody have a better idea?'

'You mean does anybody else have any clue?'

Calum could not believe what was happening. His concern for his students in general was offset by any uneasy feeling about the attitude of his two most prominent students. In a moment of frustration, he opted to make his move.

'Oh, for Pete's sake. I will check out the commons. There can't be too many places to conceal a bomb in the highly unlikely event that there actually is one.'

A cheer went up followed by chants of 'Calum, Calum'.

The Vice-Presidents both reminded Calum that he did not have the authority, but he replied that it was not authority that was required but simple common sense.

'You needn't think that our liability insurance will cover you if you are blown to pieces,' was all Calum heard from Donald MacDonald as he entered the commons.

The next ten minutes passed in almost complete silence in the courtyard, save for some hushed whispers like 'Good old Calum' and 'bugger it, I bet he finds nothing and the exam goes on' and 'goddamn faculty, they are always out to make us look bad.'

Calum stared around the large open room. There was nothing on the floor except about two hundred tables and chairs arranged in rows. It would not be very easy to hide anything on the floor. And, a quick visual check of what was beneath each table and chair should satisfy his needs. By the time he had finished stooping to observe each table and chair, Calum was dripping wet with perspiration. Whether it was caused by the physical effort or sheer terror gradually building within him, was not clear. That part completed; he turned his attention to the small stage at the back of the room. That was pretty easy too. It was obvious that there was nothing lying on the stage floor and a careful look under and behind the curtains at each side of the stage did not reveal anything either.

That just left the large storage room to the left of the stage. This was going to be the most nerve-wracking part. The room had a door which was currently closed. He knew the room contained the makeshift bar, when it was not in use, but beyond that he knew not what. Even opening the door was very difficult. If there were a bomb, it could be connected to the door and detonated when it was opened. For what seemed like an eternity, his hand remained on the door-knob while the tension built up and the perspiration intensified. Finally, he turned the knob and the door opened outward to reveal a fairly large storage room with the bar and all sorts of other materials, additional folding chairs, and boxes of glasses but no alcohol. It must be stored elsewhere. Fortunately, a good deal of the room was empty because most of the tables and chairs currently outside were normally stored in here. He was able to ascertain that there was no bomb or even suspicious package in the room.

As he returned to the main commons room, Calum had to stop for a moment just to stabilize his breathing and vainly attempt to quell the running torrents of perspiration on his head and torso.

Just when it seemed the blast would never come or Calum would never return as an alternative, the door was thrown open and he emerged in somewhat dramatic fashion while desperately blinking as his eyes got accustomed to the bright sunlight.

'There is no bomb in there. I have looked everywhere.'

Amid cheers, the Vice-President of Student Affairs announced loudly that the exam would begin in fifteen minutes, and in a quieter voice to the Vice-President for Business Affairs, 'You better get working on a policy for cancelling and rescheduling exams. You have not looked too good today and Eisenhower will be after your hide when he gets back.'

Eventually the exams took place without any further interruption and, by the scheduled end time, the commons had emptied, and students were on their way to enjoy the holiday break. Calum had tried to catch as many of his students as possible to wish them well. Several were quite profuse in their thanks to him for saving the day, and enabling them to register for their next course. That was assuming they passed the exam; and that was what Calum would be earnestly engaged in over the weekend—marking papers. He did not get a chance to speak to Erica and Carlton. They had finished the exam early and had been among the very first to leave the commons, before the scheduled end.

===000===

That night, Calum had returned to Riverside and looked forward to Nerys' arrival the next morning. He had decided on two things. He would get up very early and get a good start on marking the papers before she arrived. And, he would make no mention of his little exploit that afternoon. Even he realized, it was much out of character for him and he did not want Nerys to be forming the wrong opinion about him.

Next morning, Calum was well into the second hour of his marking when the phone rang at about eight o'clock. He expected it to be Nerys confirming that she was setting out from Santa Barbara. Instead, he was surprised to hear the voice of the President's Personal Assistant and to learn that he had called a meeting for 10:00 am today to review yesterday's debacle, as she described it. Calum was expected to attend, along with the members of the President's Cabinet.

After a quick shower, he dressed and left a note for Nerys before jumping into his car. Saturday traffic should not be as bad as workdays and he reckoned he should make it to Temecula just in time for the meeting. He had suggested to Nerys in the note that she make her way down to Temecula, if she felt like it, and they would have a day of visiting a winery and enjoying a nice lunch after he got rid of the meeting.

Calum arrived at the President's private meeting room with five minutes to spare, but was still the last to arrive. He could not help but feel the eyes of everyone turning to stare at him as he took the remaining chair.

'You know everyone, don't you, Dr Davies? Provost Jack Campbell, Vice-President Margarita Delgado, Vice-President Donald MacDonald, and my assistant, Sherrie.'

'Yes, I do. Good morning.'

'I want to say at the outset--the others have already heard this--I am not at all pleased with what happened yesterday and how it was dealt with. If there was anything at all that went well, it was your selfless act, Dr Davies. Calum, I should say. You should not have had to do what you did; but I am very glad that you did. It seems your colleagues were less willing to put themselves on the line.'

'That is kind of unfair, Mr President. Donald and I were put in a very difficult position. The police were recommending cancellation. Donald was prepared to cancel. Only I was advocating the students' position, as I am expected to do. But I do not think my responsibilities include searching out bombs.'

Before MacDonald could present his position, Campbell interceded.

'Don't get yourself all in a twist Margarita. I think what Dale is saying is that the indecision that seems to have gripped Donald and you was not a good thing. Ensuring that the exams took place was obviously very important to the University; but you had not come up with a way of making that happen. And Donald, quite frankly, cancellation was not an option.'

'Thanks Jack. That is exactly what I was trying to convey. If we have learned anything from this, it is that we need to allow some time after the last scheduled exam before the closure of the campus. That is a matter for the Faculty Senate to take on board next semester. And, Margarita and Donald, we need a policy and procedures on how to deal with a threat of some sort, how to make a decision as to whether to cancel an exam or not, and how to carry out that decision quickly and effectively.'

'I agree Dale,' MacDonald got in before Delgado could respond. However, she would not be silenced and followed up, 'Exactly what I said to you yesterday, Donald.'

154

'I expect both of you to take this on. I would like to see a draft on the first day back after the holidays. We are damned lucky we got away with things yesterday. We cannot depend on Calum to be around to do the dirty work, if there is a next time. In fact, if the truth be known, we are very beholden to you; but it is something you should never have done. And, you must never consider doing something like that again. When this gets out, you may well be in trouble with the faculty union and I will not be able to protect you. I will have to say that you were acting completely of your own volition, without authority, and at odds with what will be embodied in the policy and procedures. Otherwise, the union will be all over this as loss of academic freedom and an expectation way beyond what they are hired for; what *you* are hired for.'

'Quite so, Dale, quite so,' came the sage concurrence from the Provost, a man not known for relishing confrontation of any kind, especially with union or senate.

Calum felt he had to respond. Was he being thanked or admonished? However, before he could speak, a quiet knock came on the door and a head popped around and asked for a quick word with Vice-President MacDonald if it was not too much of an intrusion. As MacDonald disappeared outside, Eisenhower made it clear that the intrusion was not acceptable and the matter for discussion had better be of the utmost importance.

'Who was at the door anyway?' he asked.

'It looked like one of his janitorial staff. One of the supervisors, I think,' his assistant replied.

'Really! How ridiculous.'

MacDonald burst back into the room, his face florid and his words spluttering out his mouth in the company of spittle.

'My guys have found the bomb.'

'What?' A cacophony of sound echoed around the table from all present.

'You ass, Davies. You missed it. We might have lost two hundred students.'

'I looked everywhere, under every table and chair, on the stage, in the storage room. Where was it found?'

'Did you look in the storage area under the stage? That's where it is.'

'I did not know there was any storage under the stage. I did not see any indication of storage, like knobs or handles, or hinges.'

'There are no knobs or handles. You just push on the door and it pops open. When you want to close it, you just push it again. The janitors keep their supplies there.'

'How was I supposed to know that? You would have known it if you had been prepared to go in.'

'Exactly, Donald,' came the follow up from Delgado before the President slammed his hand on the table.

'Enough. Donald, have you called the police?'

'Not yet, Dale.'

'Well get the hell on with it. And make sure they bring their sniffer dog this time.'

'You mean Sniffer?'

'Is that not what I said? Get on with it.'

The group made their way out to the courtyard where President Eisenhower did his best to settle down the unnerved janitorial staff and told them to take an early lunch break and come back in two hours. There were no other people on campus today, at least.

MacDonald reappeared and confirmed the police were on their way. He suggested he call in his campus police, who were now on a skeleton shift over the holidays, but was told by the President not to bother. The fewer people on campus, the better.

Eisenhower took Calum aside and quietly spoke to him.

'This makes a bad situation worse in my opinion. You should not have been foolhardy enough to go looking for the bomb but, having done so, you should have located it. I am not sure how this is all going to play out in the media or, as I said before, with the union. I may not be able to protect you.'

'If the media wants to speak to me, I will give them the full story as to why I felt compelled to do something. I do not think I can be blamed for missing an almost hidden cupboard. MacDonald could have alerted me to the cupboard; but he was too busy denying me liability coverage.'

'Now now, Calum. There is no need to take that somewhat truculent position. We do not want to be airing our dirty laundry in public, as it were. Do we?'

The police arrived with the illustrious Sniffer in tow. It was the same sergeant as yesterday. They were briefed by the President as to what had been discovered and where, but were a little put out that the janitorial staff had been stood down. There would need to be statements taken from them.

'Surely that can be done later. Confirmation of the bomb and its safe disarming are surely the priorities of the day. Will you do the disarming?'

'You have to be joking, President. We will call in the military once we have confirmed the bomb.'

Calum felt move to ask, 'How long will that take?'

'Who knows? Were you going to suggest that you took on the disarming, sir?'

'Not likely.'

'Sergeant! Please. Can you get on with it? I would prefer that this were dealt with as soon as possible. Perhaps we can avoid the media.'

'Too late I'm afraid, Dale. That looks like Harris from the local rag parking his car over there. Why don't you Vice-Presidents intercept him and look after him?'

The three police officers consulted with each other further before it was decided the young K-9 handler and his dog would be the only ones to enter the commons and would examine what had been found beneath the stage, then report back out, before checking the rest of the facility, in case there was more than one bomb.

As they waited for results, Eisenhower wiped his sweating brow and bemoaned the fact that nothing like this had ever happened before in his career.

'Nor in mine, Dale,' came the echo from the Provost.

'Actually, I have had a couple of experiences like this in Canada. But they were, of course, bogus calls, just to try to get the exams cancelled. The administration just ignored the calls. There is not the same propensity for guns and presumably bombs up there, of course. Here is a different matter.'

'Davies, I am not sure I like that kind of comment. You will not be speaking to the media, I think.'

There seemed to be the same length of tense drama that there had been yesterday. Then the handler and a much friskier Sniffer emerged from the commons.

'There is no bomb in there.'

At least half a dozen voices cried, 'What?'

'You can look for yourself. There is no danger.'

A bemused group of administrators, faculty member, police officers and journalist stooped to peer into the below stage cupboard. It obviously contained something that resembled a bomb, even though Sniffer and his handler had rejected it.

'What on earth is it,' exclaimed the President.

'Looks like a home-made job. Are you absolutely sure it is safe, officer?' MacDonald demanded.

'I know exactly what it is.' Calum stood up and laughed. 'And what's more, I know who did it.'

'That is enough, Davies. Your bravado has gotten us into enough problems. I do not want your idle speculations. I suggest you take off now. There is nothing more for you to do here. Happy Holidays to you. You are getting married, are you not? Best wishes for that, and to your bride.'

Eisenhower almost frog-marched Calum out into the courtyard where they ran straight into Nerys, who had just arrived.

'What is going on, Calum?'

'President Eisenhower, are you sure you don't want me to be involved any further or to share my theory as to what has happened?'

'Absolutely sure. You have served me well. I mean you have served the University well. Leave it to the senior staff now. Happy Holidays and all the best for your wedding, the two of you. Now, off you go and enjoy the day.'

As they walked towards their cars, Calum turned to Nerys and said, 'Well I tried. You heard me try, didn't you? You can only try.'

'Will you please tell me what the hell is going on? Why are the police here? Why were you getting thanked then dismissed?'

'It is a long story. Let's go for a nice lunch and I will tell you all about it.'

They stopped at a pleasant winery on the outskirts of Temecula and, after tasting some interesting samples, invested in a case of really top-class Tatria Meritage. Then, as they sat down to lunch, Calum relayed the story from its very beginning yesterday, when he had returned from a much more modest lunch.

When he got to the bit where, frustrated by the indecisive Vice-Presidents, he took it upon himself to check out the commons for the bomb, Nerys went ballistic. No sharing of the frustration; no pride in her man taking charge; instead she berated him for being so foolhardy, irrespective of his good intentions. Such erratic behaviour might prompt her to reconsider whether this wedding was indeed a good idea. It took Calum a good fifteen minutes to calm her down as he insisted that, in the end, he had found no trace of the bomb. He tried his 'no harm, no foul' saying of which he was fond, but it cut little ice. It was only as it sunk in that he had not found a bomb and the exams had been able to take place, that she calmed down.

The story continued into today and to the very mixed messages he had been getting from the President, as in 'well done, but you had absolutely no authority to do it', as well as the inept Vice-Presidents and Provost falling over themselves to avoid any blame, but to make sure that Calum got no credit. This caused Nerys to adopt a much more sympathetic position toward Calum. She bemoaned the all so typical behaviour of university administrators—paid large amounts of money to achieve absolutely nothing. Calum would have done well to stop the story right there.

When he moved on to the janitor's discovery of what was thought to be a bomb, Nerys starting to lay into him once again. Not only was it a stupid foolhardy thing to do but, by failing to locate the bomb, he would have been blamed if it had gone off and students had been injured, or even lost their lives. Again, it took him quite a while to calm her down and he only succeeded when he got to the climax of his story.

'You may well be correct if there had been a bomb, but there wasn't. It does, however, cause me, with the benefit of hindsight, to reconsider my actions. I was doing what I thought was best for students and quite frankly, I was fed up with the administrators. Maybe I just wanted to show them up.'

'How can you be so sure there was no bomb? What was it that the janitor found that he thought was a bomb?'

'Oh, it was sort of made to look like a bomb; but I recognized it for what it was immediately, which is more than I can say for the administrators. They are probably still trying to persuade the police to persuade the military to detonate it safely.'

'What was it?'

'It was a very clever assembly of two large melons, with curly wires coming out of them, seated on a pair of very striking yellow sneakers.'

'My God,' exclaimed Nerys, and dissolved in a fit of laughter. Calum could not help shaking his head and eventually joined her in the outpouring of mirth, so audible and indeed visible, that it attracted much attention from the other diners.

Eventually, Nerys stopped laughing and wanted to know more.

'How did you recognize it and how do you know who placed it there?'

'That, my dear, is another very long story and not one I am prepared to relay until at least we order another bottle of wine!'

S'been A While!

'Hello, Little Sister. S'been a while.'

'Roger, you came! My, oh my. I was not sure you would show up even when you confirmed that you were going to be in town.'

'Such confidence, Nerys.'

'Well, what do you expect? How long has it been? It must have been in Toronto when I was just finishing my master's degree. That was a long time ago.'

'Might well have been. Certainly, it was in the mists of time.'

'Well, no matter about when. You are here now. Sit down, sit down. You are making the place look untidy as you always do. I see your dress sense has not improved. Forget that. What do you want to drink?'

'Umm. A water would be good. Just tap water. None of the fancy stuff.'

'Roger! This is Los Angeles. Nobody drinks tap water and survives. I am not even sure any water comes out of the tap any more since this endless drought hit us. Who knows where tap water actually comes from now? You should have a bottle of Evian.'

'Tap water please 'Rys.'

'You heard him, waiter. I will have another G&T too.'

'What made you pick this place? It is way too Hollywood for my taste.'

'That just might be because it is in Hollywood, nuthead. I am on my way to a meeting at UC Santa Barbara this afternoon. This is on the way. You could have knocked me down with a feather when I got your snail mail saying you were in California. Snail mail? Do you still not trust email?'

'I would not trust email anywhere in the world and especially in the US of A. Who knows who is monitoring it and leaking it to other parties?'

'Same old brother, my dear 'Ger. Just because I'm paranoid doesn't mean they are not out to get me! Ho ho.'

'With good reason. I much prefer to keep my business to myself or to someone that I choose to communicate with. I don't need anybody looking over my shoulder at what I am up to.'

'And, what are you up to these days, 'Ger?'

'Oh, same old, same old. I do a bit of writing. I do a bit of activism if the cause is right...'

'You mean if the cause is left, I take it.'

'Quick. Always quick, 'Rys.'

'I have gotten a whole lot quicker since I met Calum, but more of him later. Go on.'

'Well, I write articles for independent journals and newspapers when I feel the urge. I even do a bit of consulting these days. Doesn't pay much and sometimes I end up not getting paid at all. But I get by. You know my needs are not that great, unlike your expensive lifestyle.'

'Are you still on the anti-nuclear kick?'

'You have obviously not been reading my stuff or you would know. I am surprised. We are almost in the same business these days. The only thing is you seem prepared to tolerate the damned stuff in power stations as long it follows your policies and procedures. Me, I am against all forms of nuclear application because they are all going to lead to war, sometime, somewhere.'

'I am glad you are aware of my research. It has really taken off and the book is just about to go to a second print. No, I am sorry to say I have not caught any of your work. Is it mainly published in the UK?'

'No. I now have articles going pretty much world-wide. But, mainly in the underground press. That is the difference. You have gone all mainstream. There was a time when we both saw eye-to-eye on the nuclear threat.'

'Yes. That was when we were both in middle school in Sacramento. And, I mostly did it to annoy our parents. Most of us eventually grow up, 'Ger. It is just that you have never seemed to get around to it.'

'It is not a case of growing up. It is a case of whether you want to chase the almighty dollar or not. I didn't and you obviously do.'

'That is kind of obvious from your clothes. Goodwill Boutique I detect?'

'Appearance has never been important unless you only care about impressing.'

'Ok. Ok. Truce, Dear Brother! How do you manage to eke out a living? When you left me all alone to wind up Mum and Dad's estate, I remember sending you various amounts to a bank account in London. You can't still be living off that. I know I have long since blown most of my share.'

'My needs are more modest. I still have a fair bit left and I am able to put a bit away when I am earning. I am also quite proud to admit that I am able to accept social service payments when I am in the UK.'

'You mean welfare? Mum and Dad must be spinning in their graves. They were such snobs, remember?'

'They were cremated as I recall so they are more likely to be blowing in the wind than spinning. But you are right, they were snobs. The unacceptable face of capitalism. I forget who said that, but it fitted Dad to a "t" when I suggested it. They both dedicated their lives to making money.'

'And, spending it as well. That is why the estate was not as big as it should have been.'

'It was enough for me, even though it tortured me at the time to even accept any of their money. It was just that I was particularly broke at that point and it kept me off the street.'

'Do you not think they left anything worthwhile to you? You would never even guess you were their son. They did not pass anything on to you about career or lifestyle. You seem to have delighted in going the exact opposite direction in everything you have touched. I thought when you left home, you would have changed.'

'Not me! University taught me exactly why I was reluctant to go there in the first place. I have no desire for a career. Can you just see me being 'something big in the City' as Dad always went on about? No. I am happy doing what I do. I can look at myself in the mirror without cringing or regretting my actions.'

'By the look of that beard, it is quite a while since you last looked in any mirror. Do you actually have a permanent abode? I only have that PO Box number in London when I want to reach you.'

'I have abodes in various places around the world. None permanent. None owned. None mortgaged. None even rented as a matter of fact. I just have a series of addresses where I can crash until someone suggests I move on. It is a very cooperative existence.'

'Sounds a bit like my life in Boston after uni. But that only lasted six months and then I decided I was not cut out to be a bohemian.'

'The quest for the almighty dollar was on!'

'I am not ashamed of it, Roger. I have progressed up the academic tree and now I am a tenured prof. at only 52. Not bad going, don't you think?'

'You chose to play the game. You are winning the game. But it is still the game.'

'Ohhhh. Shit! Sorry, I did not mean to say that so loudly. That waiter is giving us a funny look. It is just that I wish, after all this time, we had more in common or could at least find some level we could both relate to. The last time that happened, I had just followed you to Willows Middle School.'

'S'been a while. That's for sure.'

'Are you really happy, 'Ger?'

'As a clam, 'Rys. Tell me about this Calum. I couldn't make your wedding in Palm Springs. Grand affair no doubt!'

'It was a very small and beautiful wedding actually. And, yes, I was sorry too when you ignored it. You know I offered to pay your fare out.'

'I know you did, and it wouldn't have cost you much because I was actually in Arizona in a commune at the time. I just did not fancy the Palm Springs setting. Was Frank Sinatra doing the disco?'

'He was not. He was dead by then. Palm Springs is reinventing itself. It is not all just about the Rat Pack and dirty weekends for the Hollywood set. What was this commune all about?'

'It only lasted about five minutes, I thought it was about a group of like-minded people wanting to get back to nature and practise the simple life. Turned out there were some expensive drug habits and trust funds were pretty much the admission price to keep the whole scene going. I split for Asia not long after your wedding. Tell me about the illustrious Calum. Sounds to me like the kind of conservative Dad would have latched on to with relish.'

'I think they would have gotten on with relish....and sauce. They share a great love of brandy; which I am sure they would have consumed in vast quantities if they had ever met. Too bad that Mom and Dad passed away long before their time.'

'Methinks the brandy might have had something to do with that. They both liked to tipple.'

'They sure did. They have passed it on to me but not to you. Funny that. But I have a hard time keeping up with Calum. He is just what I was looking for in a husband, second time around. He is loving, attentive, fit in spite of his age, supportive of me, very funny, and intelligent. He gets himself into scrapes because he will just not ignore things he thinks are wrong; but he seems to come out of them ok. And, in a strange sort of way, some of them have actually helped my research.'

'I read something about what he got up to in Scotland.'

'That seems funny now but, at that time, it was deadly serious. Surely, you must have been supportive of what he did?'

'Him personally, perhaps. But the circumstances were all wrong. The problem with getting rid of nuclear waste is exactly why there should not be any nuclear power stations in the first place.'

'Well, I thought he did a great job. And, I was able to include some of the background in my research papers and then in the book.'

'And, thereby helping in the quest for the almighty dollar!'

'Roger! You will never change. Calum is a great guy. I just wish you could meet him. If anybody could persuade you to change your ways, it might be him. Unfortunately, he is not around now. He has gone off on a quick visit to his beloved island, Cumbrae. What about you? Is there no Mrs Jones ever to appear from the wings? You are not getting any younger, you know.'

'I have too much of an eclectic lifestyle to accommodate a woman. There have been one or two over the years that I thought might be the one but they either let me down on the beliefs side or they just could not keep up with the pace of my travel.'

'When you get into a real relationship, you have to make big compromises. I know I have had to. Do you ever think about that?'

'Compromise is the first sign of weakness.'

'I can't believe you just said that! Calum says that all the time and I am never sure whether it is in jest or not. In your case, I know. What about dear Jane de Lawney from high school? She was your first love. I thought you were destined to be with her forever. We all did.'

'Ah, dear Jane. She has lived in Perth in Western Australia for many years.'

'You still know her?'

'…..where she is married with four children and quite happy, I assume. But that does not mean we have lost touch altogether. Every few years, we manage to steal some time together. One time, she came to London on her own to visit her parents, who are back staying there now. Another time, she and her husband took a business trip to New York when I just happened to be there. I also managed to spend some time out in Oz doing an article for a Perth publication so that worked out quite well too.'

'Oh 'Ger, you are hopeless. Is that the best you can do after forty years of chasing Jane de Lawney? Sneaking around here and there. How does she view you? I can imagine her saying "just a bit on the side," in that toffee-nosed Home Counties accent of hers. Does she still have it even though she left England when she was about three years old?'

'Ha, ha. Yes, she still speaks that way. But it is a bit unkind of you to see us in that way. I don't know why, but a lasting relationship has just never seemed to materialize and now she has all the commitments of a husband and the children.'

'Surely her children are grown up?'

'Yes, but you know what I mean.'

'No. I don't know what you mean. For someone who has such fervent views of politics and causes, you are absolutely fickle when it comes to yourself personally. I really should take you under my wing.'

'I very much doubt that would be a good thing.'

'You and I are almost polar opposites. Yet we came from the same stock. There must be some similarities, hidden away inside of us, just dying to get out.'

'Hmm.'

'I have sooooo enjoyed seeing you again after all this time. We simply must build on this. Why don't you spend some time here in

California? Calum will be home in a week. You two will get on like a house on fire once you both dismantle your defences. I will introduce you to some single friends on campus. This could turn out to be great. I will transform you! No, that is not right. You will transform yourself. I can even get you a temporary teaching position. You have so much to offer. You can stay with us for as long as you like. We have a big house, at least by UK standards. And, you can continue to write. Maybe, we can even write something together. The yin and the yang of the nuclear question. Oh, it could be such fun......stop frowning, in fact you are going a little pale. Does the prospect of stepping out of your own shadow worry you that much? Say you will do it. Say you will at least think about it. Can you stay on after you finish what you are doing here? You never actually said what it is you are doing in California.'

'I need to get going, Nerys. I have a bus to catch to San Francisco.'

'Why are you going there? What are you going to do?'

'I am attending an anti-nuke conference at various locations and a concert in Panhandle Park.'

'Oh, that sounds interesting. Who is putting it on the conference?'

'NOTANA.'

'The National Opposition to All Nuclear Applications?'

'That's them.'

'My God. They have been the most vocal opposition to my research. They are always putting me down.'

'I know.'

'But, how are you involved?'

'I am the keynote speaker...on your research......and other things.'

'Roger, how could you?'

'Well, we all have beliefs and we need to hold on to them, family or not. S'been a while, Nerys. It was good to see you. I'd better get going now.'

You Know Too
Much About
This Place!

Dr Calum Davies rushed out of the departmental meeting leaving four other professors to shrug and shift their conversation to something else. It was not that he was in a rush to get anywhere else. His next meeting with the Campus President was not for another full hour. He was just in a rush to get out of that particular meeting, a meeting with his so-called colleagues that was anything but collegial.

Calum had now been employed by the California University (CU) at Temecula for just over eight years, his first and only major

172

stint in California after moving down from Canada. First employed there in the professional accounting sector, he had shifted over to the academic sector when he took up a teaching position. That had come to an end when divorce had persuaded him that he needed a fresh new environment. After some demeaning work as an adjunct faculty, he had been offered a non-tenure track position in the Faculty of Business as an Accounting professor just as the new campus was opening. After eight years, he was now one of relatively few originals still around. Tenure track, as the name suggests, the track toward tenure and permanence of employment, was generally awarded to younger academics with an established research record. Calum was well into his fifties at the time of hiring, with a background in professional accounting and not much research on his record. He had never actively sought tenure thereafter, nor had it been offered to him.

Although the University itself had established a strong reputation as a credible private alternative to the public powerhouses of the University of California and the California State University, this particular campus had experienced a bit of a bumpy ride throughout its existence. Its strength, but often its weakness, was the philosophy around which it had been created. The campus was intended to be an independent self-supporting, corporate-sponsored model entity within the overall privately-funded university, which consisted of six other campuses. In truth, Temecula had not really been on the University Board of Directors' radar as a potential site, but the community had made a strong enough case after the public universities had turned it down, for the Board to agree to a campus on one straight and unbending condition. Temecula had to find and maintain its own funding. Over its history, that had resulted in Temecula having good years and bad years in terms of fund-raising, irrespective of how the parent university was doing. The latter was consistently successful, in fact it ranked very highly in league tables for private university revenue generation and in league tables for academic performance of private and public universities combined. But to this day, not a drop of its resources had been channelled into

Temecula. As a result of the absence of funding continuity, turnover of faculty had been higher than average for universities in California.

Calum shook his head as he strode toward his office and played back the substance of this latest meeting. Five years ago, he had been elected by his colleagues in Accounting as Department Head, when the original head moved on to another campus. It was something of a surprise that he, without tenure, should be so recognized, but it probably said a lot about his colleagues and their collective lack of leadership skills. It was proving to be a dubious honour, however. The administrative requirements of the department head position were easily managed; management of the politics was an entirely different kettle of fish. Calum was in the habit of quoting Henry Kissenger's celebrated observation "The reason that university politics is so vicious is because stakes are so low!"

His four colleagues, all tenured, and he, comprised the Department of Accounting for official meeting purposes. The several other non-tenure track and adjunct faculty in the department were denied the opportunity to sit at the high table in a strange contradiction of democracy. And, those four colleagues used just about every meeting to further two causes, improvement of their own workload and conditions and the denial of any rights or privileges to the others in the department. The campus was deeply in the throes of a funding crisis and no pay increases had been granted, other than to tenured faculty. That had been a campus-wide decision. However, the Accounting foursome had deemed the increases to be totally unsatisfactory and had set about looking for compensatory improvements in their benefits, research opportunities, and teaching loads. And those were the very areas where Calum, as Department Head, had to balance desires against the reality of a reducing annual budget. And, all of this he had to do in the knowledge that he, personally, had not received any pay increase in recent years, along with the other lesser mortals in the department.

Today's meeting had begun and ended on workload, forever the contentious issue. Tenured faculty were required to teach two classes per semester, although some could be released from one or even both if they were assigned to a special research or administrative project. Tenured faculty could, however, in theory, teach three or four classes per semester according to the labour agreement. It was up to Calum to persuade them to increase their workload, even on a temporary basis, and thereby reduce the number of adjuncts required in order to squeeze the payroll into the newly established budget while serving the expected number of students. This was the third meeting in as many weeks where the topic had been raised and vehemently rejected by his colleagues. It was the first, however, where dissatisfaction with campus working conditions had been pointedly directed toward President Jerome Dale Eisenhower, the campus founding president. Calum, who was by now accustomed to having his own reputation impugned by his colleagues, had learned that there was a growing campus-wide movement to oust Eisenhower and the Accounting professors were obviously intent on being at the forefront of the mob.

He slumped down in his chair and wondered if that was why Eisenhower had scheduled their one-on-one meeting today. Surely not. The Accounting Department was a relatively small player on campus. He could not help thinking back to an incident when he first joined CU and got involved in leading the search for an alleged bomb. Eisenhower had been both thankful and quite critical of his efforts. Their relationship had improved a little over the years, particularly since he had been elected Department Head. Was Eisenhower looking for him to deal with another bomb? Surely not!

As the time passed, his intended task of catching up on unanswered emails had been forsaken and he continued to ponder what he could do to calm down the tenured faculty without disadvantaging the already disadvantaged non-tenure and adjunct faculty. It was an exercise in creative thinking, mixed with no little diplomacy that he normally relished, and frequently succeeded in. However, when he thought back to his long career, prior to academia, in the professional world of accountancy with major firms, he noted, and not for the first time either, the difference between the two worlds---it was loyalty. In the accountancy world, loyalty to the firm and one's colleagues was a prerequisite, and failure to exhibit it meant no career prospects. In the academic world, loyalty was not expected, nor extended to anyone, or even to the university. It was a very self-centred world.

He had not solved his dilemma when later he looked up at the office clock and saw it was time to make his way over to the presidential suite on the top floor of the library.

===OOO===

'Ah, there you are, Calum, come on in. I have asked Sherrie to bring in some coffee; have a seat,' Dr Jerome Dale Eisenhower jumped up and welcomed Calum, almost a little too profusely for Calum's liking.

'Hi Dale. How goes the battle?'

'Battle? What have you heard?'

'I haven't heard anything. It is just a saying. No battle going on that I have heard about. Unless you are talking about academia in general.'

'I might be. I might well be.'

The pert and always friendly Sherrie entered the room bearing a tray with coffee pot, two cups, and a plate of British digestive biscuits.

'Your favourite Dr Davies. Digestive biscuits. I never forget that, and now Dr Eisenhower likes them too. For me, they taste a bit like placemats.'

'Really, Sherrie! And when did you last eat a placemat?

Eisenhower did not allow Sherrie to respond to Calum's question as he ushered her out with a request to hold his calls.

Calum sat and savoured his biscuit and coffee and awaited revelation of the purpose of the meeting. The more he thought about it, it had to be something to do with the faculty unrest.

'How long have you been with us now, Calum? You were one of the originals, weren't you? Just like me.'

'That is so, Dale.'

'I fully realize now that I should have offered you tenure when you were hired, that was when I had the freedom to do so, before the Faculty Senate was set up. Once it got going, there was no chance of it for an old codger like you. You must be about the same age as me.'

'Exactly the same age, if I remember correctly.'

'Well, here is what I want to put to you. Non-tenure track is inherently unfair; no surprise there! You teach more than the adjuncts and you do research that they don't do, but you don't get paid that much more. You teach more than most tenured faculty and you get paid a darn sight less. On top of that, you are the department head doing all the administrative work.'

'Are you about to give me raise?'

'Not exactly. You know I cannot do that. I would if I could, but the faculty union would be down on me like a ton of bricks.'

'Yes, the good old union, protecting the rights of its members. At least, protecting the rights of the tenured members. It does not really want to know about non-tenured animals like myself.'

'I know, I know. And that is exactly why I have a proposition I want to put to you. Have you ever thought about becoming an administrator?'

'You mean going over to the dark side? Wow! I think about it all the time….not'

'Well you should. Having no tenure is meant to be an academic expression associated with academic freedom, but it really means having no job security. If budgets ever got a lot worse and we were looking at downsizing, guess who would be first to go? We could not get rid of tenured faculty, even if they committed a capital offence; the union would see to that, so a budget shortfall is certainly no justification. We would have to look at the adjuncts and the non-tenured. Guess who costs more? Yes, you would be on the firing line. Now, I am not saying we are anywhere near the stage of looking at downsizing, but this is longest money drought in our history, and it leaves you vulnerable.'

'Hmm. I have to confess, I have not given that prospect much thought.'

'That is why I am interested in you becoming an administrator. They are slightly safer than your lot in a downsizing and, in any case, you are ready for it.'

'How so?'

'You have been here the best part of eight years. You know too much about this place! I mean you know too much about it to just muck along as a faculty member. We need you to move into the management side where you can put your knowledge to good use.'

'What do you have in mind?' Calum asked, as he helped himself to another coffee and two biscuits. This was getting interesting.

'I have it on good authority that my long and dear friend, but next to useless colleague, Donald MacDonald, is going to retire at the end of the semester. Not a moment too soon. He should have done it years ago. I want you to apply for his job as VP for Business Affairs.'

'Donald is going, is he? The faculty will be happy.'

'Yes, they will. He has constantly annoyed the faculty and their union as if it were some kind of sport. That seems to be the only thing he actually does with some enthusiasm. Now, that is another good reason that I want you. You are sort of one of them, have a good relationship with most faculty, as far as I can see. The union relationship thing is not too bad either, all things considered. No, you are just the man for those reasons, and you are a financial man and you are a practical beast.'

'Don't forget the ability to search out bombs.'

'Don't remind me of that; but in a funny way, it is true. You showed Donald up that day. A good VP for Business Affairs needs to be an accountant who has the ability and motivation to build a good team of experts around him, lead them well and let them do their jobs. Donald is forever interfering and getting in the way, bless his soul. It is some form of insecurity complex, I am convinced. He is afraid to admit that any of his underlings actually know more about their area of expertise than he does. I don't think you would have that problem. You are a leader.'

'I have watched that going on over the years. There are some good managers in Business Affairs. They just need to be given the room to spread their wings.'

'Exactly what I was just saying; only you said in that engagingly flowery language that betrays your English roots.'

179

'Away with you Dale, I am Scottish through and through.'

'Exactly.'

'You are giving me food for thought, I must admit.'

'Exactly what I intended. Can you be persuaded? 'Course you can. At your stage of life, you should be up for an adventure.'

'What would be the next steps?'

'Hiring the four vice presidents is about the only thing they let me do on my own these days without interference from the mother ship, or the unions, or the Academic Senate. I am just about ready to post the vacancy, once Donald gives me the final decision on his retirement. I am sorely tempted just to make it an internal posting. There are a couple of Donald's managers and maybe a couple of deans who can make up an acceptable list of candidates, along with you, of course. You will walk into the job, which is precisely the object of the exercise. You will just have to apply when the posting comes out. I will get Sherrie to tip you off when I do it.'

'Wow. This is not what I expected to come out of today's meeting. I thought you were going to want some help on the faculty rumblings I am hearing about.'

'The faculty revolt! I hear about it every day. The faculty can be as revolting as they like, it does not matter a darn as long as the Board of Directors at the mothership continues to support me.'

'So, you are not unnerved by it at all.'

'Not in the least. Some university presidents actually relish a good faculty revolt with the inevitable vote of no confidence by the faculty being seen as the ultimate badge of honour!'

'Do you know the quote from Henry Kissenger?'

'Indeed, I do. And, he got it right even though he was an academic himself. Now get out of here! Keep this quiet on campus right now but make sure you talk about it to your lovely wife Nerys.

She is one of the good guys on faculty. And, you might as well take those last two digestives with you as well. You have eaten the rest of them while I was busy doing the talking, but it was worth it!'

===OOO===

A lot happened in the next few weeks!

At the California University headquarters, there was a bit of a boardroom shuffle. The fifteen-member Board comprised major shareholders of the privately funded university, who had each attained a seat according to the size of their investment. The Board nominally reported to other smaller investors of whom there were many. The Chair of the Board had been in office for almost as long as the University had existed and, while it had been very much his vision that had seen CU develop the way it had, he had been showing his age of late. A minority of his fellow directors had made increasing noises about change, and eventually the minority became a majority and a new Chair was elected. Walker Thomson had made millions in real estate and happened to come from Temecula, where he had been the driving force behind getting the campus established there. He had made two promises in his election speech—to be an active Chair and to get Temecula on a more solid financial footing.

Donald MacDonald announced his retirement with some fanfare and after a hastily-arranged campus celebratory dinner, which Walker Thomson attended, he essentially vanished from the University, even though his retirement was not effective until the end of the semester. This is a practice not unheard of in academia. When you decide are going, you are gone! Similarly, when someone else decides that you are going, you are gone!

His internal job posting surfaced the day after his dinner. There was some comment circulating after that concerning Walker Thomson's unease with the fact that the job was not being advertised externally, but allegedly President Eisenhower had put his foot down and it went ahead as he had planned.

Calum had long discussions with Nerys about his intention to apply as directed by Eisenhower. She was nervous about it. Being a well-engaged faculty member, she was picking up the escalating faculty unrest toward the President and she feared what the consequences might be of Eisenhower being perceived to just give the job to Calum. Calum's apt description of the President's attitude as "damn the torpedoes" was at the root of the problem. Even Nerys, who could not be described as your typical self-serving, self-important academic, called it an anti-academic attitude to want to just parachute someone into the job. And, she worried about Calum being associated with it.

She probably should have known better. Sound advice as it was that she had provided, it was not what Calum wanted to hear, and so the application for the VP job was duly submitted. Then, that hiring process seemed to slow down almost immediately and did not follow the timelines mentioned in the job posting.

Walker Thomson embarked on a visit to each CU campus, which comprised separate meetings with the President, senior administrators' group, and the Academic Senate. Reports filtered back from each campus of constructive meetings where he demonstrated an ability to listen, learn, and make no solid promises. When he arrived at Temecula, on the final stage of his tour, the three meetings took place as they had done elsewhere. Calum had no entry to any of them, not being an elected member of Senate, but the feedback he got was pretty much what had come out of the other campuses. There was a suggestion that some members of the Senate had tried to raise the performance of the President in their meeting, but they had actually been ruled out of order by the Senate Chair, herself a faculty member. The bombshell occurred the morning

182

following the final meeting. Instead of returning to CU corporate headquarters in San Francisco as planned, word spread around campus like wildfire that Thomson had agreed to attend an all-faculty meeting in a local hotel that night. All tenured faculty were invited but no non-tenured or adjunct faculty, or staff, and certainly no administrators would be admitted. The President was considered just like any other administrator and would not be there.

That afternoon, Calum happened to be in the cafeteria meeting with some students, who were working on a research project. That was often his approach to make such meetings informal over Cokes and burgers. They were just breaking up when he noticed Sherrie, the President's Personal Assistant, leaving the cashier area having purchased a sandwich that probably meant she was working late. When her eyes met Calum's, she motioned to him to move over to a quiet area of the cafeteria.

'Working late tonight, Sherrie?' Calum asked, nodding toward the sandwich.

'No, it is not for me. It is for Dr Eisenhower. I think he intends to just stay on here into the evening but, for the life of me, I can't imagine why. You heard about the faculty meeting with Mr Thomson tonight?'

'I did. I don't like the sound of it. Thomson must be out of his mind.'

'It is worse than that, I suspect. He came to see Dr Eisenhower just a little while ago. I normally can't hear what goes on in his room and I didn't hear what the President was saying, but I certainly heard some of what Mr Thomson was saying, because in the end he was shouting.'

Calum looked around him to make sure that nobody was within earshot; but the cafeteria was quite quiet before the supper rush of students arriving for night classes.

'What did you hear?'

'I heard "Don't you tell me how to do my job, Eisenhower. The faculty want to speak to me and that is what a board chair does, he listens. You told me to keep out of your job when I challenged your decision to just post MacDonald's job internally. Well, now it is me telling you the same," and then Dr Eisenhower must have said a lot because I did not hear anything for a few minutes, but the silence was followed by Mr Thomson bellowing again. "That is a bad attitude to have, but quite frankly I am not surprised. It is exactly that attitude that has been dragging this campus down for the last couple of years. People and corporations will not put money into a university where the faculty are unhappy; you should know that. If I hear tonight that you are the problem…well, you better be prepared for some serious soul-searching when you next meet with me. That could be very soon." He then came out through the door and slammed it behind him.'

'Did you go in to see the boss?'

'I was scared to, but he eventually called me in. He looked terrible. He looked like he had suddenly grown quite old. All he did was to ask me to get him a sandwich.'

'You better get back; he will be looking for you and being seen talking to me might not help anyone.'

'What do you think is going to happen, Calum?'

Calum noted the familiarity. Sherrie was a sweet girl and very competent. She must be well aware of the tendency for personal assistants to be linked together with presidents in good times…and in bad times. She appeared to be rightly nervous.

In the following days, news of the all-faculty meeting leaked out like toxic sewage in one of Nerys' research projects. It had been one long character-assassination, and Calum's accounting colleagues had played an active part. The meeting Chair, who just happened to be the head of the faculty union, although this was not an official union meeting, had simply let it flow without any attempt

184

to moderate or temper the language or behaviour. Walker Thomson acted nothing like he had in any of his other meetings. Apparently, he commented on things being said, encouraged speakers to say more, and at the conclusion was alleged to have said that he valued hearing the truth from the faculty, something he had suspected for quite some time; they had bravely done their bit; and now he must do his. He received a standing ovation before the meeting broke up.

Meetings seemed to spring up all over campus to encourage wildly-varying rumours. The administrators' group met without the President and was alleged to already be discussing contingency plans for continuing business while there was a vacancy at the top. The faculty and staff unions seemed to suddenly be motivated to raise grievances over countless perceived violations of their collective agreements, that consumed a lot of the President's time because he had to fill in for the absent Donald MacDonald. The Academic Senate unusually cancelled its monthly meeting, on the grounds that it did not have any pressing business, although cynics commented that maintaining the pristine image of the academic body was more in mind. The same faculty members who served on it, could always do their dirty work in different venues, especially if they had the ear of the board chair. That last suggestion had been made so often as to have now become a fact.

Calum, at first, felt a grim sense of isolation. He had no organized body to interact with. He even tried getting to meet with Eisenhower, but he was almost perpetually engaged and unavailable for meetings. The hiring process for the VP for Business Affairs had ground to a halt. No interviews had been scheduled; in fact, no acknowledgement of the applications had even gone out. Nerys had picked up in faculty chatter that the process was to be abandoned on the order of Walker Thomson, but nothing had been made official.

There was a foreboding sense that things could not continue in this state of flux and something would have to break. The escalating prediction was that Eisenhower would be squeezed out, rather than simply fired. The only question to be answered was when.

Calum was surprised to get a phone call from a faculty member in the English Department, and he was even more surprised to learn what was said. Seamus O'Flaherty was an eminent academic in English literature as well as a larger than life character. Unlike many of their colleagues, Seamus tended to focus on the wellbeing of students and their studies and enjoying a riotous personal social life, in equal measures. In that respect, he was not too different from Calum, but a whole lot louder. He did not beat around the bush once pleasantries were dispensed with, he came out and said that what was happening to Eisenhower was morally, if not legally, wrong and the man and the campus deserved better. He guessed that Calum might be of the same mind and Calum was quick to agree, but the problem was he had no voice.

'Oh, but I do, boyo,' Seamus boomed, 'and I am of a mind to help create one for you too.'

'How so? I am not a member of anything. I am just a humble non-tenure.'

'You are a Scot and I have never ever found them to be humble. A wee bit like the Irish! Listen up, here is what is happening. A few, and we are only a few, mind you, tenured faculty are of the mind that we need to speak out now before it is too late to try and save Eisenhower. Word about us has percolated around campus, you know what it is like, and now we have been joined by some administrators, adjuncts, and staff, all with the same concerns and intentions. We might even be on the cusp of getting some endorsement from the Students' Union. Your name has come up as one who does not blindly follow the faculty party line but is an independent thinker with a sense of what is right and what is not. Do I have that correct?'

'I like to think so.'

'Well, are you in?'

'I am not sure. How many of you rebels are there?'

'There were twenty-five of us, as of yesterday.'

'Jeez. That is not exactly enough to make a big splash.'

'Maybe today, it might only cause a ripple, but who knows tomorrow. Are you in, man?'

'Why not, what do I have to lose? That VP job seems to be disappearing fast.'

'Aye, I heard you were in for that. You would do a good job, if it ever gets filled. But I would think it must be in your interests to have Eisenhower calling the shots, rather than who knows who else, and certainly rather than *Mr Real Estate*, who might even put himself in as president on a temporary basis. That is the latest rumour.'

'Surely not!'

'I gather there is precedent for it and a bunch of those self-serving colleagues of mine would be happy to feed his ego if they thought there was something in it for them.'

A silence prevailed and Seamus had to enquire if Calum was still there.

'Count me in. What happens next?'

'Meet tonight in the back room of the Irish Rover in town at 8 pm.'

'Do I wear a mask?'

'No need, but just watch who you tell about it. I don't suppose there is any chance of bringing Nerys along?'

'She seems determined to keep out of the politics, even though she now has the much-valued tenure.

'A wise as well as beautiful woman. Too bad. At least, we will have you!'

Thus, it was that Calum found himself on the side of the President, against what seemed like a huge majority of the campus personnel. Nevertheless, their small disparate group gradually grew in numbers as they became more visible and started to make statements in writing. All the while, the conspiracy to remove Eisenhower never actually produced any statement of intent officially; it just ground along on rumour and innuendo. The good guys, for they had failed to come up with a name for themselves, had decided that the only way to draw out the dark intentions of the other side was to go as public as possible with their concerns. That meant engaging the media. Most journalists and broadcasters seldom professed to understand academic politics and were incapable of determining the right cause from the wrong cause, but in this one they could relate to President Eisenhower, who had been in the community for a long time, was credited with the growth of the University, and always had an open door for the media, particularly if it helped fund-raising efforts.

Articles and news clips tried to capture the concerns of Seamus' group, but it was difficult to convey it in cohesive form, when the other side constantly declined to make any public comments. And, it was certainly not helped by the persistent quoting of Walker Thomson that he sensed something was not quite right at the Temecula campus and that he was listening and learning as a good board chair should do. The media comments, together with the frequent statements put out by the group, did serve a purpose, however, of informing the uncommitted and ill-informed, of which there seemed to be more than a few, once the hot heads were separated out from the rest of faculty. Some more tenured faculty members expressed support for the group's sentiments but declined to be associated with it, in spite of the strength of their academic freedom to speak out on all matters under the sun that came with tenure. Meanwhile, the President's office remained virtually closed

188

to all but a very few. Eisenhower seemed to have adopted a siege mentality and did not reach out to the group that was attempting to save him. Poor Sherrie had only been able to bear the tension for so long and then had been sent on sick leave by the President. Now, a temporary administrative assistant was the first line of defence in the office, with the strict orders to admit nobody and put through no calls. Taking messages was her only duty.

The tension had mounted over almost a full month. Something had to give. It did.

Both sides learned about the same time that Eisenhower had been ordered to attend corporate headquarters in San Francisco. Two days later, in a televised press conference, Walker Thomson, on behalf of a reportedly unanimous Board of Directors, announced that Dr Imelda Ramirez would be assuming the presidency of the Temecula campus on an acting basis, effective immediately. Furthermore, Dr Jerome Dale Eisenhower would be entering a richly-deserved retirement, effective immediately. When pressed by the media during a question session that followed the prepared statement, Thomson revealed that Dr Ramirez was an eminent academic, researcher, and fund-raiser, who had spent her career to date in colleges and universities in New England and was now moving to California to share her talents. This boded well for the Temecula campus, so much so that Thomson was moved to declare heartily 'the recovery begins today!'. Even when pressed, he was reluctant to say much about Eisenhower's presidency and not prepared to say anything about the nature of his retirement, other than to say, 'everybody has to retire eventually!'.

===OOO===

Dr Imelda Ramirez arrived on campus in something akin to a whirlwind. Not for her the gradual listening and learning philosophy; she worked on the assumption that she already knew all she needed to know about how to steer the good ship Temecula. Meetings were immediately arranged with what she called 'the key stakeholders' and those individuals, a mix of senior administrators and tenured faculty, almost universally reported that they were quite overwhelmed by the vision and energy of the new President, and left their meetings with a renewed enthusiasm for the campus along with their own particular marching orders. Within a week of her arrival, all functions of the education business were operating as if there had never been any interruption.

Calum was reminded that he did not enjoy the special status of others, when he had not actually met Dr Ramirez one-on-one yet. That was further emphasized when he learned that she had brought in a long-retired university administrator to serve as acting VP for Business Affairs and announced that the process of eventually filling the position permanently would be an open process, meaning external and internal applications would be sought.

He, as always, discussed how events were playing out with Nerys. She, personally, felt unaffected by the change, as she continued to focus on her teaching and particularly on her research. She did, however, opine that most faculty she spoke with were quite pleased with the new President. In fact, there was already a sort of grass-roots movement developing in favour of Dr Ramirez assuming the position on a permanent basis. In theory, she had a one-year temporary contract, but the situation could always change as the campus population was now well aware. Calum had also decided just to keep his head down and do what he was paid to do. This year, he had a good group of attentive students, which is so essential to success in an oft-cited dry subject like Accounting, and so he put even more energy into his work when he was getting good results.

The administrative work was another matter. His colleagues made it quite clear that Calum had backed the wrong horse when he had chosen to lend his support to Eisenhower. That meant that he was no longer suitable to fulfil the role of Department Head. His response was that any time they wanted to vote in a replacement was fine with him but, in the meantime, he would continue to try and resolve the issues that had been consuming all the committee time. As he suspected, no vote was proposed, but that did not make it any easier to get business done, notably to revise the workloads to fit within the reduced budget. Eventually he was able to hammer out a compromise that got some more work out of the tenured faculty but did not disadvantage the non-tenures and adjuncts. It was more a case of everybody being equally unhappy then equally happy, but at least it was equally felt, and next semester could be planned with some certainty.

As the end of semester fast approached, nothing had been announced about the VP job. Calum had not had much to do with the interim administrator but had commented to Nerys that he seemed decrepit and probably only capable of keeping the seat warm for a short period of time. Over a pleasant dinner one night with the O'Flahertys, the conversation had turned to a review of the new regime. Seamus was of a view that neither the VP nor the President would last any length of time and life would go on as it always did. He, of course, had not suffered any lasting damage on account of his supporting Eisenhower, he had merely been exercising his academic freedom as a tenured faculty member! He was of the view that Calum should sit tight, and the VP opportunity would come up again for him. If he had to compete with outside applicants, so what, he would still be a strong candidate. However, Calum's mood that was lifted by this assessment, was soon deflated when Nerys offered the opposite view completely. She thought that Ramirez was well on the way to a permanent appointment because she had created allies everywhere on campus and was now getting known in the outside community. She agreed that the acting VP should not stay, but she was by no means certain that Ramirez would favour appointing Calum after his support for Eisenhower. His academic freedom was nowhere near as strong as Seamus'. Her advice to Calum was that he should focus on his teaching, maybe do a little more research, and forget about administrative aspirations. As an alternative, he should contemplate retirement now that he was getting into that age range.

That last comment staggered Calum. They had never had more than passing discussions about his retirement. The fact that Nerys was ten years younger and really just starting out on her career, in terms of gaining tenure and research reputation, had led them previously to conclude that he would probably work for a longer time rather than a shorter time, until they could retire roughly about the same time. He found himself protesting rather loudly about being put out to graze by his own wife. He did not even have ten years' service in yet and would not qualify for a pension from the University.

Nerys knew that she had unintentionally hurt him, but she also felt that all options had to be considered. Before she could even try to placate her husband, Seamus had intervened to suggest a round of liqueurs to round off a splendid meal. It caused peace to break out but did not solve the problem.

Calum often made general reference to the need to read the "writing on the wall", and how calamities could frequently be avoided if people paid attention to the signs. If he were practising his own philosophy, he would surely understand where things were headed when he learned of a memo from the President sent out on the last day of semester to all tenured faculty. It stated that, at the beginning of the next semester, all departments should ensure that their department head position was filled through election by a tenured faculty member. He well knew that his status as a non-tenured department head was one of only two on the entire campus, the other department being Religious Studies, where there was only one tenured faculty member and she had declared no interest in administrative matters. The writing was on the wall.

It was an awkward summer for Nerys and Calum, as they struggled to find common ground on whether he should pursue his career, either staying at CU Temecula or looking for another job, or consider retirement. No particular headway had been made and it was probably fortunate that Nerys had to spend several weeks on the road doing her research. At least that put the discussion on the back-burner for a short while. Towards the end of the summer break, they were able to travel to Scotland to spend two weeks on the Isle of Cumbrae, Calum's self-declared spiritual home. They had both acknowledged, time and time again, how the short ferry ride from the mainland to the island seemed to have a therapeutic effect on Calum, and any worries he arrived with simply washed away. Nerys had hoped that would continue to be the case and a more relaxed Calum would be able to approach some more practical discussion about his future as they slipped into their favourite activities and places to visit. However, Calum had announced that he did not want to spoil their holiday with any more depressing talk about the CU and so no progress was made at all!

===OOO===

It was standard practice for faculty to return to campus one week before the start of classes in order to make curriculum adjustments, solve last-minute scheduling issues, and generally get ready for new semester. In reality, it was more of an opportunity to gossip with colleagues about what one had got up to over the summer break. There was as much talk about taking water-skiing lessons as there was about any startling research findings. Calum usually enjoyed what he called the "lull before the storm" and a pleasant first week was often the indicator of a good semester ahead. The opposite could also be true.

He had not been in his office for fifteen minutes when one of the four tenured Accounting professors, Dr Carlos Delgado, probably the one that he got on best with, popped his head around the door. With only a little sign of embarrassment, he announced that the tenured faculty had held a vote and he, Carlos, was the new department head. He was sure the others joined him in thanking Calum for all his efforts and hoped he understood that they were only complying with the directive from the President. As he made to quickly disappear, Calum ushered to him to come in properly and have a seat, if he had five minutes to spare.

'Carlos, you have not caused me too much grief with your news. It was something of a poisoned chalice. I wish you well this semester. I assume I will now not be on the department committee, but if I can help you in any way, you only have to ask.'

'Thanks for that, Calum. This is awkward. I need this job like a hole in the head. I would have been just as happy to see you continue. You were probably a better department head then I will ever be. I hate confrontation, as you probably know.'

'I know, I know. You are only obeying orders.'

'Exactly!'

'Many a crime has been committed under that pretence.'

'Aw, c'mon Calum. You know what it is like. I don't know why you don't have tenure and then there would be no problem.'

'I am not sure I know either, but one thing is for sure, it is not going to happen now. And as Dr Eisenhower said to me, in what was probably the last conversation I had with him, that puts me in a position of vulnerability.''

'Surely not! You think that? No, I can't believe that.'

'Hmmm.'

'No. I am sure you will be just fine. I imagine you will not be regretting the loss of all the extra work that comes the way of the department head. I really appreciate your offer of help, but I will try very hard not to impose on you. As it happens, however, I have been given a task this morning on which I could do with some advice. Apparently, I have to try to find an additional couple of adjuncts at this very late stage, just days before the start of classes.'

'Wow, that is late. Good luck. Do we have more students than we were told to prepare for last semester? I thought they capped the intake at the agreed number.'

'I don't know. I was just told to find two more teachers.'

'Well, all I can suggest is that you call the nearest community colleges. They are already in session and some of their adjuncts might jump at the opportunity. They are not called the Freeway Flyers for nothing. They will travel any distance just to earn a living wage.'

'Fantastic. I would never have thought of that. I will get right on it. You don't happen to have the college phone numbers?'

'Not on the tip of my tongue, but I am sure they can be obtained on the internet. Ask for the HR Department or Academic Office'

'Right. Great. Gotta run now. I assume you have seen the VP for Business Affairs job is posted. I know you were interested in that one.'

'I haven't. I will take a look. See you later, Carlos.'

The first thing Calum did was to go onto the CU website and bring up the job vacancies screen. There it was, front and centre, the largest advertisement of the many listed. He read the details, which were considerably more than had appeared in the original posting. The focus on potential candidates was very wide and touched on administrators and faculty members of universities and also on management-types from the business world. Calum scanned all the required and desired qualities and experiences of the ideal candidate and decided that he ticked all the boxes. In spite of all the ups and downs of the previous semester, he started to get excited again about the prospect of moving into this role. He could be an effective business leader, he liked the managers and could work with them, and it would be no bad thing to be get out of the faculty firing line (no pun intended, he thought to himself). Yes, this might well be the change he was looking for.

He immediately referred to his application form and curriculum vitae he had previously submitted, which were also saved on his computer, and started to check carefully that the wording responded to the new posting. He made some changes and added a bit of more of his private sector accounting experience. Once he was satisfied that he had captured the candidate he wanted to portray, he was tempted to just hit the send button and fire it off to the HR Department. At the last moment, he hesitated and decided to have one last discussion with Nerys that night. They had been talking on and off about this opportunity for weeks now and had not always seen eye-to-eye. Perhaps it was a good idea to have one last review.

Nerys settled down in her study to carefully review the paper copies of the posting, application, and CV, which Calum had thrust into her hand the minute she had got into the car to come home. Now, he was clearing up the dinner dishes and making a racket washing pots and pans. He must be serious about this application to make such a sacrifice, she thought.

She knew she had to tread warily when he finally burst into the study looking for her reaction. She took time to work through the advertisement and connect each of the requirements to his application and particularly his CV. He actually listened closely to what she was saying, for once, without interrupting. She pointed out that there were only a couple of areas where she felt he could tighten up the wording or say a little more. He eventually enquired if all of this meant that she now saw him as a legitimate candidate. Something churned in her stomach and it was not the recently consumed goulash.

'That is a difficult question to answer. Of course, you are a legitimate candidate. You are more than that. You are a first-class candidate. Your CV likely stacks up there with anybody who applies; and you should have the advantage of inside knowledge. But you know how this racket works. There is more politics in it than anything else. In that regard, I just don't know. I don't really think that anybody truly knows how Imelda Ramirez's mind works yet and she will be calling the shots. I would hate for you to be terribly disappointed if you don't get it. You need to go into it with the belief that if you are not successful, it is no reflection on your ability, it is just down to those dark factors that abound in academia.'

'I know that. I know that. I think you need to be super-positive in your outlook when you make a decision like this. I have to tell you that since I saw the new posting yesterday, I have been getting more and more enthusiastic about the prospect. In some ways, I am glad that I did not get the job the way Eisenhower was planning it. I would rather win a full-blown competition. I think that would help my credibility once I am in the job too.'

'Of course, it would. Well, if your mind is made up, go for it. As an internal candidate, you should be guaranteed an interview. Then you can knock them dead when you get to see the whites of their eyes. I wonder who will be on the interview panel. Just don't tell them any of your jokes!'

The following morning, Calum arrived early into his office with a plan to execute. He had not fired off his application last night. Instead he had tossed and turned all night and hatched a plan without sharing it with Nerys. He was convinced that it would increase his chances, which must already be pretty good.

A call to the President's office had secured him an appointment with Dr Ramirez at 4 pm and he spent all day up to that point rehearsing in his head how to establish a good rapport with someone he would be meeting one-on-one for the first time. This was his favoured approach to preparing for stressful engagements, to rehearse them endlessly in his mind, so that he knew exactly how to control the direction of the conversation.

He glanced at an all-employee email from the President that appeared on his computer screen,, just as he was about to set out for his meeting. It announced that Dr Ramirez declared a philosophical aversion to the presidential suite being located on the top floor of the library (with the view to die for, incidentally). Consequently, starting immediately, a major refitting would be undertaken on the first floor to accommodate the new presidential suite, and the top floor would be restored to library purposes. The project would hopefully be funded from special donations. Furthermore, student study space would only be affected in a minor way and only for the one semester.

Wow, he thought, that does not seem like the action of an Acting President. That seems like someone who is pretty confident they are going to be around here for a while. He concluded that he must somehow work that into his conversation. Maybe even compliment her a little on her philosophy and vision. He gulped but reassured himself that he could do this thing.

When he arrived at the President's office, his suspicion that Sherrie had not returned from her sick leave was confirmed. When he innocently asked after her wellbeing, the replacement assistant said she did not know, and the conversation petered out at that. The campus was still very quiet prior to the start of the classes and the library had been virtually empty on his way there, but Calum was made to wait for half an hour before finally the door opened and Dr Ramirez stepped out to invite him in. They could have sat at the meeting table, or they could have sat in the new comfortable armchairs in the corner of the room, but instead the President retreated behind her vast new desk and indicated to Calum to sit in the single chair located on the other side.

For some bizarre reason, digestive biscuits flashed through his mind. He had not tasted one since he had last been in this room. Was he going to today?

'Thank you for taking some time out of your no doubt busy schedule to see me, Dr Ramirez.'

'Dr Davies. I was on the verge of calling you to a meeting when I got your request. So, here you are, and I can do it now.'

'Really! What I wanted a few minutes of your time to discuss, Dr Ramirez, was my prospective candidacy for the position of Vice-President for Business Affairs. As you know, I originally applied for the job before you arrived, and I would now like to take the opportunity to........'

'Dr Davies, I am going to stop you right there. What I am going to say to you will render moot what you thought you were going to discuss with me.'

'I am not sure I understand.'

'Dr Davies, I will be perfectly frank. I do not see you playing a role in the Temecula campus under my new leadership. I am talking about in a teaching capacity. Therefore, it goes without saying that I do not see you in a senior administrative capacity either.'

'What? Are you firing me?'

'Come come, Dr Davies. Let's not be crass. You made a decision last semester to openly support the outgoing President and, by doing that, you signalled to me that you are not supportive of me.'

'I supported Dr Eisenhower in principle when he was being shafted. It is something called loyalty. It had absolutely nothing to do with you. With all due respect, I had never heard of you at the time.'

'I do not believe that you can show this loyalty to me. You are too far down another road.'

'What does any of this have to do with my teaching record? Alright, forget the VP job if you must. I could have done that job damned well and I could have got the best out of a good group of managers.'

'Could I have got the best out of you? I doubt it.'

'My teaching record is exemplary. Why would you throw that away? I guarantee that it would compare favourably with the other faculty in the Accounting department.'

'At the end of the day, it is not really much to do with teaching qualities. Teachers are plentiful. What I am looking for are teachers who are committed to me and my philosophies. You used the word loyalty; that is such an old-fashioned concept. The new reality is commitment. I could not count on your commitment. You know too much about this place. I know you would doubt and challenge every change that I intend to make. And that makes you a threat to me. One that I am not prepared to accommodate when I don't have to.'

'On what grounds would you fire me? The union will be interested, I am sure.'

'I have already cleared this with the union!'

'Well I would be interested to know on what grounds you are going to fire me.'

'You are going to retire. You are not being fired.'

'I can't retire. I only have eight years' service. I would not get a pension.'

'We will buy you two years' service. You will get your pension. You will be able start drawing it almost immediately.'

'But I don't want to retire right now.'

'We will also pay you a year's salary in a lump sum.'

'What else?'

'Nothing else. No benefits, for example. Assuming Nerys stays here and I sincerely hope she does, you can be added to her benefits. Salary pay-out and pension purchase! That is more than generous, I would say. I will give you forty-eight hours to agree to this document I am going to give you. It includes a confidentiality clause that you will be required to respect. You should sign it, and have it returned to me. Nerys can do that. Have I covered everything? Do you have any questions? Oh, by the way, if you do not accept this offer, you will be terminated with no compensation, effectively immediately. Either way, I don't expect to see you on campus again after today.'

'On what grounds could I be fired?

'Oh, we will think of something. At least, our expensive attorneys will think of something, and it will stick, even if you were thinking about a lawsuit. That, Dr Davies, would be futile.'

'So that is it? I know too much about this place and my loyalty is not transferrable.'

'Goodbye, Dr Davies. Your email privileges will cease at midnight tonight.'

I Think That Maybe I Am Dreaming; But Just in Case, Hail Caesar!

The chimes of the grandfather clock that Calum loved and Nerys loathed, resonated throughout their patio home in Irvine, California. Twelve times, no less, to signal midnight had arrived. As she had pointed out on many an occasion, if they had spent a bit more money, they would have a clock whose chimes could be turned off at night. However, this was the clock that Calum had set his heart on from the catalogue and, in truth, he had not noticed the absence of the muting feature until it was delivered, assembled, and in full action -- twenty-four hours a day.

He rubbed his eyes and declared with a sense of resignation that he would have to quit for the day. This darned genealogy! It was consuming him. Once he got started on any given day, he could easily work on it through the night and into the next day, if he were not stopped. In fact, more than once when Nerys had been off on the road doing her academic research, he had done just that. It had all begun less than two years ago when she had suggested that he needed a hobby to occupy his time now that he was a retired accountant. True, he had adopted a role sometimes described as an adventurer, and he had already had a number of such experiences; but as she had pointed out, his adventures were not always predictable and not always to be encouraged either. He needed a predictable activity and what better than to investigate and tabulate his family tree. Predictable it might be in many respects, but who could have predicted that it would begin to take him over? Almost one hundred ancestors had been discovered on the very first day of research using the computerized search engines, a thousand ancestors were identified in short order, soon it was five thousand, then ten thousand, and now it approached fifteen thousand. A virtual lifetime's work for some researchers had instead been achieved by him in twenty months and all because he was prepared to put in horrendous shifts of work; with the same enthusiasm, or perhaps it was resilience, that had previously driven his careers in accountancy and higher education. It was definitely time to close down operations for this night. Nerys had made the same observation as she had left for bed over two hours ago.

He crawled into bed with great deliberateness in order not to disturb his wife. His body was tired. His mind was tired too but that did not mean it was not alert. That had been his trouble throughout his career and frequently led to disturbed sleep patterns punctuated with long periods of lying awake and thinking; vivid dreams; and times when he was not sure whether he was awake and thinking or asleep and dreaming. Many a morning had been spent in recall, trying to work out what had been controlled thought and what had been uncontrolled dreaming. Tonight might be one of those nights, he mused. He had been wrapped up all day with his potential 55th great grandfather, the Roman Emperor Marcus Antonius Augustus Aurelius. He had examined countless sources of information in order to confirm the legitimacy of his inclusion in the Davies Family Tree and, at this point, he was 90% satisfied. Was that enough? Probably not, he needed more proof. Shut down, he told himself. Do not think about it anymore for today. Empty your mind and get a good night's sleep.

===000===

I can't understand it. I am trying to shake my head as if to do that will allow me to make sense of it. I am in some sort of garden, that much is clear, but I cannot recall how I got here. It almost feels like I am dreaming this; but I am fully awake. Am I not?

It is very warm; it feels like about noon on a mid-summer's day but the last thing I remember is heading off to bed and it was black dark outside. The humidity feels high, much higher than it should be for Southern California at this time of year. Am I in California? The garden paths are bordered by exotic plants that I am not familiar with. The sounds of insects and far-away birds seem unfamiliar too. There is no sign of any human presence in the garden. Somewhat helplessly, I call out:

'Is there anybody here? Hello. Is there anybody here?'

From behind a high hedge comes a voice:

'Ego adsum!'

I hear it but struggle to recognise the language.

'Venite ad me.'

It sounds a little like Italian, but I don't understand Italian. In fact, if I think back to my high school days, it sounds a little bit like Latin. But it surely cannot be. Nobody speaks Latin in this day and age, except doctors or biologists and even then, only to describe things; not in conversation.

I decide that the only way to trace the mystery voice is to walk up and around the high hedge to my right, which is blocking my vision in that direction. Elsewhere, my view is uninterrupted, and I can see absolutely no sign of life. When I turn at the end of the hedge and peer around the corner, I see that the garden opens up into a large square of luxurious lawn with some sort of gazebo in the centre. I walk slowly toward the building and I am startled when a curly haired, bearded man leans out from the shadows within.

'Salve!' he says with an odd salute of diagonally crossing his arm across his chest.

I am even more startled when I see he is clad in a bedsheet. What is this? Who is this? You know, rather than a bedsheet, I fancy this is some sort of toga!

'Salve! Welcome! I suppose I better speak in English, which I assume is your native tongue, from what I have heard.'

I feel like I am standing staring without the ability to say anything. He effects a smile, which suggests that I am not in any immediate danger. I try a smile too, but it does not come easily.

'Did you just address me there in Latin?'

'I did.'

'I have never heard anyone speak in Latin. Who are you?'

'My name is Caesar Marcus Aurelius. I am the Emperor of Rome.'

'Funny enough, I know of you. In fact, I know much more about you than I did just a day or two ago. I am of the strong opinion that we might actually be related.'

'I am your 55th great grandfather, or so I am told.'

'And you also died in 180AD, or so I am told. How can you be real? How can you be speaking to me?'

'Shake my hand. You will see that I am real.'

I take his hand in mine and it feels real. In fact, it is quite a firm grip; but no shaking motion takes place. I decide to initiate the full handshake.

He smiles and nods his head.

'I had forgotten how you actually shake hands. I would be more inclined to do this,' and he repeats the salute across his chest. I feel it only polite to copy him.

He laughs heartily and exclaims, 'We are going to be friends, my 55th great grandson, Calum Davies!'

Although he has the appearance of a relatively young man, Marcus seems to have some difficulty moving, so we agree to sit down together in the gazebo. I have a million questions to ask and I struggle to frame them in a coherent order so that I can encourage a flowing conversation. He is very patient, almost serene, and at times a little detached. The most obvious questions are where are we, in what time are we, and how did I get here? And the most important of all---why to almost everything that I can think of?

He smiles and nods, as if he has been asked these questions before, perhaps many times.

I learn that we are in the Hortus Odoratis at Saena in Etruria and Marcus explains we are in his Perfumed Garden and I guess it is in Siena, which is in present-day Tuscany. This is his treasured summer home and a place that he will always escape to when time permits. I learned just yesterday that he died in what is now Vienna, Austria, and his ashes are interred in the Castel Sant'Angelo in Rome. Now might not yet be the time to ask how those ashes in Rome relate to the apparent flesh and blood before me in Siena.

In fact, things get a whole lot more complicated after that when he tells me that we are in neither his time nor my time. He tells me that we are of the same direct lineage, albeit over 1800 years apart, and can come together because he has been given the knowledge to enable it to happen. He does not offer any detailed explanation of how and in some ways, I am relieved. This may be the time to just accept things at face value, even though that is not the regular Calum-approach.

We fluctuate from one direction to another in our conversation, in spite of my best efforts to maintain focus. It is all just too much to take in. Eventually however, we reach the million-dollar question, although I do not put it that way to him, why am I here?

'This is a long story, Mea Nepos, and why I want it to be just between you and me.'

I notice he has used the expression Mea Nepos several times and I am guessing it means My Grandson, forgetting the mere 57 generations between us.

'As long as time has existed, or at least as long as there have been men to understand it, there has been an ability to bring together those from different generations, once in a while, in an event called The Gathering. All the participants belong to one family tree.'

'My generation might call that a family homecoming.'

'If it helps, think of it in those terms. Only, The Gathering includes family members from multiple generations, who share one thing in common---they are all deceased, obviously.'

My immediate thought is how do I fit into The Gathering, given that I am not deceased, at least as far as I know.

I learn that each Gathering takes place about every 150 years. Marcus has been tasked for many centuries to act as the organizer; there have only been two other organizers since he passed away and became eligible for membership. At each Gathering, decisions are made on future eligibility from the many branches of the family tree to which Marcus and I belong. Thereafter, it is Marcus' responsibility to monitor the growth of the family over the next 75 years and to select a very few prospects for future membership. He has the ability to bring them to a meeting with him, just as he has done with me, to confirm their suitability.

I can't help myself, but I ask: 'How do you determine suitability?'

'There are but two criteria. Fundamental interest in the common good and belief in The Gathering. The first is a matter of fact which I can only observe if it exists. I cannot induce it. The second is up to me and you. I have to convince you to lay aside all the other beliefs you probably rely on and accept the reality of The Gathering and all it stands for.'

'When is the next Gathering due to take place?'

'There is no exact date. I will decide nearer the time; but it will be in approximately 75 years' time.'

'By which time, I will be eligible to participate? I get it.'

'Good. That was the easy part.'

'Why me? Was I nominated by someone in the same way as I was when I joined the Rotary Club?'

'I know of no such Rotary Club. It sounds like it might be an organization of chariot drivers.'

'A little more contemporary. It is an organization pledged to pursue the common good in a community.'

'Ah. Excellent! And, you are a member?'

'I was! But I could not keep up with the need to make up for absences from the monthly dinners. I was just too busy at that time of my career.'

'I understand, I think. To answer your question, you were, indeed, nominated by Margaret Page. She is your 4th great grandmother.'

'I know her. Women are allowed in?'

'Of course. Ever since the great debate and decision at the Gathering of 1640. Margaret Tudor, who was Queen of Scotland, was the catalyst of change. Her name kept coming up. There was no rule against women because there are no actual rules, but there was a long tradition of male-only membership. She was the breakthrough. Since then, there have been as many women entrants to membership as men.'

'You could teach the golf clubs in Scotland a thing or two about equality of membership!'

'You speak of strange things but golf I have heard of. It is a game where you chase a white ball with a stick. It does not sound that exciting, certainly not compared to the games that were played in my day!'

'True. But it can get a little heated if the rules are breached. Golf is probably the best example of a sport that is bound in accepted rules and it is a matter of honour to follow them.'

'Interesting. It sounds like it has much of the characteristics of the Roman credo. We probably invented the game.'

'I think not. The Scots have that one covered. Remember them, the ones your lot had to build a wall to keep in or out, depending on your viewpoint.'

'Yes, yes! Hadrian! My adoptive grandfather! I know of whom and to what you refer.'

We have been talking for what feels like a couple of hours but the sun's position in the sky and the temperature seem not to have changed since I arrived. Along with the constant background chorus of birds and insects, I am now overcome with the aroma of the flowers and shrubs that dominate the garden. It is well named.

We go on to start to talk about other members of this Gathering that may bind us together. This is largely at my behest in trying to get at the purpose of the event. Marcus goes on to explain that all members and potential members are drawn from the very long and broad family tree to which we belong. In a surprising foundation of democracy and equality, there is no particular evidence of consistent class or breeding or any other differentiator among the membership—kings and queens are eligible along with lowest levels of commoners and everybody in between. I am starting to understand why the accountant is having this conversation with the emperor!

Marcus rattles off names I am familiar with from my genealogical research, such as Charlemagne the Holy Roman Emperor; Arnulf Caroling, a king of the ancient German States; Sarah Glover a matriarch of the burgeoning southern states of the US during the early 19th century; William the Conqueror of England; and Christian Lamont, who married well into the landed-gentry of 18th century Scotland. He also mentions a number of well-known names and completely unknown-names that I assume I have yet to encounter in my research. I have this strange feeling of my family tree coming to life on two separate occasions, once during the

210

lifetime of the members and now in this bizarre Gathering in a time that I am not yet able to pinpoint.

'Of course, Mea Nepos, you must realize that the names I have mentioned are but a random selection of the membership of The Gathering. And, the membership of The Gathering is but a very small sample of all your ancestors in our family tree.'

'You have been involved in selecting all the members of The Gathering?'

'Not all of them. Two came before me and made the selections in the early days but I would think that I have chosen more than three-quarters of the current membership. That is one of the reasons that I am very tired, but more of that later.'

'Have any of my ancestors declined to join?'

'Some. But not that many. The long period between each Gathering permits me to do a great deal of research and, of course, conduct the meetings such as we are having now. By the time I extend an invitation I am pretty assured of acceptance.'

'Once you have appointed a member, can he or she later resign or be removed?'

'Good question. In theory, either can happen but, to the best of my recollection, never has.'

'So that means that all members attend all Gatherings?'

'Yes. In our particular circumstance, there is no real excuse for absence. There is no illness or other disposition among our members, which might cause them to miss out!'

I start to laugh at this matter-of-fact observation. The serious face of the Emperor of Rome looks at me and then takes on a smile followed by a hearty laugh as well. Humour bridges the generations, it appears, and makes me feel good.

'I have to ask you, Great Grandfather Marcus, how many members has The Gathering got right now?'

'I told you before, I am but Marcus to you. You have a great many great grandfathers. As to your question, I have no idea. I have had no reason to count them all. You might want to. You are the accountant, after all!'

I continue to gather as much information as I can about The Gathering. I really don't know how much time I have; I assume that is at the discretion of Marcus for I am not even sure if I am awake or asleep!

I realize that perhaps I should have asked this question at the very beginning of our conversation, but it feels easier to ask it now that I have some background information.

'Marcus, I have to ask you this. The Gathering seems like a fascinating group of fascinating people, coming together in fascinating circumstances, but I have to ask---why? What is the purpose of The Gathering?'

'It has taken you some time to come to the root of the matter. I respect that. You want to know as much as you can before you seek our purpose. The truth of the matter is the purpose is very simple. All members of The Gathering are committed to doing what they can to promote the common good. They come from a great many different times and backgrounds but in their own personal experience each has acquired knowledge. Now they come together to share that experience and work toward deciding what is best for the future. They cannot change the past, but they use the past to influence the future.'

'I understand what you are saying about the mass of experiences being brought to the group and synthesizing them into a plan for the future. I have got that right, haven't I?'

'Perfectly! But ask the question I know you want to ask.'

'Well, I have difficulty seeing how The Gathering can influence the future. Are all its members, well, are they not all dead?'

'They are not alive in the traditional sense. You can find my ashes in Rome if you know where to look. But we have been given the ability to communicate with the living. I am talking with you here and now and soon you will return to your life in America with your wife, possessing knowledge that you have uniquely acquired. As part of the test of determining your suitability to eventually join The Gathering, you will have, from this day until the day you die, to practise and preach the philosophy of pursuit of the common good. To put it bluntly, if you exhibit the necessary good habits from here on, now that you have the privileged information you have received today, you will qualify for membership and we will have succeeded in ensuring the future of our goal.'

'And, if I don't portray those good habits?'

'Then, you will never hear from me again and you will never join The Gathering. You will simply live out your life until the day you die. That should not be seen as a bad thing; you will just not have committed to our work.'

'But, does that not mean that your future plans may come to an end?'

'Our future is not dependent on any one individual. There are many such as you at this point in the proceedings. Our work will hopefully be carried forward by some, if not all, of the people that have been identified as potential members.'

I sit for a long time trying to process what I have heard. I can understand the philosophical tenet of pursuit of the common good, even if I am having difficulty understanding the vehicle for its accomplishment. The Gathering remains elusive to me and so I continue to seek information from Marcus on how it has functioned over the centuries and what he feels it has achieved.

He amazes me with stories of small acts of kindly intervention of which I have heard nothing, and giant acts of benevolence which have changed the course of history and which I am inevitably aware of. In both cases, he ties them back to the work of The Gathering. I learn that notable people from the past, such as Richard "The Fearless", Duke of Normandy; Malcolm III "Canmore", King of Scots; and Henry Sinclair, Earl of Orkney and Knight Templar, that I might be familiar with for their reported exploits, good and bad, have since made major positive contributions. But he also cites the same contributions from little-known or unknown persons who just happen to be part of the family tree. In fact, he mentions some ancestors with the name Davies, my kith and kin, who have nobly served The Gathering but will never appear in any history annals.

'One of the great things about The Gathering is that it brings together people with very different backgrounds. It also encourages them to form unlikely relationships. For example, your namesake, Hendrie Davies, who was a fisherman and lived in the 16th century, has become a close friend of Charlemagne, who was Holy Roman Emperor in the 7th century. That is not a pairing that might have been predicted but they both share a deep interest in the purpose of the organization.'

'I am very familiar with both of these men in my family tree. I could not even begin to imagine them being friends, given their backgrounds, never mind the generational gap. That is amazing. You know in my research work, I am stuck on one of my lines at Hendrie Davies; I cannot trace his father and mother and I have been searching for months.'

'If things were to work out for you, you would be able to get the information from him first-hand. That would make your research much easier!'

I smile again at another example of ancient Roman humour.

Much as I am tempted to know more and more about the people I am already familiar with, it is the people belonging to my tree that I have never otherwise heard of that really intrigue me -- the notion that people who led uneventful and unnoteworthy lives are able to make a strong contribution in this afterlife that I have discovered. I am left asking myself—do I want to be part of this? Who, in their right mind, would not want to part of it? But there is a cost of admission as I have been told. I would have to demonstrate a far greater commitment for the rest of my natural life than I have done hitherto.

I think some more. Am I prepared to make this commitment? Where is the guarantee that I will be rewarded with membership of The Gathering? Is there really such a thing as The Gathering? Am I just being encouraged to be good for goodness sake in some abstract way? Why would this Gathering be connected only to my family tree? Are there other Gatherings for other family trees?

Marcus places a hand on my shoulder and comments as if he is able to read my mind.

'We have spoken enough for now. I can tell you have more questions than answers. That is natural. I have told you what you need to know. Now, you must go back and do a good deal of thinking on whether you will join us or not. You are aware of the price of admission. It is but a small price to the committed, but well beyond the means of those who are uncommitted.'

'You are correct that I am confused. Every time I get to the point of understanding something, it just prompts another whole series of questions. Will I be able to talk with you again? If you were from my time, I would not be prepared to let you go without first obtaining your email address.'

'We will in all probability not speak again in your natural lifetime, unless I find there is something I have not covered with you. In such a case, you will be brought to another meeting similar to this. If you fear that you failed to ask me something, there is no way that you can conjure me up. You will just have to work it out for yourself. That is part of your test.'

'Must I keep this secret? Can I seek advice from anyone? Can I talk with my wife, Nerys, about it?'

'I place no restriction on you speaking with others but do not be disappointed if they don't understand what you are asking. You already have knowledge that precious few in the world of your time share. Only in the very unlikely event that you encounter such a person; or you have someone, perhaps your wife, who has absolute, unbendable faith in you, will you be able to persuade them to believe what you have learned. And even then, will they be qualified to advise you? Your future from here on will most probably be a solitary experience if you mean to see it through to membership.'

'Marcus, I am quite exhausted from taking in all I have heard. It concerns me that I will not have another opportunity to talk with you, but I must accept the conditions that you impose. You must be tired too.'

'I am tired, but it is more from the fact that I have been fulfilling this role for a very long time. However, when I get into a conversation such as the one we have had today, I am revived and filled with hope for the future. Nevertheless, I must face the fact that a new organizer of The Gathering will be called for very soon. It is long overdue. Perhaps someday, you might take on the role, you never know.'

Marcus rose from the bench and placed one hand on each of my shoulders.

'Farewell Calum. You have proven to be just the person that Margaret Page predicted you would be. I sincerely hope that the next time we meet will be at The Gathering. But for now, close your eyes and travel safely!'

===000===

Nerys woke with a start and stretched her right hand out until it made contact with Calum's body, which was curled up in a ball. He grunted recognition.

'Are you awake?'

'No.'

'You probably are still sleepy although it is almost 8 o'clock. What time did you finally come to bed? You had still not come when I got up to pee at almost 2 o'clock.'

'That can't be right. I came to bed at almost exactly midnight. I am surprised the chimes did not wake you, even if I didn't.'

'The bed was empty when I got up, I swear.'

Calum said nothing and fell deeply into recollection of all that had gone on in the Hortus Odoratus. Had he been dreaming? Had he just developed an elaborate series of thoughts because he had Marcus Aurelius on his mind when he retired to bed? Or?

He could remember absolutely everything that had passed between the Roman Emperor and himself. Dreams were seldom like that. Normally he could only remember snippets; mostly that had taken place just before he woke up. He could not remember going to sleep but he had been asleep when Nerys touched him.

This was all too much to fathom. He longed to share his experience with her. Marcus had said that could be done. Would she, however, believe him? Would he believe her, if the roles were reversed and she was relaying a most unusual night to him? He was a sceptic by nature, and he was almost certain that he would not have believed her, but he would have had fun hearing the story unfold. Nerys was different. She was less sceptical and had a degree of faith inside her, although it was not attached to any religion. She would listen. She might dismiss. She might not.

'Don't you think we ought to get up? I have research to do today and you, no doubt, have a full day of genealogy planned as well.'

'I don't know if I can get up. I am exhausted. I feel like I have had no sleep at all.'

'Well, you were asleep when I prodded you; but goodness knows when you came to bed and actually fell asleep.'

'I told you already, I came to bed at midnight. I remember the chimes.'

He fell silent again. To tell or not to tell. How was he going to handle the responsibility that the organizer had placed on him? Did he really want to be a member of The Gathering? How was it going to change the remainder of his life if he were to qualify? Nerys would have to be party to that change. He could not just change his ways to actively pursue the common good without her noticing. Should he tell her now or wait until he processed his thoughts some more?

He felt he was on the verge of starting to tell her when she threw off the duvet on her side and declared:

'I am getting up, I have too much to do. If you want to lie in, that's fine. Don't make the bed when you do get up. I am going to launder the duvet.'

'No, no. I will get up too.'

With that, Nerys, who was now standing at the foot of the bed, whipped the duvet off completely to carry it to the laundry room. The resounding clinking sound of metal connecting with the wood floor caught the attention of both of them.

'What was that?'

'I don't know,' replied Nerys as her eyes scanned the floor. Calum was now out of bed and looking as well.

'There it is. There. In the corner.'

She stooped to pick up the shiny metal piece.

'It looks like a coin. Where on earth did it come from? Do you think it is made of gold? It is certainly heavy enough. Look there, on the one side is an elephant. What does that signify, I wonder? And, on the other side is a curly haired guy with a curly beard to match.'

'That is Marcus Aurelius. He is my 55th great grandfather, you know!'

Cruz Cruise Crew's Big Adventure

Doctors Nerys Jones-Davies and Calum Davies, educator and retired educator-now-turned-adventurer respectively, were not pursuing either of their current vocations. They were on an ocean cruise for purely vacational purposes. Though neither of them professed to be an avid cruiser, this was by no means their first time on the ocean waves. They considered this mode of transportation to be a convenient way to see lots of new places in a short burst of time. If one or more places were to become potential favourites, they could always revisit them later and stay awhile. Thus, they came to be cruising in the Mediterranean and East Atlantic in mid-winter, with the weather better than they had been experiencing in California and a good deal better than at their other home in Scotland.

Alas, with the voyage only half completed and the island of Tenerife beckoning, the strain of cruising was beginning to make an appearance and cause tension between them. Cruising was supposed to be the most relaxing form of vacation that existed, where one is left to eat and drink with unfettered abandon, especially if one holds the unlimited drinks package (which they generally did), lie in the sun around the pool on the top deck, and on every second day troop ashore for a quick tour around a new exotic (as described in the brochure) location. There are even a host of light activities on board for those days when the ship remains at sea. However, Calum, who was generally the one who brought up the suggestion about going on another cruise, was also the one who quickly got bored with the set routine and was ready to head for home about mid-way through. This cruise was proving to be no exception.

They had enjoyed shore visits to Barcelona, Casablanca, and even the first two of the Canary Islands, but this current day at sea was stretching their patience. Nerys was quite content to select activities offered on board such as art appreciation, deck games, and wine tasting. She could even use up their WIFI allowance to keep in touch with email and various communications about her current research project on the ethics of nuclear waste disposal. However, Calum was finding less and less to do except prepare for and then recover from the frequent and enormous meals. He had even tired somewhat of drinking, first with Nerys and then on his own as she got involved in her activities. The solo drinking had, at least, led to him getting to know some of the crew members in each of the bars. That was not something he did as a rule, talk to bartenders, but it had become something of a necessity given that he had a particular aversion to talking to fellow cruisers and he could hardly talk to himself. Somehow, it was easier to fend off potential chatters when he was with Nerys and even to cope with their generally inane conversations if the fending off failed. However, when he was on his own his eyes were constantly examining new arrivals to the bar to determine if they looked the chatty type and were likely to sit beside him. In such case, he was ready to excuse himself, full drink or not. They did not cost anything. His strategy might only have been abandoned were he to be approached by a particularly attractive woman on her own but, thus far on the cruise, that had not happened.

On this day, was it only five o'clock, he sighed on one of the frequent looks at his watch; he was seated in the so-called tropical bar on the top deck of the ship adjacent to the swimming pool, while Nerys was catching a session on advanced computing skills. He could not quite see the attraction of the topic because she would probably already know more techniques than any of her classmates, judging by the apparent background of the average cruisers. At least, she had backed off from her first choice of the ballroom dancing lessons, which Calum had resolutely declined to even consider. That was a relief. On the other hand, perhaps she had sneaked off to the ballroom dancing to find a new partner among the many swarthy Latinos who seem to dominate the passenger demographics. Perhaps the advanced computing skills was just a cover. Calum had no more opportunity to explore this emerging hypothesis because his new-found friend, the bartender from the Philippines, offered him another opinion on the high esteem with which the President of the United States of America was held in his home country and throughout Asia. Calum caught enough of the fractured English to get the point that was being made and wished there could be a change of topic or even no topic at all. He was on the verge of slipping away with the intention of having a nap in their cabin before

222

Nerys returned; she would doubtless be brimming with equal enthusiasm for what she had been doing in her class and for the evening dinner which would be looming large. He had eased himself off his stool at the bar when one of the servers, armed with an empty tray, returned to the bar to pick up drinks for those seated around the room. He was Indian according to his little name tag and Calum knew him to be the one who spoke the best English among this team of crew members.

'Well, Mr Calum. You are still here I see. Where is that very, very beautiful wife of yours? Miss Norris? I hope she is well.'

'Nerys,' he replied as he had on each day of the cruise.

'Indeed, sir,' came the response with that odd gyration of the head upon the shoulders commonly practised by many of his culture, 'Miss Norris.'

'Nerys is either taking over the advanced computing skills class or is being taken over in the ballroom dancing class. Either way, she is not here at this point in time.'

'Ah,' said the server in a strange knowing way. 'Are you looking forward to tomorrow's day ashore in Tenerife? A very, very beautiful island, if I may say so.'

'I suppose so. Is it any different from the last two islands we have already visited, all high-rise vacation apartments and volcanos?'

'You are very, very funny, Mr Calum. That is exactly what is there on Tenerife. Very, very beautiful,' he said with another gymnastic gyration of the head.

'What do you do on such days, Harish?' Calum asked, as the server's name on his name tag came into his line of vision and reminded him. 'Do you get to go ashore?'

'Not at every port-of-call, Mr Calum, but tomorrow is a very, very special occasion. Many, many of my colleagues will be going ashore for a gathering, some would call it a party, Mr Calum, at the famous establishment in the town of Santa Cruz called The Jolly Roger; just like the pirate, you know.'

'That sounds like a good time. What is the occasion?'

Before Harish could respond, a cry from across the room invited him to get a move-on as they were all thirsty and looking for their drinks.

Harish quickly excused himself and scurried off with his tray absolutely loaded with pints of beer for the noisy group of Englishmen in the corner, that Calum might have described as 'yobbos', had he been invited to so do. Those were cruisers and were to be avoided at all costs. He was intrigued by the reference to The Jolly Roger in the middle of a Spanish island, and he decided to have one more drink before returning to the cabin, in the hope that he might be able to find out more from the server about the goings-on planned there for tomorrow.

Eventually Harish was able to stop again for a chat as peace had broken out among the punters, lapping up their beers and now engrossed in the English Premier League football match that had appeared on the bar's televisions.

'What is this Jolly Roger place like then, Harish?'

'A jolly, jolly place, Mr Calum. I like to go there each time we are in Tenerife and I do not even drink the alcoholic drinks, you know. I just like to see my friends laughing and having a good time. We have to work very hard on the ship, you know Mr Calum, and it does them good to blow off the smoke, you know.'

'Blow off some steam.'

'Exactly, that is what I said.'

'How far away is this place from where the ship berths?'

'It is on the outskirts of the town of Santa Cruz. It takes about half an hour by taxi or the tram. I like going by tram. Very, very exciting, climbing up the hills. The Jolly Roger is at the top of the hills around the city and looks down over the bay. You can see our ship in the distance'

'You know, I just might try to negotiate a deal with Miss Norris so that we look in on The Jolly Roger at the end of the day tomorrow. That would be after we have seen and done all the things that she has listed for us, of course.'

'I think you and Miss Nerys would be most, most welcome, Mr Calum.'

The night thereafter went fairly smoothly, that is until the big disintegration at the conclusion of dinner. Nerys had returned from her class totally pumped up and extolling its virtues. She insisted on sharing with Calum the several new procedures and techniques she had learned, even though he tried as hard as he could to concentrate on the Sky News which was being carried on the ship's television service. At one point, he stopped to think either she did actually go to that advanced computing skills class after all or else she is a wonderful actor.

Later, they dressed up in a semi-formal fashion. When they had first gone cruising, there were official formal evenings when Calum could wear his tuxedo and Nerys would wear a classic gown. However, there had been a tendency for cruise lines to make the dress code less formal because many of the cruisers did not like dressing up. That was another good reason to avoid fraternizing with cruisers. Tonight, being the conclusion of a day-at-sea, they guessed that dress standards would be slightly better than days when the passengers staggered back on board after an exhausting day ashore and were less inclined to dress up. They had got that guess correct and Nerys remarked that they both looked rather swell and just right for the part. They both liked dressing up, perhaps because they seldom got the opportunity at home in California.

This seventh dinner of the cruise was pretty much the same as the first six had been. The menu consisted of a wide array of appetizers, main dishes, and desserts. Most were admittedly slightly smaller portions than one would generally encounter in a regular restaurant and, therefore, there seemed to be a tradition to order more than one plate of each course. Calum could easily end with three appetizers, two main dishes, and a dessert, the latter not because he wanted it but just because it seemed like the right thing to do to finish off the meal. This display of decadence, if not outright hyperphagia, topped off by unlimited wine, meant that by the end of each dinner, they were both well and truly "pickled", as Calum was wont to observe. Tonight was no exception, but instead of cascading into a state of merriment and contentment, they had sort of crawled into a state of tension. Next day's plans would be the cause of the growing tension suddenly exploding.

'Phew, that was some meal. Much too much food. I could not eat a single thing more. In fact, I think I have had more than enough wine too. I am just going to order a nightcap and take it back to our cabin, once you are ready to turn in. Does that work for you?'

'If you did not persist in ordering most of the items on the menu, you would not be so full. Have your nightcap here in the dining room. I will have one too. One of those nice Brazilian caipirinhas, I think. We have not talked yet about what we are going to do tomorrow in Tenerife. I hope you are going to be a bit more interested in that than you were in my newly acquired computer skills'

'Yes, well, I did not come on a cruise to polish up my computer skills. In fact, I would not be very interested in polishing them up ashore either. Computing is, in my humble opinion, a necessary evil, developed to stretch my patience at every turn. I don't know why they claim it is based on logic. I am a very logical person and everything about it seems illogical to me. Whenever I try to solve a problem, I just succeed in creating another.'

'I probably know the solution to that now after my class but, never mind, you will never change, I fear. Here is what I have planned for tomorrow. It will help you take your mind off your lack of computing skills. We need to be ashore at the crack of dawn, literally as soon as we berth, because we have a lot to do before we get back on the ship at 3 o'clock in the afternoon. It sails at 3:30 for Madeira but we will be back in plenty of time.'

'What is there to see on Tenerife? I only know about the capital Santa Cruz. In fact, I have an idea for doing something there.'

'I doubt we will have time for that! We will walk off the ship and into the centre of Santa Cruz. It will take about half an hour but will save us the price of a taxi. They always prey on the cruise ships and fleece the passengers. There, we will get on the tram to San Cristobal de La Laguna and spend some time walking around there. It is a UNESCO World Heritage Site and it will be worthwhile seeing the preserved buildings. From there, we will hop on a local bus that takes us to the La Oratava Valley and give it a quick look. It is supposed to be nice. If we had more time, we would try to fit in a lunch there; but we don't as we have to then get to the chairlift base. We might need to catch a taxi to take us there because I am not quite sure how far it is from where the bus drops us. We will then ride the chairlift up to the top of Mount Teide. I want to spend as much time as possible at the crater of the volcano. You should try to read about it before we leave tomorrow so you know what to look for. Then, it is back down on the chairlift and onto the public bus back to Cruz. A swift walk from the city centre to the ship should see us back on board by 3 pm, precisely. Now does that sound like a rewarding day or what?'

'Sounds ok and I know you have done a lot of research for each port-of-call, Nerys. However, I was chatting to some of the bar staff this afternoon and they have invited us for drinks at a jolly place on the outskirts of Cruz. Do you think you could shave some time off the other things to allow us to look in on them? They are a good bunch of chaps and it is probably some kind of honour for we humble passengers to be invited by the crew to join them!'

'Absolutely not!'

Now when you think about it, it would be easy to place the blame on either of them for how the argument blew up—she for being inflexible and he for being insensitive—and it is probably just as easy to place the blame on either of them for how it all went downhill after that. Nevertheless, the outcome, after a good deal of noise that attracted the interest of several fellow diners, was dramatic, not open to renegotiation, and lacked much in the way of cooperation or compromise. She would proceed with her carefully planned day, all on her own, and he would have a lie-in and then catch a taxi to the terminal for a tram to The Jolly Roger and an afternoon's revelry with the crew. They would get together again at 3 pm, perhaps to compare notes!

===OOO===

Calum had barely stirred as Nerys, without a great deal of effort to keep the noise level down, prepared herself for the day's outing. In a final shameless act of vengeance, she shook him awake just as she about to leave the cabin to enquire if he had changed his mind about coming. He must have already been awake for he politely and quietly responded in the negative.

It was a good two hours later that he finally woke up again and, by this time, he had to move quickly in order to get to the dining room before they stopped serving breakfast. Once he got there, however, there was no rush to complete it; the dining room was fairly empty, and the servers were not rushing to and from the kitchen as they normally did. This was a completely different atmosphere and one that met Calum's approval, so he enjoyed a long leisurely breakfast, prolonged by an extensive review of the Scottish, English, Canadian, and American newspapers on his tablet. This was his standard practice at home but the first time he had been granted the opportunity on the cruise. Any guilt he felt at being party to the decision to split up for the day was offset by the pleasure of catching up with all the news.

Meanwhile, Nerys was making good progress on her carefully planned trip and was already at the chairlift base and looking forward to the exciting journey up the mountain. She was determined to maintain a feeling of serenity, not think of Calum, and she even managed to keep calm when suddenly swarmed upon by a large group of Chinese tourists determined to make the transition, as if by right, from last to first in the queue to board the large gondola. Several trips to China on research projects had, however, not only broadened her mind on her chosen subject matter but also taught her how to use her elbows in such confrontations and no appreciable ground was lost, despite the inequity in numbers of combatants. Soon, she was safely established in a window seat with her phone/camera at the ready for the ascent.

Calum still had a bit of time to kill when he finally left the dining room; so, he decided to take a leisurely walk around the ship on the top deck. Normally, the walking track was clogged with Olympic-standard athletes and idle strollers jostling for space, causing collisions and traffic jams along the way, but today being an in-port day, the track was deserted. He did ten laps at an even pace and then stopped to check the step count on his watch. Satisfied that he would have an appropriate response to Nerys, who would inevitably accuse him of doing very little all day, he returned to the cabin to have a second shower of the morning and then he was ready for his solo adventure. He was in a good, relaxed frame of mind.

Even the absence of any taxis on the pier, because all the cruisers who intended to go ashore had long since done so, did not faze him. He simply enquired as to the direction of the tram terminal and set out to walk to it with a growing pleasure at the additional number of steps currently being logged on his watch. Nerys would be more than surprised. They enjoyed a friendly rivalry on who could achieve the greater number of steps in any given day, but Nerys was the more conscientious of the two and had even been known to go out for a necessary walk before bedtime if she was lagging behind him in the evening count.

By this time, she too was logging steps up ferociously as she made her way around the narrow winding paths framing the edge and dropping into the dormant crater of Mount Teide. The Chinese group had long since disappeared after a flurry of photograph-taking upon arrival and the crater was not really very busy with tourists at all, probably because today there was only one cruise ship berthed way down in Santa Cruz. On some days in the high season, there could be as many as four or five. This suited her perfectly as she examined all sorts of natural phenomena and carefully recorded photographic images for posterity. However, as was almost always the case after a disagreement, Nerys now regretted it and wished that Calum was with her. She was almost at the point of hoping he was having a good time on his own.

Calum had purchased a ticket for the tram but had been thwarted in his attempt to buy the return version because of a lack of cash and the fact that the dispenser did not accept credit cards. No problem at all he concluded, he would simply purchase another single ticket on the way back, by which time he would have more coins because he would have bought drinks. Nothing was going to spoil his day, he confidently predicted.

The tram ride was quite exhilarating as it wound its way back and forth in a steep climb out of the city centre. Calum had always loved trains since he was a small child, and this was the next best thing. He marvelled as the tram stopped at rudimentary stations every few minutes to let people climb off and on -- once the doors had automatically opened. They did not stay open long, he noticed, which necessitated swift movement by the passengers. All the while from the comfort of his seat, he chuckled at the many riders who could not find a seat and had to stand, desperately holding on to straps and poles as the tram lurched along. It reminded him of San Francisco and the wild rides on the cable cars. He carefully counted the stations that came and went until the station closest to The Jolly Roger appeared on the next stop indicator. He simply joined the scrum of passengers leaving and joining and within seconds he found himself on the platform, being carried along toward the station exit. Let the fun begin, he thought!

The Jolly Roger was not difficult to locate but Calum wondered if he had found the right place when he opened the door. The bar, at just minutes after noon, was packed with all nationalities and not a soul seemed to have a cruise ship uniform on. He squeezed his way through the standing crowd, looking from person to person and also at those who had been lucky enough to have acquired seats around the perimeter. It was not a large facility but there must have been well over a hundred patrons jammed in. He still did not recognize anyone and was about to abandon his adventure because it seemed impossible to actually find a way up to the bar for a drink, when a familiar sing-song voice rang out from the farthest corner of the room.

'Mr Calum, Mr Calum, you made it. We are over here in the corner!'

Calum struggled again through the crowd to finally arrive at a group of around a dozen happy faces, mostly Philippinos with a couple of Indians and a standout, probably of Scandinavian origin. They ushered him to come and sit down on one of the several chairs generously surrendered by crew members. Almost immediately, a small glass of the beer which most of the group were drinking, was conjured up out of nowhere and placed in front of him. A toast was then raised to the honorary crew member amid much laughter.

Within minutes, Calum was demanding to know how a round of drinks could be acquired in the seething mass.

'No problem, Mr Calum,' replied an excited Harish and, upon accepting Calum's 50 euro note, dived into the mass with all the skill of a scrum half in a rugby maul. Minutes later, he re-emerged with a tray bearing drinks for everyone and not a drop had been spilled. There was a great advantage, thought Calum, to being in the company of a group who largely made their living as waiters!

Thereafter, rounds and rounds of drinks fuelled hilarious stories delivered in a mixture of broken English interspersed with native languages. Calum was able to just about follow what was being said but, in that respect, he was probably just the same as everyone else in the group. He noticed that none of the crew members talked about their work or the cruise in general and he imagined that this gathering was about getting a break from what was very hard work every day and there was no need for anyone to be reminded of it. Calum took the hint and refrained from making any reference to the cruise from a passenger perspective. The crew members seemed to only want to talk about home, a place most of them had not seen in many months, and sharing lively tales of home and family seemed to bring a sparkle to their eyes. Calum jumped in and regaled them with some funny tales of life in California and some of the very odd things that had happened to him since he retired from being an accountant and university professor. He also introduced them to the Isle of Cumbrae in Scotland, the place where he had become embroiled in some more serious adventures. None of the group had heard of the island but by the time Calum had translated the serious adventures into amusing escapades from which he escaped unscathed, not only was everybody laughing noisily but many were now vowing to visit this Cumbrae. Calum was always at his happiest when he was talking about his beloved Cumbrae and at one point he sat back and smiled, trying to remember when he last had such fun, and then wondered how Nerys was getting on.

By this time, she had descended from the mount on the cable car, an experience that was little more unnerving than the ascent, partly due to the gondola lurching to an unplanned stop half way down, causing another Chinese group she had been paired with to scream uncontrollably. Just as she was beginning to worry that the Chinese were jumping up and down and causing the gondola to sway and might actually cause it to malfunction permanently, it lurched back into action and continued toward the base station. Upon reaching the terminus, the Chinese applauded mightily and Nerys was inclined to join them with no little relief.

Now she had to wait for the bus back to Santa Cruz for she had chosen to travel by public transport and the next one was not due for twenty minutes. She had chosen this mode because she thought the scheduled tour buses were overpriced, no doubt especially targeted at the cruise ship passengers. However, as she saw the Chinese pile onto their tour bus and take off leaving her standing on her own, she began to wonder if she had made the correct call. No doubt, Calum would have had a comment to make about her thrifty nature, had he been there. Still, she had planned this trip almost to the minute and, assuming the bus was on time, she would be back to the cruise ship comfortably before the 3 pm deadline that had been set.

But the bus was not on time. In fact, a good fifteen minutes after it should have arrived and had not, a taxi arrived to deliver a corpulent American couple. In the milliseconds it took for Nerys to wonder how the gondola would handle the weight challenge of the Americans, she also made the decision to ask the driver if he was going back to Santa Cruz. He replied that he was commissioned to wait the two hours at the cable car terminus for his clients to return from their trip to the mountain top. However, he was confident that he could ferry the good lady to Cruz and be back in time for his pick-up and he would do it for the very reasonable rate of 75 euros.

Nerys spluttered in a most un-good-lady-like manner and protested the highway robbery being proposed to exploit an unfortunate visitor to his island. On being reminded that he bore an obligation to appropriately represent that island, both parties reluctantly agreed on a fare of 60 euros and soon they were on their way back at a healthy clip. 3 pm arrival would not be a problem. The unexpected outlay of euros could be quite easily concealed from her husband.

Calum was returning from a trip to the washroom and noticed that the crowd in the bar was beginning to thin out a little. As he sat down, he also noticed that his group had diminished somewhat, no doubt some of the crew needed to be back earlier to prepare for the departure. He sat down and had a charming conversation with Harish about India. Harish had maintained his stance of not drinking the 'the evil alcohol', as he referred to it; but somehow, he seemed just as merry as the others who had now consumed quite a bit.

In what felt like only a few minutes, Calum had to excuse himself again to go to the washroom. How was it he could drink large volumes of beer without a visit to the washroom (to Nerys' astonishment) but once he finally succumbed, he was on repeated visits regularly thereafter. Something to do with the aging process, he lamented.

This time, he encountered the only Scandinavian-looking person in the group, who turned out be a Norwegian called Roald. Their conversation quickly turned to a common interest in football. Calum was delighted to learn that Roald's home town was Stavanger and started to reminisce about the time in 1964 when his favourite team from Scotland, Edinburgh Waverley, had played Stavanger SK in the European Cup-Winners' Cup. Instead of returning to their group, they stood at the bar where there was now some space. Calum immediately ordered schnapps for both, on hearing it was Roald's preferred tipple, and waxed eloquently about the two matches. He remembered they had been of great interest to him as a young teenager. He learned that the younger Roald was also very familiar with the encounter, having been told about it by his father who had been in attendance. The fact that both teams had won their home game; but Waverley had triumphed on the aggregate score, stimulated Calum to prolong the discussion on this topic.

When they finally made their way back to their group, it had noticeably shrunk again with only two Philippinos remaining and no sign of either Indian. Calum took this to be more of the gradual return to the ship for crew members. However, he still concluded that he had some time left as did, obviously, the remaining crew members.

Roald was on something of a rebound and had managed to swing the conversation to the unforgettable (for him) match of 1970 between Norway and Scotland, which the former had won comfortably to record their first victory in the history of matches between the two countries. Roald seemed to have acquired a photographic memory of all three home goals and described them in great detail over many minutes. Calum nodded with understanding and tried, unsuccessfully, to blend the equally famous Scottish victories of 1959 and 1974, the only two he was vaguely familiar with, into this sporting treatise. The Philippinos tried manfully to understand the significance of the great series of matches and did little more than smile and nod.

Calum was keen to get them involved in a conversation, if only to derail Roald and asked, slowly and deliberately:

'Enough of this European stuff. How about, you chaps? Is football popular in the Philippines?'

That proved to be a bit of a mistake as the conversation immediately swung toward several unforgettable games in the Trans-Asian Cup and prompted animated reports from both crew members which Calum, and presumably Roald, just about followed with great difficulty. The frenzied discussion went on for quite a while and was only finally interrupted when a server came to enquire if the foursome wanted more drinks.

As they awaited their arrival, the football dialogue appeared to finally be exhausted.

'Tell me, Calum. Are you enjoying your holiday in Tenerife? I assume you are staying in one of the hotels, or have you rented an apartment?'

'Me? I am not staying here. I am on the cruise ship, just like you guys.'

'Oh, dear me. I think we might have a problem here. I just assumed you were staying locally and had somehow become acquainted with Harish. We are all from the cruise ship, that is true, but the reason for our little get-together today is because my two fine Philippino colleagues and I are leaving the cruise at this port and will pick up our sister ship in a few days' time. We are able to spend a little time on shore leave. The others were saying goodbye to us. We may not meet up again for many months.'

'What a hoot! I had no idea. So, you are not making your way back to the ship today?'

'Nor, my friend, are you, I fear. The time is almost a quarter to three o'clock and I have grave doubts that you will make it back in time before it sails unless you leave this very minute!'

'Oh shit!,' echoed around the bar as Calum grabbed his jacket and fled through the doors, causing an incoming couple to be scattered like pins in a bowling alley.

===OOO===

Calum had a good natural sense of direction, unlike Nerys who was always dependent on research and notes, and he quickly retraced his steps to the tram station. And there before him was something that presented a dilemma. A tram was sitting at the station but, judging by the last of the passengers disappearing on board, it was on the verge of closing its doors and taking off. What to do? Calum was all too aware that he did not have a ticket for the return trip. Did he risk missing the tram in order to buy one or risk the 400 euro fine he had read about on the trip up from the city centre?

As is often the case, the decision made in the heat of the moment turned out to be the wrong one. Calum was not unfamiliar with the maxim. He leapt on board just as the doors were automatically shutting. The tram was not as busy as the earlier one and he quickly found a seat. Glancing at the advancing time on his watch, he decided he could still make it but might have to grab a taxi at the tram terminus. Somewhat guiltily, he leaned out of his seat to scan the centre aisleway in both directions in search of a conductor, in the knowledge that he did not have a ticket and might have to prepare an eloquent explanation. He had not seen any sign of a conductor on the way up and none was in evidence now, thankfully. That reassured him a little and he settled back down in his seat and glanced at his watch again and did the quick mental arithmetic with which he was quite accomplished. Still looking ok.

He decided to seek further assurance and turned to the person behind him, who had the look of an expatriate Brit about him.

'Excuse me, any idea of how long the tram will take to make it to the terminus in the city centre?'

The person was indeed just as Calum had speculated and answered in a plummy English accent:

'Oh, best part of an hour going this way, old boy. It has to go all the way up to La Laguna before it turns around and heads back to the city. You would have been much better catching a tram heading in the opposite direction if you are in hurry!'

237

For the second time in not that many minutes, a resounding 'shit' was uttered, and Calum alighted from his seat to stand by the door awaiting the next station. On the way up, those stations had seemed to arrive every few minutes but, on this occasion in full demonstration of Murphy's Law, it took an age to appear. He leapt out, ran to the end of the line of carriages, and crossed behind them to the track going in the opposite direction. After straining his eyes to see if he could spy a tram on the line coming into the station, he walked to the entrance/exit to consult a posted timetable.

'Damn it! Ten more minutes. I can't afford that much time. I would be better looking for a taxi. It will cost a bomb from here but will be quicker than the tram in any case and can take me right to the cruise ship terminal,' he exclaimed to no-one in particular.

He strode out on to the street to search in either direction for a distinctive yellow taxi. He had no joy for several minutes and then one appeared out of nowhere from a side-street and started to slow down in response to his frantic beckoning. Just as it began to pull up in front of him, he noticed to his horror that the taxi was not responding to him at all, but rather to a tall, erect man, not ten yards away from him, who was hailing it with obvious authority. Another heat of the moment decision was called for, there was no time to worry about the possible ramifications of it.

Calum raced up to the gentleman as he was starting to stoop in order to enter the taxi. He grabbed him by the arm, pulled him aside, and made to get into the taxi while trying to explain his more compelling need.

'I am sorry. Truly sorry. I just have to have this taxi. I am desperately short of time if I am going to get back to the cruise ship before it sails. Please excuse my rudeness.'

The tall, erect gentleman took a step backward, then a step forward before emitting a long stream of obscenities and protests in a language not familiar to Calum but which he guessed to be German.

As the gentleman now grabbed his arm, Calum tried again to explain his dilemma but all he got in return was a further stream of indignation. Deciding that this was a debate that could not be won, he shook the hand off his arm, turned and dived into the taxi all in one movement and yelled to the startled driver:

'To the cruise ship terminal and fast as you can make it. There is an extra fifty in it for you if you get me there before that ship sails!'

The driver was totally confused over the competing clients arguing outside his taxi and had more than a little sympathy for the other gentleman, who was the one he had first spotted hailing him. But 50 euros was 50 euros and would not appear on the meter so it would not be payable to the owner of the taxi company.

'Right away, sir, Does the ship leave at 4 pm?'

'3:30,' was all that Calum could splutter.

'Oh!' said the driver and, crashing the gears of his taxi, took off down a steep winding side-street at an alarming speed.

As they descended the hills at a velocity that made Calum's ears pop, the driver exhibited all the skills that Calum had only seen in F1 racing and by Steve McQueen in the film 'Bullitt'. At precisely 3:29 according to his endlessly consulted watch, they finally slowed down as they appeared at the control gate for the pier from which the cruise ship was due to leave. There was nobody outside the checkpoint, probably officialdom had made the safe assumption that all traffic had already been cleared, but the driver applied the brakes to come to a stop where he was supposed to, in line with the office.

'No. no. Just drive through!'

'I must not, sir. I am required to stop here in order to get clearance to proceed.'

'Just do it, man. There is nobody on duty. Drive through!'

The sentence that the driver was about to deliver in support of the contention that he must not break the rules was suddenly aborted when not one, but two, US fifty-dollar bills fluttered onto the seat beside him. With an excruciating screech and smell of burning rubber, they were off again and headed to the foot of the long line of steps up to where passengers had re-joined the ship.

With all that noise and unmistakable smell, a good many passengers who had simply been idling away the time leaning over the handrails watching the proceedings of cast off, were now intently watching the race against time. Included among the growing number of watchers, but the only one with the background knowledge, was Nerys, who had grown fed up waiting for Calum in the cabin and had stepped out to look for him, but with the unshakeable certainty that he was about to miss the boat. He had done a good number of silly things in his time; but this might be the tops. She was already considering how he would get from Tenerife to Madeira to catch up with her. Suddenly, her musings were disturbed by goings-on down on the pier and she leant over like everyone else to bear witness.

With another screech, this time of brakes, the taxi ground to a halt and Calum alighted and started to run up the steps, all in one motion. The audience was well aware that his troubles were not yet over, alas. They could see that the ropes had been cast off the capstans and the gangplank unit was now separating from the ship. A gap between the two was clearly visible and increasing slowly, but perhaps not slowly enough.

Amid frenzied yells of encouragement, Calum, the former athletics champion in high school, belied his advancing age and took the steps two and even three at a time to teach the top. Only then did he notice the gap! No time for hesitation, he employed his long jump skills and took off into the air. Long jump had never been his strongest event but, nevertheless, his somewhat inelegant flight ended with him landing on the deck of the ship. As cheers went up; he might even have achieved the perfect landing and simply walked off to accept the adulation of the surrounding audience, but the momentum of landing overcame him, amid his fatigue, and he instead lost his footing, went down and tumbled over, and ended up flat on his back.

Did he momentarily lose consciousness? Or, was it just a reaction to his difficulty in breathing, having consumed all of the oxygen available to him? He just lay still, as emotions of differing kinds passed over him. Eventually, he was left with a heaving chest and a silly smile on this face. The passengers had clustered around him with some concern but when they saw the face, more cheers erupted. Nerys fought her way through to him with even more determination than she had exhibited in fending off the Chinese. When she saw him, she stopped and stared, eyes bulging, and mouth locked open. Then, the recriminations began! He lay contemplating the replacement of the smile with a look of contrition, but that seldom helped. In any case, it was not required because at the end of a long tirade about stupidity, stubbornness, and sheer irresponsibility, Nerys collapsed onto her knees and held him in her arms and offered soothing words. The cheers of the audience were augmented by widespread applause as if signalling an end of one of the entertainment shows offered on the cruise.

No more than a few of the closest passengers would have heard Calum abandon his smile and whisper:

'Phew. Left that a bit short, didn't I! I might need a bit of a nap before dinner. How was your day?'

He resumed his smile in spite of the nipping sensation of a tightening hand in the proximity of his throat.

Floating the Idea of a New Home

Dr Nerys Jones-Davies was trying desperately to finish an article that simply had to be done before they took off for Scotland. Dr Calum Davies, with no such academic or any other commitments, was merely excited about the latest trip to their favourite island, which would spark off a new phase in their lives

242

and most probably present him with a new adventure or two. He could not keep quiet, even though he was well aware that Nerys was trying to concentrate.

'I can't believe we are about to put down roots, after all this time. That is if the mobile home has roots to keep it secured during those south-westerly gales. Otherwise, we might wake up in the morning and find we have floated over to Wee Cumbrae. Ha, ha, ha!'

'Calum! Can you please keep quiet for just another half hour and then I will be finished this thing? I am almost there.'

Calum shrugged and again picked up the tourist brochure for the Isle of Cumbrae in the Firth of Clyde; the location of their soon-to-be second home. It was not as if he needed to learn about the island. He had been visiting it on an almost annual basis since he was a small child. In fact, he could almost recite by heart the text of the brochure. But he never tired of looking at the pictures. He always chuckled at how the Tourist Office tried to update the photographs every year or so when a new edition came out, and yet the photographs looked exactly the same as in the previous editions. That was the beauty of the island for him, the more it changed the more it stayed the same.

He quietly went through to the kitchen to pour them each a glass of wine and even more quietly returned to surreptitiously place one in front of her. He was about to slip back into his chair when Nerys exclaimed:

'There! Done! That should wow them in the nuclear waste board-rooms of the civilized world!'

Calum gave a cheer. Her research focus on the safe disposal of nuclear waste had attracted interest, much support, and some opposition, but always interest around the world. He was tremendously proud of what she had done in a short academic career to establish her name. Although it contrasted somewhat with his own academic record, he was highly supportive of her. As long as it did not get in the way of their travels and adventures!

'Now! What was it you were saying, Calum? No doubt, you were rambling on about Cumbrae. Tell me what you were saying.'

'Oh, I was not saying anything new. You know me! I was just going over everything that led us to decide to get the mobile home brought to the island and located in what is probably the best spot on the island for views to the other islands. It is going to be sensational. Probably a better idea than buying an existing house because we could never get such a view. Though, God knows, we have looked at enough houses. Especially since Anna and Jacko showed a similar interest. And, you know, the best part of all was when Jacko hoodwinked Scotty Green into selling him a share of the Westview Hotel. That so pissed me off that I was tempted to disown the island altogether. Then Scotty must have guessed he had pissed me off and when he gave us that piece of land, we were off in a completely new direction.'

'You are good at going in a different direction, but somehow you get to the right destination in the end. Cheers,' expressed Nerys and raised her glass.

'Very droll. But you are correct, it is the right destination.'

Calum went on to reminisce for the next hour about the very well-trodden path that led to their impending journey.

Anna Salisbury had been Nerys' dean at the California University prior to her surprise retirement. Jacko Irving-Brand was her husband, an entrepreneur of some repute in California and throughout the United States, although Calum had tagged him as somewhat-shady. A couple of years ago, Calum had got himself embroiled in an adventure, during his first-ever extended stay on the island, involving disposal of nuclear waste from the Farland Power Station located just across the firth from the island. Ironically, the American backers of what turned out to be modern-day piracy also happened to be behind the sponsorship of Nerys' fledgling research program. As Calum got deeper and deeper into the mystery, he not only put himself at physical risk, but also placed Nerys' academic career in jeopardy. It was then that Anna Salisbury came through with strategic support for her to save the day and pave the way for that prestigious academic record of today. And, during this time, Anna became familiar with the islands of Great Cumbrae and Little Cumbrae. That was where the housing problem all began. You could even read all about it now. Some bounder had copped Calum's story and put it in a book called 'Crises on The Cumbraes'!

Anna and Jacko had accompanied Nerys and Calum to a conference at the University of Cambridge and of course, Calum had insisted that they all visit Cumbrae as, to use his words, "they were already in the neighbourhood". Although he had missed most of the island visit through getting entangled in another adventure involving spies in high places, that had not stopped Anna and Jock falling in love with the island. That was not the problem. They were allowed to fall in love with the island; in fact, they were expected to. But it could not have been predicted that they would declare an immediate intention to buy a home there. Just like that. Over a long weekend. In addition, Anna suddenly announced that she would be retiring in order to spend more time travelling, especially to the island! All this after Nerys and Calum had been procrastinating for months, if not years, about acquiring a property, deciding to go ahead one day and thinking better of it the next; their friends just decided to dive in. But it got worse. After exhaustive and exhausting visits to every property for sale on the island, and a good few more that weren't, Anna and Jacko appeared to have come up dry. They could not find exactly what they wanted. Calum would have been satisfied if the story had ended just there.

The bombshell that Jacko presented to Nerys and Calum at the end of their trip to the UK had just about laid Calum flat. They had all been staying at the Westview Hotel, which was in Calum's opinion the best on the island, and its owner, Scotty Green, had become Calum's best friend among all the islanders. Jacko had been disappointed with the failure to locate a suitable property and had sat down over drinks with Scotty seeking commiseration. By the end of the not-short session, Scotty had offered Jacko a 20% share in the Westview as part of his gradual transition into retirement from the hotel business. With the investment came the right of use of one of the two best suites in the building, looking westward with a view to die for. When Jacko casually mentioned his new acquisition, it was all Calum could do to resist decking him and laying him flat instead. Nerys could immediately spot the surprise, disappointment, hurt, anger, and probably another couple of emotions that welled up in Calum before he was able to compose himself and say 'well done' with negligible enthusiasm.

Thus, they had spent the next year and more on very different paths.

Jacko and Anna, who had followed through on her intention to retire, were free to travel extensively and every trip seemed to involve a visit to Cumbrae to make use of their suite. It had been said by some observant islanders, and most tended to be quite observant, that Anna and Jacko took on the characteristics of royalty when they were in residence at the Westview. All that was lacking was flying the American flag to announce each arrival; but Scotty had never got around to installing a flag pole.

Anna made some effort to get to know the islanders on each visit but Jacko just settled into the hotel, alternating between their suite, the dining room, and the bar, and all the while running his various business ventures in the US and around the world. A laptop and powerful mobile phone were all he needed; and, in truth, he could have operated from anywhere. However, being in residence at his *island place* appealed to his sense of purpose and image!

Over that same period, without consciously announcing they were going into exile, Nerys and Calum spent very little time on the island and any travelling they did was generally connected with her research and mostly involved Asia and mainland Europe. No more popping over to Cumbrae "as they were in the neighbourhood". Nerys had begun to wonder if Calum was really serious about giving the island a miss for a while. He had never been like that in the time she had known him and clearly Jacko's move continued to bother him. Jacko had intimated that Scotty wanted to talk to Calum about a similar investment, but Calum had professed it would be the last thing he would want to do. Even when Nerys had suggested at least keeping in touch with Scotty during their self-enforced absence, Calum had shown no inclination whatsoever. It was with great surprise one day, therefore, when Calum came bounding through their patio home looking for Nerys to announce with much excitement:

'Scotty is going to subdivide that land next to the hotel and wants us to have the best parcel of land. And, the best part is it that it will be free, gratis, and for nothing!'

So, it transpired that Nerys and Calum would become houseowners on the island, not just folks that had the use of a hotel room.

Scotty had owned the land to the east of the hotel for years but had done nothing with it. The hotel sat in its own grounds and was fringed on the north and west sides by an eclectic mix of cottages, mobile homes, and caravans. But the pristine east side had remained undeveloped. Now, he had decided to subdivide into six small plots, each capable of taking a small cottage. They were arranged in three rows of two and he had earmarked one of the front ones for his dear American friend who had seemed a little out of sorts of late. The site had an uninterrupted and truly breath-taking. view over to the islands of Little Cumbrae, Arran, and Bute and the mainland peninsulas of Kintyre and Cowal. With only the around island road and a field of cows between the site and the foreshore, there was little, or no chance, of that view ever being interrupted in the future. Calum and Nerys were ecstatic.

Much discussion had gone into what kind of house they should build on their property. There were definite challenges to any kind of construction on islands, with all materials and labour having to be brought over from the mainland. Building projects were notoriously slow on this island and many others around, and completion dates were prone to being extended on numerous occasions. It was perhaps for that reason, along with Calum's well-known lack of patience, that when Nerys came up one day with a brochure for luxury mobile homes pre-fabricated in Central Scotland, that Calum immediately jumped on the idea. They were extremely well fitted out and would make the most effective use of the site area available to them. There was only the issue of transporting the finished home from Airdrie to Cumbrae, by way of the ferry. That should not present much of a problem. The manufacturer must be doing that all the time. When it was confirmed that the mobile home could be delivered and made fully operational within six months or less of placing an order, the decision was made on the spot. As Calum pointed out, if they had insisted on regular construction, it would take more than six months to get planning permission from the distant county council to which Cumbrae belonged. Then they would be at the mercy of distant contractors. They would be lucky to be finished in two years. Mobile was the way to go. An instant dream house. And, they would be there to witness its arrival next week!

===000===

It was mid-morning on an early day in March. Unsurprisingly, it was still very chilly because the sun had barely peeked through the heavy cloud cover. But this was Scotland after all, so the weather was acceptable because the rain had not appeared today, unlike the previous seven days in a row. What was more of a worry was the wind, which had abated for now but had already blown up into mini-gales twice this morning. Wind, more than any of the other elements that could be thrown at it, was the nemesis of the ferry to and from the Isle of Cumbrae. If the wind got up to a certain velocity, the ferry simply went off for a while. A while could be an hour, a day, or several days.

Calum and Nerys had parked their rental car in the lot adjacent to the ferry slip and were awaiting sight of the ferry setting out from Largs across on the mainland. Its appearance out of the harbour would signal the commencement of the eight-minute sail to the island. They remained in the car meantime to keep warm, in expectation of what was going to be a memorable return voyage. They would walk onto the ferry for the trip to Largs along with other islanders, some with their vehicles. However, on the immediate trip back, there would be walk-on passengers including themselves but only one vehicle. The 11 o'clock sailing was reserved solely for a truck and low-bed trailer bearing one complete mobile home. Yes, the mobile home was almost home. So far, the logistics from the factory in Airdrie to the ferry slip on the Largs' side had worked out perfectly. That much Calum knew because he had been in constant touch with the driver after the latter had made the mistake of calling him at the outset of road journey almost five hours ago. Once mobile phone contact had been established, Calum sought updates every half hour or so.

Calum let out a trademark whoop as he sighted the ferry emerging from the mainland harbour.

'There it is. Two minutes late just to tease us. Eight minutes to go!'

Nerys smiled at her husband and thought of the excitement of Christmas mornings.

249

The light traffic from the mainland disembarked quickly and soon Calum and Nerys were aboard and the ramp of the ferry was being raised while the safety message, taped in a lilting Highland voice, was playing. As usual, nobody listened to it. What could happen in eight minutes? Nobody, at least none of the islanders, ever stopped to think about it. Calum insisted on standing outside, as if that might hasten on the voyage, while Nerys retreated into the warm, if not comfortable, salon along with the rest of the passengers.

She was chatting to two acquaintances bound for their regular shopping expedition to the mainland, where a better selection of foods and prices was considered to be available, much to the chagrin in all probability of the island grocery store. Calum burst into the salon just as the ferry was starting to enter the harbour.

'Wow, that wind has started to blow up again. I hope this darned ferry does not go off!'

A local worthy, who was well aware of the purpose of their journey, in fact most islanders were, sought to reassure him.

'Away wi ye. It is no blowin' anything at all. Nah, nut at all. See yon sea oot there, it is hardly movin', man. The ferry will run back just fine, ye mark ma wurds.'

Calum nodded at the sage observation and, nevertheless, blew on his frozen hands.

A little later, Nerys and Calum stood by and watched with a mixture of tension and admiration as the seemingly oversized truck and flat-bed trailer inched its way down the long, steep slipway (it would have to be low tide just at this minute, wouldn't it!) and on to the suddenly smaller-looking ferry. But thanks to the driver's skills and precise directions from the ferry crew members, the vehicle eventually made it on to the ferry, with not very much space to spare on either side or at the front and back for that matter. Only then were the foot passengers allowed on and there were relatively few. It was too early for islanders to make their return and potential day-trippers had probably been unconvinced by the weather prospects. Talking about the weather, the wind gusts had died down and the sun had actually come out momentarily.

Calum had persuaded Nerys that they ought to remain outside the salon to supervise the delicate crossing, although the driver had not paid attention to the suggestion and had retired into the salon for the duration. Although Calum thought the decision a little cavalier on the part of the driver, he assumed at least that the truck brakes had been set. He was wise enough not to bother asking the driver to confirm this.

It must be recorded that the first four minutes of the voyage went exactly to plan. However, at roughly the mid-way point in the channel, it all suddenly went wrong. There was a horrendously loud grinding sound, the ferry visibly lurched forward and very quickly stopped. The crew and passengers, including the driver, flooded out on to the vehicle deck to investigate. Nerys and Calum, who had been standing on that deck, had both been thrown forward and she had actually collided with her mobile home. While rubbing a painful shoulder, she joined the melee and asked the same question that everybody else was asking:

'What the hell happened?'

The ferry was now not moving at all and it felt like it was bobbing around in that water in spite of its heavy load. Suggestions were flowing from the passengers, ranging from abandon ship to just leave it to the crew to get to the bottom of the problem. The crew, however, seemed to be running around to little purpose and without giving any direction to the passengers.

Eventually a shaky voice came over the tannoy system, not the lilting Highland voice of regular announcements it must be said.

'Attention all passengers. We appear to have a mechanical malfunction. We are presently investigating its cause. At this point, we are unable to be under power, but we hope to rectify that very quickly. This is not an emergency. No emergency procedures are necessary. Please just return to the passenger salon and await further announcements.'

As is the case with the British race, in contrast to many of their European cousins, no panic emerged and universal compliance with the suggestion to go back inside ensued. Calum, being of that stock, shrugged and followed suit. Nerys, who was not as a rule averse to causing a fuss when she disagreed with bureaucratic orders, on this occasion hesitated for a moment and then joined the retreat without comment.

Once inside, the truck driver was the first to comment that his schedule for the day did not allow for delays. Someone else said suggested that the reason for the stoppage might be to rescue someone in the water, as this had happened once before when she was aboard, but she was quickly shouted down. The elderly and somewhat delicate machinery that ran the ferry was clearly pinpointed as the reason for stoppage. And stopped they were. Unfortunately, at this point in time, the wind had chosen to rear its ugly head again and strong gusts from the north east could be seen and felt to be having an impact. The sea was now noticeably choppier, and the ferry was visibly bobbing about like the proverbial cork in water.

Minutes passed with no announcement forthcoming. Calum looked at his watch and reckoned they were now about twenty minutes behind schedule. The driver observed him looking at his watch and started to moan again about his schedule. Finally, the tannoy system crackled into action again. This time, the lilting Highlander was back:

'Caledonian MacBrayne Ferries apologises for the delay in today's voyage, which is due to reasons beyond the control of the company. Passengers are advised to......'

The lilting Highlander was replaced by the hesitant Lowlander, with much clearing of his throat.

252

'I have to apologize, ladies and gentlemen and of course boys and girls, for this unfortunate delay. It looks like we are not going to be able to fix the problem on our own; so, I have radioed for assistance. That should be here from Gourock very quickly. In the meantime, please just sit tight. You are in no danger.'

The announcement had not done much to satisfy the occupants of the passenger salon, and numerous conversations were taking place. A local who had been staring out of the window toward the island declared with some solemnity that the ferry was drifting; it was not standing still; the whipped-up current caused by the wind was causing it to drift. He added for affect that they were drifting in a south-westerly direction.

At that point, a crew member came in the door, ostensibly to pour himself a cup of coffee, but he also took the opportunity to provide an unofficial, but perhaps more illuminating, report.

'Aye, damnedest thing ye could imagine. We have lost a propeller. Seems like it just came loose, messed up things down below, and caused us to grind to halt. I dinna think we can fire up the engines again. Mind ye, I'm no an engineer.'

With that, he disappeared out the door with his coffee.

Time dragged on. The self-appointed observer gave drifting reports by the yard every few minutes from his staked position by the window looking out toward the island. Eventually, the rest of the passengers decided to abandon the salon and move out to the car deck and tiny upper deck where they could better see what was happening. In reality, to the naked eye, very little was happening, at least very fast. The ferry was gradually drifting downstream and toward the long, thin stretch of land that extended outward from the island. The land was part of the National Water Sports Centre and served as a breakwater for their various watercraft lessons and safe sailing ventures. The Centre was about half a mile from the ferry terminal by the coastal road. With the ferry now slowly heading toward the stretch of land and seemingly incapable of altering its course, those who knew about such matters must have been trying to determine if the land represented a dangerous obstacle or a convenient stopping place for a runaway craft. Those with an interest in the mobile home situated on the ferry were wondering the same thing!

The drifting observer had joined the other passengers on deck and immediately proclaimed that the wind speed was increasing and, therefore, the rate of the drift was also increasing. The former was obvious, but the latter was not to everyone else and Calum concluded that the observer was just one of those typical Scots who come into their own during a mild crisis and wish it along to disaster status with gloomy predictions.

The crew had become more prominent again and the consensus among them was that a couple of tug boats were needed and had been requested from Gourock. The only question remaining was how long it would take them to sail down the Clyde. With little else to do except chat with the passengers, it was noticeable that they all had availed themselves of a coffee. No doubt chaos was ensuing at both ferry terminals now that the ferry had gone walkabout, observed one cheerful wit, perhaps relishing this alternative to the regular routine eight-minute journey, back and forth all day long.

Calum and Nerys were huddled with the truck driver trying to work out alternative plans, should the mobile home be successfully landed. The latter's schedule was fast disappearing and a night on the island would have to be contemplated as well. That was all assuming a successful landing. The prospect of a crash landing on the stretch of land now appearing closer at every turn did not bear thinking about. The driver could only envisage a very costly rescue for the mobile home involving barges, cranes, and insurance companies.

The animated conversations everywhere were interrupted when crackling signalled another message was forthcoming on the tannoy system. Somewhat bizarrely, the lilting Highlander returned

254

with the now-standard apology on behalf of Caledonian MacBrayne, then the now-familiar other voice appeared. He explained that great efforts were being made to come up with tugboats. Two had been dispatched from Gourock and were making their way down river as fast as they could. In addition, he had discovered that a nuclear submarine from Her Majesty's Naval Base Clyde at Faslane, further up the river, had been passing down the west side of the island today on its way to the open sea and was being escorted by three tugs. Those tugs had now been excused from their duties and were making their way back toward the island too. The captain's doleful voice accentuated the seriousness of the situation, but even he could not help but paint a potentially amusing scenario of two set of tugs, approaching in haste, from different directions in an effort to save the day. One could only hope that the race did not end in a head-on-collision to further add to the drama. A cheer went up from some passengers at the news.

Calum had called Scotty Green to let him know what was happening and to ensure that he would have a room for the driver as it became increasingly likely that an overnight stop would be required. That was not a problem for Scotty as Calum's room was the only one occupied this early in the season. The driver could have his pick of the others. That accomplished, Calum returned to the group of passengers and crew, many now on a first name basis, as friendships were established during the time of crisis

Everyone was located on the port side of the ferry and their eyes were firmly focussed on the narrow land stretching out from the Water Sports Centre. The drifting observer confidently predicted they would have fifteen minutes until they ran aground. The wind had actually died down again, but the momentum of the current was enough to maintain the drift.

Nerys took Calum's hand and attempted an encouraging smile to keep up their morale. Who could have predicted this? What would happen to their brand-new luxury mobile home when they ran aground? Would it be damaged on impact? Would it be damaged if an effort was made to remove it from the stranded ferry? They went through all these issues again as they had at least five times before. No definitive answers could be found. They were just about to talk to the driver again, for he was a bit high-maintenance and needed constant reassuring, when the tannoy crackled.

No formalities this time, just an excited captain yelling at the top of his voice.

'Here they come. Look up there beyond the top of the island, just by Inverkip. Here they come.'

Everybody rushed over to the starboard side and, sure enough, to the north just off Inverkip point, where the landmark power station chimney used to be before it was demolished, could be clearly seen two tugs majestically cutting through the waves.

A great cheer was raised by passengers and crew. And then it was followed by an even greater cheer because, just at that very moment, three tugs sailing close together as if they were in a synchronized demonstration team came hurtling round the top of the island from the west. They would win the race by a short head! One up to the navy!

In very short order, all the tugs got involved, first in stopping the drift toward the immovable object and then in shooting lines onto the ferry to take it under control. One could not help but be impressed with the team work among those in control of each tug, no doubt with radios crackling as they coordinated the salvage effort. In no time, the tugs had the ferry turned around and heading along the coast toward the island terminal.

The tannoy crackled again and an elated captain offered his thanks to the tugboat crews and announced that they would be towed back to Largs and from there to Gourock. That meant the passengers would have to wait at Largs for the replacement ferry to bring them to the island. The replacement ferry was already on its way from Gourock.

Groans were heard from the passengers at this news. So near and yet so far, they could almost wade ashore to the island now, they were so close. However, Calum was thinking about much more than just the inconvenience facing the foot passengers. What about his precious cargo?

Protocol be damned. He raced across the car deck, up the stairs to the tiny upper deck, and mounted the strictly-out-of-bounds-to-passengers ladder up to the wheelhouse where the captain resided in imperious fashion. Nerys shouted his name without really knowing what she intended to say. Some of the passengers, at least the quick-witted ones, guessed what was afoot and yelled shouts of encouragement. A crew member yelled, 'Ye canna gang up there......aw, what the hell, gang yersel, Yank. Give the skipper whit fir!'

The captain, who was just finally settling down a bit after an extremely stressful experience, was startled when a head appeared in his wheelhouse followed by a body from the ladder.

'Captain, you cannot take us back. Not with our home on your ferry! Surely these clever tugs can help you land at the island slip and allow everything and everybody to disembark. Then you can go back to Largs and Gourock.'

'Sir, you're no allowed up here. It is against the rules.'

'Fuck the rules! See sense, man.'

'I understand your wee dilemma. If it were up to me, I would do what you ask. But I have my orders from Gourock, you see.'

'No, I don't see. Call Gourock and put me on to whomever can change your orders.'

The captain leapt back a little at this suggestion and inadvertently engaged the tannoy switch with his posterior.

'I'm sorry. I'm sorry. No, I can't do that. No, not at all! He would never give permission. Especially when he has already made a decision for us to go straight back to Largs.'

'Have you ever heard of the saying that it is easier to gain forgiveness than it is permission?'

'No, I can't say I have ever heard of that one. I understand what you are saying but I would not know how to go about it.'

'Here's an idea,' replied Calum in a somewhat conspiratorial voice while he stepped back out of the wheelhouse onto the top of the ladder in order to give the captain the feeling of being in command of his own space: 'Why don't you get on the radio to whomever is in charge overall of the tugboats and ask him if it even feasible for the tugs to guide the ferry onto the slipway to allow for us all to get off?'

And so, a relatively muted radio conversation went on, which was, of course, transmitted over the tannoy for all onboard to hear and even any islanders listening on the coast road because they were less than 100 yards from the action. The captain seemed to wonder why he was hearing his own voice so clearly but was too consumed with the delicate negotiation to do anything about it. The tug skipper initially said it could not be done but was further prompted by the ferry skipper, upon Calum's subtle prompting; then he said it could be done, but should not be done (was this a rules conspiracy among the mariners?), then he finally agreed that they could give it one try as they were so close to the terminal and the wind had now completely dropped away.

The ferry captain gave a final response with his now more formal voice restored, 'Understood. Let's get on with it. Over and out!' He then winked to Calum as if it had been his own idea all along. All the passengers below cheered; and the captain looked out and wondered how the news had got around so fast. Now, fully in command again, he addressed Calum, 'Thank you for your help. I would now appreciate you vacating my wheelhouse. Go and prepare for disembarkation.' Shortly after that, he would notice the tannoy switch in the open position.

The flotilla of tugs took on the task of guiding the ferry onto the landing slipway, as if this were a rare opportunity to demonstrate their admirable manoeuvrability skills, not only to the passengers and crew but also to the sizeable group of islanders waiting to get off the island, or who had just gathered at the terminal as news of the excitement had spread far and fast. The challenge was always going to be to get the ferry far enough up the slipway in order to safely lower the ramp. This was achieved in almost comical fashion by three of the tugs buzzing around like industrious worker bees to the rear of the craft and giving it a good old push! Up she went and when the captain was satisfied they had got to the point where he would have taken it had they been under steam, he ordered the ramp lowered. Ferries do not tie up, except at the end of the day, and usually maintain their place on the slipway through judicious use of the engines. In the absence of those today, the worker bees at the stern did the next best thing.

The passengers flowed off, some casually walking as if nothing had happened and others vacating as if they had just earned a great reprieve on the Titanic. Calum and Nerys were among the first onto terra firma and immediately turned to offer encouragement to the truck driver. It was as if he sensed that the mariners had had their big day in the spotlight and now it was his turn, for he negotiated his considerable load off the ferry, up the slipway, and onto the coastal road with considerable aplomb, and amid appropriate applause from the watching crowds.

Calum immediately ran up to the truck cabin, knocked on the window and informed the driver, 'Best go around by the west side of the island as that is the way you are facing. I don't think you want to try a U-turn on this road. I am just going to thank the captain and then we will get going too, down the east side. We will be at Westview before you. Take care!'

The driver kind of felt that Calum's humour was a bit inappropriate after the demonstration of his skills and just rolled up his window and nodded.

Meanwhile, vehicles and walk-on passengers were hastily boarding the ferry for its final voyage to Largs, before anyone changed their mind or the man from Gourock appeared on the scene. It would mean that some vehicles were left waiting for the replacement ferry, whenever it appeared, but at least there were a good number of happy islanders, and visiting drivers and contractors who were relieved to be getting off the island.

Calum tried to get back on the ferry in his quest to thank the captain, who remained like a true leader in his wheelhouse surveying all that was happening below, but Nerys yelled:

'Don't you dare. Do you want to get stuck on that ferry again? You can thank him the next time you see him!'

Calum, for once obeyed the order, and luckily caught the captain's eye as he scanned the slipway to confirm that everybody who was getting onboard had, in fact, got onboard and he could raise the ramp. On seeing Calum, they exchanged thumbs up signals that all was well that ended well. Calum was already mulling over how he could make public the captain's decision to put ashore without getting him and the worker bees into trouble. But that was for another day.

The truck and flat-bed trailer pulled up to the vacant lot adjacent to The Westview Hotel almost exactly three hours later than scheduled. That was not bad, all things considered. The driver, with help only from Scotty Green's odd-job man, then set about the not inconsiderable task of removing the mobile home from the trailer and landing it precisely on the concrete pad that had already been laid in advance. This they achieved, though it was an extremely slow business, under the watchful gaze of Calum, Nerys, and Scotty. In the absence of a crane, there was no margin for error, but the driver knew his stuff and the odd-job man knew when to get involved and when not. Within an hour, their home had landed exactly where it needed to be for lining up with the already installed and capped services. All that was left to do was secure the home to the concrete pad with formidable chains, connect up the services, and test that everything was working. They discussed the amount of time that would be needed and whether the driver would be able to catch the last ferry at eight o'clock. In the end, because they could not even be assured that there would be a ferry at eight, it was decided that he would complete his work and then enjoy the hospitality of the Westview for the night. His only request was for Calum to join him in his telephone conversation with his wife in Airdrie to assure her that he was not bound for a night-out in Glasgow and the one night's absence from home was unavoidable!

The complete mission was accomplished in total darkness at almost 8:30 pm, making the earlier decision the correct one. Nerys insisted on trying everything inside the mobile home even though the driver had assured her it was completely operational. She was delighted at the design and functionality of the lighting, heating, and kitchen appliances. The kitchen was relatively spartan compared to her kitchen in California, but to hear her exclaim, it might have been a far superior model. Calum left her to her triumphant discoveries, chatted to the odd-job man before he left for home, then escorted the driver into the hotel. They would enjoy a tasty dinner, if it were anywhere near Scotty's standards, and then they would all sleep in the hotel tonight. What little Nerys had brought over from the United States and bought on the way down from the airport to the island, could be moved into the new home in the morning. Then the real buying spree would begin, thought Calum, as Nerys would identify the one hundred and one things that the new home simply had to have that were not already built in. Oh well! He would have to buy some tools, of course, for those odd-jobs needing to be done around any home.

Dinner was splendid, as predicted, and copious amounts of wine was offered as was Scotty's regular habit. The driver enjoyed

261

himself so much that he declared a night-out in Glasgow could have come nowhere near tonight's event. There were only the three of them at the dinner table along with a local couple on a bit of a night-out themselves. Much talk focussed on the adventures on the ferry and by late in the meal, the already palpable excitement had been enhanced with tall tales and observations from the participants and the islanders alike.

As was his custom, Scotty appeared with unordered liqueurs and joined his guests for that *wee nightcap* he so enjoyed.

At Calum's request, Scotty waxed lyrically on all the things that had been happening on the island since Nerys and he had last been there. In his typically loquacious manner, he gave the facts and his opinion on potential developments, like the new public housing for the elderly, the higher than average number of properties for sale, something that he as Chair of the Community Council for the Cumbraes had concern over if it signalled a diminishment in popularity of the isles, and the hottest topic of all to affect the community in recent times: a proposal to introduce fish farming to Great Cumbrae. This idea, in keeping with many that came along, had appeared to split the island population right down the middle, with half in favour and half dead-set against. Calum was keen to know more about it all, but it was Nerys that suggested it had been a long, long day and there would be plenty of time tomorrow and beyond to find out all the nuances of the arguments for and against. Calum did not welcome the adjournment but had to confess he was feeling tired. That warm and fuzzy feeling after such a good dinner, was, however, shaken out of him with Scotty's late pronouncement as they were heading up the staircase to bed.

'Good night to you both. It was a pleasure as always. Remind me how long you are staying on in your new home.'

'We leave on Friday so that is four days. Unfortunately, we just have to go back home to California after that. But we will back to our other home, our new home here, just as quickly as we can,' replied Nerys.

'I look forward to that. But you are in for a treat before you leave. I just got an email while you were eating dinner. Guess who is breezing in for a few days, starting Wednesday? Jacko and Anna! So, you will have two nights together to catch up and show off your new abode. Great news, eh!'

It was difficult to tell Nerys' reaction; but Calum felt like he had just received the proverbial good news and bad news, all wrapped in one!

===000===

Two days after its eventful arrival, the new mobile home had settled in well in its new surroundings and the Davies' had settled in well inside it. They were both amazed just how functional the living, cooking, and sleeping quarters were. The home might total fewer than 500 square feet but there was plenty of room for them. And, even for visiting guests!

Jacko and Anna had arrived in the afternoon and quickly acted like they had never been gone. Anna and Nerys got together almost immediately and set off on a long walk around to Fintry Bay and then over the hill by the farm and golf course and back to the only town of Millport. The walk was dedicated to catching up on all the gossip at California University at Temecula, and the Isle of Cumbrae, their areas of strong common interest.

Jacko had been on the road for several days before getting there and so cried off doing anything until dinner time, while he caught up on his countless business ventures. Whenever he was coming to Scotland, which these days was often, his partner in California, Jackson Hanley, would prompt him to look for business opportunities in order to diversify their already heavily diversified portfolio. Since he first came to Scotland, Jacko had been working with another American, Joel Wannamaker, who was based in Glasgow. They had dabbled in a few ventures, which had not exactly made them rich and Jacko was beginning to tire of the decidedly shady entrepreneur. That would undoubtedly please Calum Davies, who had grave misgivings about Wannamaker, based on his experience during the great nuclear-waste adventure of a few years past. However, now that Jacko was working on a project that would not involve Wannamaker, that would not necessarily please Dr Davies either. He would have to tread warily over the next couple of days.

Left to his own devices for the afternoon, Calum was experimenting with the electric scooter he had bought in Millport from the shop that operated a rental service. An electric scooter, more of a moped than a trendy '60s Vespa, was ideal for island travel. He had already ascertained that two full circuits of the island were possible on an overnight charge and perhaps even three. He had not wanted to push his luck and be left with a push home if he miscalculated. He was very pleased with his latest toy. It was possible to carry a passenger and Nerys would be enlisted tomorrow to begin a new round of testing. The island now had no petrol station, it being a victim of the economic slowdown around the arrival of the new millennium, and so a nightly charge at minimal cost was just the thing.

Nerys had insisted on dinner at their new place and the two women, newly refreshed from an invigorating walk, stimulating conversation, and a quick drink in Frasers Bar on the way home, had set to work in the small kitchen. They only had a bare minimum of ingredients and a limited number of cooking utensils to work with, but they succeeded in producing a memorable meal. As was customary with this foursome, there was ample high-end wine to compliment the food. The conversation that went along with the meal was a little stilted at the beginning, largely on account of Jacko and to a lesser degree Calum; but by the time the cheeseboard and crackers indicated the meal was reaching a conclusion, everyone was engaged in the animated discussions. It took Calum to suggest their customary conclusion in a not-so-customary setting.

'That was a fabulous meal, ladies. One wonders what you might have been able to come up with in your kitchens back home that would have bettered what we had tonight!'

'Thank you, kind sir, 'Nerys replied, 'and in the time-honoured tradition, I assume you two will be washing the dishes. Remember, there is no dishwasher here. You will have to do it the Scottish way, in a sink of soapy water.'

'Plenty of time for that, my precious. I was going to invoke our normal tradition of nightcaps all round, and I was also going to suggest that we take them outside on the deck. There is no wind and the temperature seemed bearable when I poked my nose out just now.'

'Outside? You must be kidding. It will be freezing,' complained Jacko.

'Let's give it a try, we can always don our parkas if we have to,' Anna diplomatically suggested.

'I have some brandy that will stave off the cold, no problem. Let's do it. It is black dark out there; but it will be a good rehearsal for the long summer nights when it will be daylight at eleven o'clock,' said Calum with gusto.

They were soon spread out in the Adirondack chairs, sipping their drinks, and staring out into the sheer blackness except for some twinkling lights from villages on the isles of Arran and Bute.

Talk turned to the new abode.

'I must say I am thrilled with how it has worked out. The journey over on Monday was highly eventful but it was all worth it,' said Nerys.

'I love it,' said Anna.

'It is a bit too small for my liking,' said Jacko in a typically undiplomatic manner, 'even out here is tight. There is probably more space in our suite in the hotel if you measured it out.'

Calum jumped in, just a little too quickly. 'I seriously doubt that. In any case, slim guys like the three of us don't need as much space as you do, so we will manage fine in here.'

Anna was quick to respond. 'Naughty, Calum. You must have noticed that Jacko has been on a health regimen since you last saw him and has dropped almost thirty pounds. His svelte new body will manage just fine here as well.'

'Go, girl. You tell him. Don't be so touchy, Calum. I am just saying that it is a pity Scotty did not give you some more land and you could have built or shipped in a bigger house. You should have offered to buy the vacant plot next door.'

'For the relatively few weeks that we will spend here each year, we were happy to accept Scotty's gift, but we were never going put out any more of our own money. This will suit us…..just fine!'

Nerys stepped in when she thought she should.

'Look, if you two are going to bicker all night, I think Anna and I will step back inside before my toes fall off. Have you had enough of this wonderful darkened vista, Anna?'

Anna's answer was expressed by quickly rising and leading Nerys through the sliding doors and back into the living room. The doors shut quite firmly behind them; the two men were left with the bottle of brandy and their thoughts to share.

Jacko was mulling over when and if to bring up his new project when Calum gave him the perfect opportunity.

'At dinner the other night, Scotty was taking about this fish farm proposal. It seems to have riled the islanders up no end. These sorts of things usually do. Do you know about it?'

'Oh, indeed I do!'

'Really. I know a bit about fish farming from my time in Canada. They were big there at first but there was as much opposition as there was support for them. Lots of people used to say they caused contamination and lowered the wild fish stocks. The First Nations, in particular, were against them. I think a lot of them have since closed up.'

'The environmental concerns are always exaggerated in any kind of business venture, but particularly in fish farming. You know that. It will take good, well-compensated business scientists to make the case to shoot down the well-compensated green scientists in order to get a project like this through all the planning hoops. Scotland has a reputation of being a bit too green, compared to England, and therefore less business-friendly.'

'You are well-informed for an American.'

'It is always a wise business practice to keep informed. I think the rock on which the proposal may founder is the location. Right in the West Bay in front of all those big expensive houses. The Nimby lobby on top of the environmental lobby might just kill it, or at least condemn it to years and decades of discussions and study groups.'

'But those houses in the West Bay already face the Farland Nuclear Power Station on the mainland. That is the ultimate eyesore and it does not seem that it is going to be demolished any time soon, even though it was suggested a few years back.'

'True, but people have got used to suffering that blight on their view and there is next to nothing they can do about it, even if they wanted to. But a fish farm proposal is a different kettle of fish, ho-bloody-ho, precisely because it is just a proposal. Those house owners will work themselves up into a frenzy about their view being impaired by the much closer fish cages and infrastructure, and once they get going on the inevitable smell, it will be case closed.'

'So, you think the proposal will ultimately fail?'

'It probably will, but just to make sure, someone has to come up with a better alternative proposal.'

'Is there one in the works?'

'I think you could safely assume that.'

Calum turned and, even in the darkness, he could sense a broad smile on the face of the wily entrepreneur.

'You bugger! You have an alternative plan, don't you?'

'I do.'

'Tell me about it.'

'Well it is not quite finalized. And, it will not be made public until the West Bay proposal dies or gets irretrievably bogged down. Then I will ride in on a white horse and save the day for everyone.'

'How is it better than the West Bay one?'

'Because it takes out the Nimby factor or at least takes it out of the hands of a large number of powerful, influential people, and drops it into the hands of fewer small people who will not have the same clout. That is why my proposal will succeed where the West Bay fails.'

'Wow! Where are you going to locate your farm?'

'Right out there in front of you. It is a perfect location. It is actually a better environmental site and the view is not so important!'

'What do you mean, ass-hole. That is my view! And, yours too for that matter. Even if you don't care about us, why would you deliberately destroy Scotty's lifework and your own investment?'

'Business is always about losing a little to win a lot. I can live with the impact on Westview in return for the profits I am estimating!'

Jacko immediately jumped to his feet, slid open the doors and called to Anna that Calum felt it was time for them to go.

It's Murder On The Waverley!

This was the first summer that Nerys Jones-Davies and Calum Davies had spent a full three months on the Isle of Cumbrae, in the Firth of Clyde, just off the west coast of Scotland. A lot had occurred in order for that to happen. Nerys, with her tenure confirmed at the California University at Temecula, had declined to be considered for the position of Dean upon the sudden retirement of her friend Anna Salisbury. That meant that Nerys could continue to enjoy the privilege of almost four months of vacation and research time when she was not required to be on campus and could spend it on Cumbrae. Calum, as the now not-so-recently retired accountant and academic, had no such demands on his time and was totally free to spend his summer wherever his desire took him. Not surprisingly, they ended up on Cumbrae.

It was interesting, however, that Nerys, who had only first visited the island a few years before, was the driving force for making this shift, albeit temporary, from the sunny climes of California to the challenging climes of Scotland. Calum had an obsession about Cumbrae and had visited it at least once in most years of his life. Yet, when it came to make the commitment to a whole summer residency, he was the reluctant one at first. Perhaps it was the thought of that weather change, for he was much more aware of what Scotland would probably throw at them than she. Perhaps he was uncertain about where they would stay for such a protracted period and was still a bit miffed that his friend, Sandy Green, the owner of the Westview Hotel on the west side of the island just beyond the only town of Millport, had sold a share in the hotel not to him but to their friends, Anna Salisbury and Jacko Irving-Brand. One thing for sure was that they would not stay in their friends' courtesy suite that came with their investment!

That particular conundrum had disappeared when Sandy had offered to gift Nerys and Calum a piece of land adjacent to the hotel, thereby allowing them to place a prefabricated home on the prime site, with a view to die for, out over the western islands. In very short order, they went from worrying over where they might stay to having their very own home. Nerys was delighted because it effectively enabled her plan to spend the summers there, and Calum was delighted because he now had a permanent address on the island of his dreams and adventures, and so he might as well spend the summer there too. Funny how common interests come together when you least expect it!

The summer had been joyous but was now drawing to a close. It had even started with something of a heatwave. Now, a Scottish heatwave is a lot different from a California heatwave, but it had been most enjoyable all the same. With the safe prediction from Calum that it would not last, they had spent almost all of the long daylight hours out of doors doing everything conceivable that the island had to offer. They had even ventured into the sea on several occasions for a swim, something they never did in the Pacific Ocean because they considered it too cold! The heatwave did not last, and it was soon replaced by the normal changeable weather that could include calm and windy, dry and wet, warm and cold, sunny and overcast; and sometimes all in the same day. Their new life just adjusted to the reality. When it made sense to go out, they did as before and gradually integrated with the island community. When it did not make sense to go out, they stayed in their home and she did research of an academic nature and he ventured into research of a genealogical nature. Oh, and always they ate and drank well of the local products and never tired of looking out their picture window to the sight of the other islands, whether they be clear as a bell, partially shrouded in mist, or totally invisible, when a little imagination was called for.

Nerys had got involved in island causes as Calum might have predicted and there were many of them, including the movement to raise the necessary public funding to save the old pier, which had been condemned due to its neglected condition. That was why today they were joining a cruise on the last sea-going side-paddle steamer in the world, named The Waverley just like Calum's favourite football team in Edinburgh. In light of the state of the old pier, the cruise would leave from the other island pier at Keppel, which belonged to the Cumbraes Environmental Research Station. The cruise would take them around the much larger Isle of Arran, stopping at several ports-of call, on the way to publicize the Save-Millport-Pier campaign, and back in time for supper.

The sailing had begun in mid-morning under a chilly, bright-blue sky but alas, by the time they had reached Whiting Bay on the south of Arran, their third stop, the weather had totally closed in and driving rain made for very little visibility. Future planned stops were now very much in doubt because of the difficulty in negotiating the small, and in most cases aging, piers. There was nothing else to do but enjoy the amenities of the fine old steamer Waverley.

Nerys had taken the opportunity to engage in endless mobile phone calls with friends, near and far. Calum had grown tired of overhearing while trying not to overhear, the animated conversations.

'I think I will just pop along to the bar for a small sensation,' he announced quietly.

Nerys surprisingly heard this but did not break off her conversation. Instead, she waved a hand, somewhat regally.

Apparently, most of the male passengers had arrived at the same idea, and the bar was quite congested. Calum could not initially get a seat and so he stood, from time to time being buffeted to the right or left, and supped his Tennent's lager, the most popular lager in the country and quite acceptable to him although, it was not his favourite.

He was eventually able to grab a seat and sat for a while without ordering a second beer or even the small sensation, i.e. a large scotch, that he had first promised himself. He could not help thinking about how the weather impacted so heavily on anything that you wanted to do in Scotland if it involved venturing out of your home. Plans always had to be flexible because the all the weather forecasts were inaccurate and unreliable. That was particularly so of the BBC, which ironically seemed to be one that most people consulted. Today was predicted to be cloudy with sunny breaks and

273

.

a 20% chance of rain! But, what the heck; he was still glad they had made the decision to spend the summers here, even if he could no longer see the coastline of Arran. It was out there somewhere.

If he had been expecting Nerys to join him in the bar at the conclusion of her call, he would have been disappointed. When he eventually made his way back to the aft salon, there she was with her mobile phone apparently glued to her left ear and right hand continuing to wave in the air.

'I know, I know'

'____'

'Hm. It is just as bad here on many days and today is one of them.'

'____'

'Well that would be preferable to our present plight. We are on a paddle steamer.'

'____'

'It is called The Waverley and we are on a day-cruise on the Clyde. But it is pouring rain and we can't stop anywhere. That is why I am catching up on my calls.'

'____'

'Right now, I can honestly say, it is murder on the Waverley'

Calum tapped Nerys on the arm. He could not restrain himself.

He tugged at her sleeve when he got no response.

'What did you just say, Nerys?'

'Hold on a minute, Sally. What is it, Calum? Can't you see I am on the phone. I said it is murder on the Waverley'

'I thought you did. That would make a grand title for a tale of adventure!'

Her eyes rolled and his did too as he sighed, 'Hmmm.'

The Author

Edwin Deas is a retired accountant with a doctoral degree but neither status has ever enabled him to have any adventures in his lifetime. Therefore, he has to imagine them through the eyes of a character called Calum, whom he has never really met.

This is his third novel and gathers together the motley crew who have been associated with Calum in the first two novels---**Crises on The Cumbraes** and **Six at Cambridge? Calum's Shorts** has little to do with his underwear and more to do with a series of short stories in which Calum and acquaintances get involved in what we will call mini-adventures. The outcomes are essentially the same, very few characters are sacrificed or harmed, and society does not really move forward much.

Edwin Deas was born in Edinburgh, Scotland an increasing number of years ago and has split his life between Scotland; British Columbia, Canada; and California. Indicative of successful times spent in all three locations; he now owns homes with his wife in each. He is often unsure which nationality to own up to and tends to use whichever suits the circumstance or gets him through Customs quicker. He does, however, confess a deep and lasting love for a certain island back in Scotland.

Edwin Deas is a Chartered Certified Accountant from the UK; a Chartered Professional Accountant from Canada; and holds a Doctorate in Educational Leadership from the University of San Diego, California. He strenuously denies, however, that writing financial statements prepared him for writing works of fiction and he enjoys the necessary learning experience he gains from doing the latter.

Edwin Deas lives more of the time in Oceanside, California with his wife Bronwyn Jenkins-Deas, who puts up with a lot but is never anything other than loyal and supportive. Jasper the dog completes the household. They are never entirely sure of his commitment to the cause, but he appreciates two good meals per day.

Back Cover Pictures

Top: Millport, Isle of Cumbrae, Scotland

Bottom: Temecula, California, USA

22945102R00163

Printed in Great Britain
by Amazon